AIMING
for LOVE

Books by Mary Connealy

From Bethany House Publishers

THE KINCAID BRIDES

Out of Control
In Too Deep
Over the Edge

TROUBLE IN TEXAS

Swept Away
Fired Up
Stuck Together

WILD AT HEART

Tried and True
Now and Forever
Fire and Ice

THE CIMARRON LEGACY

No Way Up
Long Time Gone
Too Far Down

HIGH SIERRA SWEETHEARTS

The Accidental Guardian
The Reluctant Warrior
The Unexpected Champion

BRIDES OF HOPE MOUNTAIN

Aiming for Love

The Boden Birthright:
A CIMARRON LEGACY *Novella*

Meeting Her Match:
A MATCH MADE IN TEXAS
Novella

Runaway Bride:
A KINCAID BRIDES
and TROUBLE IN TEXAS *Novella*
(*With This Ring? Collection*)

The Tangled Ties That Bind:
A KINCAID BRIDES *Novella*
(Hearts Entwined *Collection*)

BRIDES *of* HOPE MOUNTAIN • 1

AIMING *for* LOVE

MARY CONNEALY

BETHANYHOUSE

a division of Baker Publishing Group
Minneapolis, Minnesota

Published by Bethany House Publishers
11400 Hampshire Avenue South
Bloomington, Minnesota 55438
www.bethanyhouse.com

Bethany House Publishers is a division of
Baker Publishing Group, Grand Rapids, Michigan

Printed in the United States of America

Library of Congress Cataloging-in-Publication Data
Names: Connealy, Mary, author.
Title: Aiming for love / Mary Connealy.
Description: Bloomington, Minnesota : Bethany House Publishers, [2019] |
    Series: Brides of Hope Mountain ; 1
Identifiers: LCCN 2019016547| ISBN 9780764232589 (softcover) | ISBN
    9781493421671 (e-book)
Subjects: | GSAFD: Christian fiction. | Love stories.
Classification: LCC PS3603.O544 A78 2019 | DDC 813/.6—dc23
LC record available at https://lccn.loc.gov/2019016547

ISBN 978-0-7642-3485-9 (cloth)

Scripture quotations are from the King James Version of the Bible.

Cover design by Dan Thornberg, Design Source Creative Services

Author is represented by the Natasha Kern Literary Agency.

19 20 21 22 23 24 25   7 6 5 4 3 2 1

Aiming for Love is dedicated to Sabre Sage Burns,
a young woman I met when I traveled
to the area where *Aiming for Love* is set.

She has struggles in her life, but she has faced them
and remains a woman of beautiful faith,
generous smiles, and a loving heart.

You inspired me, Sage.
It was wonderful to meet you.

1

October 1873
Hope Mountain
Near Bucksnort, Colorado, Near Grizzly Peak, Colorado

Josephine Nordegren floated through the woodland silent as a ghost.

She smiled inside, but kept the emotion tucked away. Strong feelings almost had a sound. Maybe animals had hearing sharp enough to pick up a pounding heart.

She inched closer to the doe nursing her fawn. But *inched* wasn't the right word. Playing games in her head, she tried to do better. Not *inched*. *Floated* maybe.

Drifted was good. *Glided*.

She entertained herself with her thoughts as she glided closer, her goal was another little game she played. One she'd gotten almighty good at. Not as good as her little sister, Ilsa, but good.

She'd sneak up on the doe, slap her on the rump, and watch her run.

But not until the baby had its belly full. No sense inter-rupting the meal.

Settling in, only a few feet from the unaware wild critters, Jo waited in utter silence.

The doe's head jerked up. Her white tail flew high. She whirled, graceful as the wind, and charged straight at Jo . . . then ran right past her, close enough Jo could've gotten in her slap. The fawn stumbled, then, almost as fleet, dashed after its mama into the woods only inches from Jo.

She let herself smile then. Right out in the open. Because on the breeze came the scent of woodsmoke.

Very faint.

And a lot more interesting than a deer.

She moved toward it. The smell got stronger. She had a moment of envy for the deer that smelled it before she could. Ah, to be that good. Maybe the doe heard it, too. Jo had ambitions to beat every woodland creature at noticing the world around her.

She'd have known it was a campfire even if she wasn't ex-pecting one—and she was expecting one. A campfire smelled different than if the forest in her Colorado Rockies home was on fire.

But after only a few days, she believed these men knew to take care of the woods. They seemed wise and cautious in their actions.

Knowing.

They wouldn't want the forest to burn any more than she did. Their care helped lure her. Even knowing her big sister, Ursula, would want her to stay well clear.

Instead, Jo floated through the fall woods. Leaves drifted

down from overhead, driven by a cool breeze that could turn mean and bring heavy snow at any time.

When she got close, she pushed the smile back inside.

Sitting only a few feet back in the lush forest, she was invisible. She'd chosen her clothes carefully. She'd made them just for this purpose. The different shades of dull earth tones sewn out of fabric scraps on her leather jerkin and trousers. She touched the spot on her chest where the strap of her quiver crisscrossed with the string of her bow. The clothing itself was made from deer hide, shot, tanned, and sewn by her own hand, though Ursula was the best at it.

The trousers were tight enough to not catch on bushes and mark her path with noise. But not too tight—she didn't want the fabric she'd so painstakingly patched with forest colors of gold, green, and brown to reveal the shape of a leg or arm.

The men worked diligently setting up the camp. They'd come for the first time only four days ago.

Jo hadn't seen a man since Grandpa died many years ago.

Now she couldn't look away.

She carefully took her bow off her shoulder and set it aside, along with the quiver, so they didn't rustle any branches. But she kept them within grabbing distance.

She inched closer so she could listen to the men speak. They were interesting, and she watched greedily. How they handled their horses. How they treated those pretty spotted cows with horns as long as tree branches.

The men were skilled with the fire, quick to put on coffee. She'd never tasted it, but Grandma had talked about how much Grandpa loved his coffee, and Grandpa had brought some home from time to time. Then, after Grandma died,

Grandpa made coffee on his own and talked of campfires . . . probably just like this one.

But Jo was too little then to have a taste, and heaven knew there was no such thing as coffee available for her and her sisters now.

She cast off the memories the coffee woke up and watched the men. It was almost impossible to keep from going out in the open and speaking to them.

The lure of it was matched by terror. It must have been men like this who killed her parents. Grandma and Grandpa had said it often enough.

The outside world had killed their son and his wife. Mama and Papa. Dead so long now that Jo could only catch glimpses of a memory of them.

And here now was the outside world, come nearly to her doorstep.

Had her parents been fascinated like she was? Was that why they were dead? The men seemed quiet and calm, but men must kill.

She should slip away. But she didn't.

Because she was waiting for the tall man. And then she saw him.

She sat up and leaned forward.

Then she caught herself. That kind of movement drew the eye of a deer. Since she hadn't seen a man since Grandpa died, she couldn't know if a man was as alert as a wild animal. But she had to be careful, just in case they were.

She forced her body to relax, but still her mind rabbited around.

The men were all sizes. Mostly lean as a strip of pemmican.

She only knew men could be fat or lean because she saw these men here and could compare them to Grandpa. He'd been stout, and he'd loved to slap his belly, laugh, and say, "A fat man is a rich man."

But the tall man was different from the rest. He told the other men what to do.

She'd heard him called Dave. She'd heard Warden. She'd heard Boss.

When she saw him she thought Dave Warden Boss.

The cattle herd way up here, closer to Jo and her sisters than anyone had ever come before, must be his. They spread out across the vast, open meadow surrounded by forest. Deer and elk herds, wild boar, mountain goats, and bighorn sheep wandered and grazed here. But no one had used this perfect mountain valley for cattle before.

Jo and her sisters had a few cattle, but they stayed in the narrow-necked canyon that hid Jo's house. And they were almost pets. They gave milk and had babies, but Jo couldn't stand the thought of eating one of them. She hunted instead, and she was very good at it.

The men, even as they sat and drank coffee and talked, were alert. They were comfortable out here with woods and wind, cattle and horses, campfires and wilderness food, but still always listening, testing the air for scent, and looking around.

Jo considered herself to be the same.

Dave Warden Boss had eyes sharper than the others. He spoke quietly, but when he spoke, the men listened. There would be stories told around the campfire as the meal ended and the dark closed in. They'd all laugh, but Dave Warden

Boss wasn't loud about it. He laughed and his eyes flashed with humor that she remembered from Grandpa. But when Grandpa's blue eyes flashed with humor, he joined it with a roaring laugh. Not Dave Warden Boss. He was a quiet man.

She watched them drink from tin cups. She and her two sisters only had two. Through the years the others had rusted through. Ursula had carved out a cup from a knot of wood, and it worked fine, but Jo longed for a tin cup she could take home to her sister. What a treat that would be.

Oh, Ursula would demand answers. She'd be fierce and scared. Jo wouldn't do it anyway—it was stealing. But she could think on it. She knew true temptation, maybe for the first time in her life.

It didn't matter if there was an unexplained cup to upset Ursula anyway. If the men were here to stay, Ursula would have to know about it. A tin cup would be the least of their worries.

Jo watched the comings and goings of the men.

Seven in all. Three rode herd while three slept. Then the first half would return and sleep, while the others rode out among the cattle. The extra man was Dave Warden Boss. He was out riding for part of the first watch and part of the second. He slept an hour at a time, rode out, came back and slept, woke and rode out. A restless man. A watchful man. She couldn't be sure when he'd go, but she'd watched every one of the three nights they'd been here, and she knew he'd stay away awhile.

She bided her time. Her sisters wouldn't worry if she didn't come home. She commonly wandered the woods at night.

Patient as a stalking cougar, she waited for the first three men to ride out and the second three men to sleep. Then she waited for Dave to ride out. When he left, she floated toward the campfire, silent as a ghost.

No one woke. They didn't even stir.

The first night she'd only studied.

She'd watched them strike a fire with a magical wave of their hand and was in awe. She remembered matches, but their last one had been gone for years.

Grandpa had taught them to get by without a match, but watching that fire leap to life so easily was a near miracle.

She'd slipped in the second night and picked up a small tin full of matches. Studying them, she wanted to take them, but she set them aside. They hadn't noticed her in their camp that night, so the next one she'd hunted around and looked at more of the wonders they carried. She'd found a small tool they used to poke a hole in leather for stitching. They had one, an awl, Grandpa had called it. But to have two, so more work could be done, what a wonder that would be.

Now, tonight, the fourth night, she eased in again. The men slept, one of them making a ragged noise from his throat that had scared her the first night, but now she was used to it and congratulated herself for her courage.

She'd heard Dave Warden Boss say this was the last night up here. The herd had settled. Now they'd just need to come daily and ride through, counting and checking for trouble. She'd heard someone talk of building a cabin, but she wasn't sure when, where, or for whom.

Reaching the campsite, Jo lifted the cup where it sat by a coffeepot. It was the one she'd seen Dave Warden Boss holding. It gave her a thrill to hold something that was definitely

13

his. Not a spot of rust anywhere. She was so tempted to take a sip of coffee, just to see what it tasted like.

The sound of hoofbeats startled her. Dave Warden Boss usually stayed out longer. Moving faster than usual—silent but swift—she dashed into the forest, turned, and crouched. Waited.

Three men came in, three went out. It wasn't the man she'd expected. She relaxed as she watched the camp settle down again. When the ragged noise started, she knew they were asleep, and she smiled, ready to go home. Then she reached for her bow and quiver only to realize she still held the cup.

She'd taken it in her haste to avoid the approaching men. She had to put it back. But when would Dave Warden Boss be back? Did she dare slip into the camp twice?

A hard hand landed on her shoulder.

"I've got him."

Dave Warden Boss had her.

Jo whirled to dive away, run.

His grip was unbreakable.

Six men swarmed around her as she fought for her freedom.

She couldn't escape. Dave Warden Boss had a grip that seemed like he'd seen it all before.

2

Dave had never seen anything like this before. A child up here in these highlands. Who was this?

Dave hung on tightly as the small, wiry thief exploded into motion. If Dave hadn't been angry enough to have a mighty firm grip, he'd've lost hold and let the youngster get away.

"Got the thief, boss?"

Jimmy Joe, a talkative man. Always eager to say out loud something anyone could see if they owned two working eyeballs.

"Yep." Dave had his hands full. A fist swung, and he jerked his head back in time to miss out on a black eye. Dave started dragging the little hombre toward the fire. He wanted to get a good look at him.

"Are we haulin' him in to jail, boss?"

Six men, only one given to yammering.

"Let's see who we've got here." Dave noticed the odd clothing. He'd've never seen him if that match tin hadn't been moved and left partly open two nights ago. The next night he'd been watching, and he'd seen the slight form slip in, study the camp, then vanish.

But Dave had just barely seen him. An almost ghostly figure so quiet it gave him chills.

Tonight, though, he'd been ready when the scoundrel had stolen a tin cup. Dave had money in his saddlebags, but the ragged little filcher hadn't gone searching for that. This here wasn't a real desperado, but a sneak and a thief, and Dave had no use for such as that.

Twisting, hollering, kicking, the kid came along. With a high voice that made him even more sure he was dealing with a half-grown boy. Dave dragged the youngster to the campfire, not as sure what to do as he'd been earlier. A thief was a thief, and Dave had planned to haul the man in to the sheriff—and that was a long haul. But maybe it would put the fear of God into him . . . and if not God . . . the fear of the law of the state of Colorado.

But a kid? What was Dave going to do about a kid? A kid, moreover, who'd stolen a single cup.

If the kid had stolen food, Dave would've seen if he needed more. The kid did a wild twist, and Dave almost lost him. He tightened his grip.

The new tighter hold knocked the kid's hat off, and long pale hair cascaded out from under a scarf tied over the youngster's head.

"Let me go!" Not a boy whose voice hadn't gotten deep, a young girl.

Dave was so stunned by what was adding up in his head, he forgot to duck and got swatted right in the mouth by the tin cup. He looked into her eyes in the firelight and realized the cup was wielded by—by—

Not a boy or girl.

A woman.

A fully adult woman. Dressed in what? A fluttery . . . something? Strange clothes. A foot whizzed by his face, and he almost got kicked in the teeth by a woman wearing trousers for sure.

The fire danced and hissed, casting shadows over everything, but the clothes were definitely strange. Brown, he thought, but not one color; instead, her clothes were patched with different shades of brown and gold, hard to judge in firelight.

The cup swung toward him again, and when it hit him, it bounced off Dave's face and went flying. Good, she was disarmed.

Jimmy Joe snagged the flying cup out of the air.

Talkative, but a handy kid.

"A woman?" That wasn't Jimmy Joe. That was Alberto, his foreman. "What's a woman doing up here on Hope Mountain?"

And that was a question worth asking.

Because none of them had an answer.

Quietly, like he always talked, Dave said, "There aren't any women closer than Bucksnort. Not even native folks." None he'd heard of anyway. Clearly there was one. He'd come up here scouting for pastureland and found a gold mine in prairie grass.

And anyway, an Indian woman wouldn't have white hair, and they sure as certain didn't wear patched-up brown trousers.

A foot pounded on his shin. But her shoes were soft, like moccasins. None of her twisting and kicking shook his grip.

"Who are you?" Dave asked. "And if you wanted a cup, why didn't you just ask for one?"

With that, she stopped. Still as a hiding animal. Hiding animal? Now why in tarnation had that strange thought slid through his head? But it struck him that way.

Then in a voice with the thickest mountain accent he'd ever heard, she said, "You'd gimme a cup?"

She turned to face him, and, because he was angled so the fire was coming past his left arm, it cast light on her face. She had eyes so light blue it was like looking into stars shining in the night sky. Her hair white as moonlight. A moonlit rat's nest, but still, a pretty color.

"If you needed one."

There was a long silence, and the expression on her face reminded him of a friend of Alberto's who'd drifted through a couple of years ago. He spoke little English. He'd listen intently and think awhile before he responded to anything. Dave figured it was because he had to sort out an unfamiliar language.

"I need one."

And she said no more, but it was clear English, so that wasn't her excuse.

He waited, almost humming with confused irritation.

So, did he just hand her the cup and let her go?

That didn't suit him. She couldn't belong up here. Where were her people? Were there folks living around that he'd never seen during his days of scouting?

"Before I give you the cup, I want you to tell me what's going on." From the way she looked at him, her eyes narrowed in confusion, it struck him that the question was too vague. He tried something simpler. "What's your name?"

"Um . . . Jo."

Joe? A man's name. Strange business going on with this woman. But she'd answered, so simple questions were best.

"Where do you live?"

That animal stillness again. It reminded him of how a rabbit hid beneath a bush, hoping a big old wolf didn't notice him—he wasn't that thrilled with casting himself as the one who ate small critters.

This time there was no answer.

"Do you live up here?"

Silence.

Could she be in trouble with the law? Could she have a husband up here who was in hiding?

Dave's brain was starting to hurt from all the questions.

He had a diabolical idea. "All right. Well, it doesn't seem to me as if you have a home, certainly not a safe home. I can't leave you up here. I'll take you back down to my ranch. My ma and pa are there. Ma will take care of you. Find you some proper clothes. Let you drink right out of a tin cup anytime you want. It's a long, long way, and I doubt you'll ever get back up here."

Her gasp was so deep, so physical, she slipped through his fingers.

He grabbed her before she could run. He leaned close, nose-to-nose, and said, "Do you live alone?"

"N-no."

"Are you married?"

"N-no."

"So, you live with your parents?"

"N-no."

Dave fought to keep himself from shaking her. He wasn't one to play guessing games.

"Who do you live with?" There. A question without a yes or no answer.

There was a stretch of silence, and Dave wondered if he'd ever get much out of her but yes and no.

"My sisters."

That threw him like a lassoed calf at branding time. Sisters, more than one. But they would most likely be near her age. And she seemed only just full grown.

Then she blinked at him with those big blue eyes with dark blond lashes so long they fluttered in the breeze. She was a little older than his first guess. Not a barely adult girl for sure.

"Do you want to bring them down to my ma, too?"

"No."

Dave almost punched himself in the head for asking another yes or no question.

He watched her, and as he did, he realized he could see more than just what was lit up by the fire. Dawn was breaking. Should he just let her go? There was no doubt she was frightened and she'd run, vanish forever. And he just couldn't in good conscience let her do that. Her fear would make her run when her best chance of survival was coming down off the mountain with him.

His chest swelled with the rightness of it. He felt like he was saving her life. A hero. He had to get her out of here, and her sisters, too. And he would. He wasn't going to let her escape. Considering the terrified way she was watching him and the other men, he wondered if that might make him a kidnapper.

They hung men for kidnapping in Colorado.

But he decided then and there he was doing it anyway.

He sure hoped she didn't kick up a fuss about it.

3

Her fist landed hard enough on his eye that it started to swell shut.

He fell backward but hung on to her, and they fell into a tangled heap. His men shouted . . . a couple might've laughed.

"Hang on to her." Dave wasn't a yeller as a rule. He'd found he could get folks to listen just fine if he spoke quietly. But right now, he yelled. He didn't want her slipping away. He figured if she ran off now, he'd never see her again.

Jimmy Joe took a solid hold along with Parson Fred—that's what the old-timer called himself, but Dave had never noticed the man preaching a sermon. It struck Dave just how wrong it was for this young woman to be alone with him and his six men.

They had her on her feet, then he got boosted up. He touched his nose, and it wasn't bleeding, but he had a fat lip.

He took hold of her wrist and said, "I have her."

The other men let go so suddenly Dave wondered what he sounded like. His hand clamped on her, ready to dodge the next blow. She was going home with him to see his ma, even though it was a long ride through some wicked country, more up and down than flat, with stretches he'd had to force his cattle through. And that was after he'd spent the summer tearing the trail open, widening, chiseling, kicking off avalanches.

They'd've never made if it they weren't a tough bunch of mountain-born longhorns.

Just as he was trying to convince himself it was all right to tie her to a saddle, thundering hooves turned his attention to that rattlesnake of a trail they'd taken four days ago. A trail they'd broken for cattle for the first time.

And now, days after he'd been the first, what sounded like a second herd was coming at a dead run.

There were trees thick along the far side of the valley from where Dave stood, right where that trail reached this mountaintop. He couldn't see the trailhead, but he knew that's where they were coming from.

His gun filled his hand. He dragged the mystery woman with him behind a fall of rocks. The rest of his men spread out. They'd talked about defending themselves up here. The rumors about Bludgeon Pike were all over the range below. But honestly, he'd never thought he'd have to.

And then a longhorn burst out of the trees, coming straight from the trailhead. Another and another. Ten then twenty. Dave's grip on the woman was as tight as his grip on the gun, but he had no reason to fire at a bunch of cows.

And then Ma burst out of the trees and into his high valley with . . . it looked like . . . a rooster in her arms. He was so startled he almost lost his grip on everything, including his mind.

Isabelle Warden was a stout lady, but that had only happened in recent years. His ma had helped tear civilization out of this wild land. She and Pa had been at it for thirty years. She was as polite and ladylike as any woman he knew—he paused at that thought since he barely knew any women. But she seemed plenty polite and ladylike. But for all that, she could ride hard, shoot straight, and make a decent fist.

Dave put the gun back in his holster. Ma reminded him of this little spitfire he had, and suddenly, despite having no idea what Ma was doing here with cows galore, he was mighty glad to see her.

As Ma rode across the meadow, more cows came behind her. She was on the far side of a huge swath of grass. Pa thought maybe near a thousand acres in all. Ma had never been up here, but following the trail left by about two hundred cattle wasn't all that tough.

She rode through the cattle that'd come up with her and a bunch of his own. His cattle stirred around, and a stream of more cows kept coming in from that trail. Calves kicked up their heels. A low song of mooing and running hooves broke the early morning silence.

Not that Dave had been noticing the silence, what with questioning his little thief friend here.

He saw a big black bull emerge into the pasture. Pa's brand-new champion Angus. It looked like Pa had brought a big old chunk of his herd. Why would he do that? He knew even though there was a big pasture up here it wasn't near big enough to keep all of these cows fed, and with winter coming on, they'd be dealing with hungry cows in just a few days.

Everything about this invasion screamed trouble. What had happened down at the ranch for Pa to do this?

Ma galloped straight for them. Yep, that was definitely a chicken.

Another man emerged into Dave's valley. One of Pa's steady cowpokes. Of course, Pa only had steady ones around. He was a good judge of a man. Were all his cowhands coming up here? It wasn't just the cattle that'd go hungry. Dave didn't have food for all these people . . . except on the hoof.

"You men ride toward that trail, see if anyone needs help. Watch for Pa."

All his men moved fast. They were running by the time they reached their horses. He'd broken them out of a trance . . . and he'd done it just as fast as he'd broken out of his.

"What in the world is going on?" He glanced at Jo in the full light of early dawn. As if she had some answers. That almost made him snort. Nothing about the words *yes* and *no* would be much help.

"They had to be riding all night in the pitch dark to get here," Dave thought out loud. "That trail is just barely passable with great care in full daylight."

And then he saw snow on the backs of some of the cattle. He added, "In full daylight in perfect weather. It must be snowing down below."

Then Ma reached them, pulled her horse to a fast stop. Dave grabbed her reins, slapped them into the hand that still held Jo, and took the chicken.

Ma swung down with the skill of a woman who'd been riding all her life.

The chicken squawked and flapped, and Ma took the bird

24

back as soon as her feet were on the ground. Her horse shied, and she got the wings under control and put one hand on the bird's beak.

"Trouble coming, Dave, and we abandoned the ranch until things are settled."

Abandoned the ranch? Those were words that near to knocked Dave onto his backside. Pa would never do that. But all the trouble in the area was coming from one place.

"Bludgeon Pike?" The man had been pushing people off their land all year, but he went after nesters, not an established ranch like the Circle Dash.

"Yep, Pike. We heard he's coming after our land with all his men. Your pa didn't like it, but we had to get out. Maybe if you and the hands that came up here had been with us, we'd've stood and fought, but Pike has a lot of men, and hired gunmen at that. We figured he'd draw plenty of blood even if we beat him back. Pa had enough warning that we could have sent someone up here to fetch all of you, but instead we gathered the herd and came up." Ma scowled and glared back at the trail that still spilled cattle into Dave's pristine valley.

More of the hired hands showed up. Pa had kept six, and Dave had taken the same number. Pa had a bigger herd down in the lowlands, but Dave needed help getting a cabin and bunkhouse up, and a barn if there was time before the worst of the winter slammed down. Corrals, getting the herd used to new land. He needed every man he could get.

Pa's hands led strings of horses, heavily packed. Some had big wiggling gunnysacks on their backs. More chickens, Dave hoped that was what wiggled. What else could his folks have put in there?

"I had my own little war with him to convince him to fall back. He agreed to come only if he could bring his cows. We stripped the whole ranch, which is how I ended up with a chicken riding on my lap. Now we're up here, and we need to build a chicken coop. Scout more pastureland."

Dave had done a lot of scouting, there wasn't any more.

"Get a cabin and bunkhouses up fast." Ma had got the bit in her teeth and was yammering away.

"First thing we need is to build a chicken coop so I can put this stupid rooster down. We'll get—"

Dave figured she'd say it all twice more so he didn't bother to listen.

"—snowing down below, and I can't believe it's not snowing clear up—"

Dave did switch hands so he could hold the reins separate from Jo's wrist. He felt her tug now and then, no doubt still interested in escaping. Well, there was no escape for Dave, so why should she get away?

"Unpack those loaded horses and use a tarp—"

It was a waste of time to try and talk over Ma, so Dave ignored her and watched hundreds of cows fill up his valley and go to grazing on the only grass he had.

"And why do you seem to have permanent hold of a woman, son?"

He heard that.

The horse Ma rode was a good one, so Dave dropped the reins. Not all horses were well-behaved enough to ground-hitch, but this one was. It went to chomping on more of Dave's grass.

"I caught her stealing a tin cup from me this morning."

"I didn't steal it."

"Yes, you did."

"I forgot to let go of it."

"That's stealing."

"You are a liar, like the Bible story of 'The Boy Who Cried Wolf.'"

Dave froze and turned to look at her. Ma stopped fussing and pivoted to face Jo.

Ma said, "Um . . . 'The Boy Who Cried Wolf' isn't a Bible story."

Jo narrowed her eyes. "You accuse me of theft and make it worse with heresy."

"I accused you of theft because you snuck into my camp and took a cup," Dave stated matter-of-factly.

"I ran. It was in my hand, and I forgot to let it go. That is not stealing."

"That is exactly stealing."

Dave glanced at Ma, who arched one brow. "Who did you say this woman is?"

With a small shrug, Dave said, "She claims to live up here with some sisters. I don't know if her family died or if she's a little loco. She ain't answering many questions."

Jo kicked him in the shins again. But he could put up with her moccasins all day.

Ma's eyes narrowed as she looked closely at Dave for the first time in the light of dawn. "You seem to have a fat lip and an eye that's swelling shut."

"She hit me with the tin cup she stole." Dave shrugged, feeling pretty comfortable just hanging on to her. "Her name's Joe. She wants me to let loose of her, but it don't feel right to leave her up here alone with only sisters and so scared she might not think of nothing but getting away. She's a sneaky little thing and has been in our camp three nights in a row. I don't know what to do. I'm glad you're here, Ma."

Then, wary of the chicken, he managed to hug his ma. He really was glad to see her.

Ma's eyes shifted between Dave's black eye, the little sneak thief, and the grip he had on her wrist.

She finally settled on Jo. "I have to agree with my son, Joe." She paused. "Joe is no proper name for a girl. Is it JoAnne? Joan? Jolene?"

Jo shrugged. "No."

Dave's shoulders slumped. "That's mostly all she says. Though she did mention sisters at one point. I hope you enjoy questions because it'll take a powerful lot of them to get much information from little Jo here."

Ma nodded and turned to Jo. "Are you hungry? I can make something to eat. We've been working and riding all night since word reached us Pike was sending men to attack us at dawn."

Ma glanced at Dave. "Your pa is coming fast, driving all the cattle he could round up yesterday, and that's a lot of them. He's hoping the snow falls hard enough to cover the trail. But he's bringing near onto a thousand head and everything that's close to the ranch—and he'd moved most everything in. Anyone who wants to find the trail bad enough can follow a thousand cows."

Nodding, he silently watched Ma find canteens and get a pot of coffee boiling. It was breakfast time after all. Then she began pulling supplies off her horse. Cowhands led pack-horses over and started unloading.

"We'll need shelter. We can put up a tent for now, but where did you plan to build a cabin, Dave? The men might as well get going on it."

A few cows darted into the dense forest that surrounded the open glade.

"That'll take days. For now, comb those cattle out of the woods and ride herd till they're settled. We'll pitch a tent before nightfall." The cowpokes nodded and rode toward the milling herd.

"I'll holler when there's food," Ma called after them. Before long Ma had bacon sizzling.

"How far behind you is Pa?"

Ma shook her head and started a griddle heating, then whipped up flapjacks. She glanced at Dave, and he could see his steady ma looked near tears. "I just don't know, son. He was packing everything he could load on horseback. The old fool may get himself killed if he is determined to save too much. And if he waits long enough tracks will show in the snow, then he'll give us all away. But abandoning the ranch was like a knife in the gut. I couldn't convince him to abandon anything else."

Shaking his head, Dave said, "The pass—that mean, winding, tight pass about halfway up—has a good overlook. We can hold off a hundred men with a few armed sentries. I'll post two men, and if we hear gunfire, the rest of us can come a-runnin'."

Dave barked out a few orders, and two of the men rode for the trailhead.

The cows kept flooding in. His wide green valley was filling up fast. "Ma, you know I'll do anything, give anything, even my own life to keep you safe, but I don't have room in this valley for a thousand head of cows."

"I know, Dave. I know." Ma turned to give Jo a sharp-eyed look. "Jo, how old are you?"

Dave wondered if Ma might sneak a question past the quiet woman, who still tugged against his grip pretty much constantly.

"I don't rightly know. Twentysomething, I think. I sorta lost track."

A whole string of sentences. Dave was impressed.

"And do you see that my son means you no harm? He has a firm grip on you, and honestly, if he'd wanted to hurt you, he could have by now."

Jo looked down at her wrist, then up at Dave, not looking like she was feeling safe.

"How long have you lived up here?"

Jo scrunched her nose up when she looked at Ma as if the question made not a lick of sense.

"I've always lived up here, uh . . . ma'am."

"Call me Ma."

That got Dave's attention. No one called her Ma but him.

"I only 'member the littlest things about my own ma. She died when I was about . . . five or so. It don't seem right to call someone else Ma."

"Just do it." Ma's voice left no room for discussion.

"Yes, Ma."

"And are you a woman of your word?"

"Whazzat mean, M-Ma?" She sounded as if *Ma* could barely pass through her throat.

"It means if I ask you to do something and you say you will, can I trust you? Or will you say anything to get Dave to let loose of you and then run for the woods in those . . ." Ma's eyes slid down Jo's body. ". . . in those dreadful trousers."

"Don't rightly know about saying anything, but if I say something, I'll do it. We live by the Good Books up here, and I'll be keeping to them."

Dave shook her arm gently, and said quietly, "'Thou shalt not steal.'"

Ma flipped flapjacks and bacon, crouching by the fire. "Good Books? Book*s*? There's only one book that's called the Good Book."

"Then we're mighty lucky we got two of 'em. Them's the only books we got."

Dave flinched at her heavy accent and strange slurred way of speaking. He sort of wished she'd go back to just saying no. "The part that says not to bear false witness, which I take to be lying, is right next to the part where it says 'thou shalt not steal.' I don't think we can trust her, Ma."

"I didn't steal the cup."

Dave decided to hold on to her anyway.

Ma started putting the hot cakes on a plate and hollered, "Come and get it!"

Dave stepped back as the men came. Ma flipped, emptied the griddle, added more batter, flipped again. She kept shoveling out flapjacks as the men grabbed plates. Somehow Ma had butter and jam to spread. The woman really had packed up the whole house.

She fed them, cooking so fast her hands were nearly a blur. The men ate a couple of big stacks of cakes each. Then they headed back to work as Ma thrust a plate into Dave's hand.

"I don't reckon I can eat and hang on to her at the same time." Dave frowned at Jo, for the first time seriously tempted to let loose. His ma's flapjacks were his favorite.

"You sit here beside me." Ma handed a tin plate to Jo. "I'm watching you, so don't run off. Dave, you sit on the other side of her."

Ma patted Jo on the shoulder. "Much as it pains me to admit it . . . I don't think we can trust you. But if you get one bite of these flapjacks, I think you'll sit down and finish them, so Dave can let go for a while."

More cows poured in, they just kept coming and coming. More hands arrived. But it looked like they'd be awhile dismounting, so Ma filled a plate for herself and took this chance to eat.

Dave wanted his flapjacks bad, so he guided Jo to the spot Ma had pointed to and plunked her down just as Ma handed Jo a fork. Jo glared at Dave, ignored the fork, and picked up a pancake in one hand . . . one really dirty hand . . . and took a bite.

Her eyes went wide as she chewed. "What is this?"

Ma's food had taken Jo prisoner.

4

Jo had a faint memory of food something like this. Grandma died when she was eight. She remembered Grandma making food with this dry, powdery white stuff that looked like snow . . . flour. She and her sisters ground wheat and corn and called it flour, but it was coarse, nothing like this. The lady . . . Ma . . . would tell her what she was eating, but it went against so much of her training to talk easily with strangers.

Jo didn't know what question she'd ask anyway.

Instead she ate. She'd been awhile since last eating. They usually ate in the morning and at night, though Ursula said a middle of the day meal was proper, too. But Jo was usually out hunting and heaven knew what Ilsa got up to.

Ma added eggs and milk to the fine flour. Jo knew those because they had chickens and a few gentle milk cows. When Grandpa died, he'd had a bull and a few cows to provide them with milk. Now the herd had grown a bit, but they were pets. Nothing like this huge herd of spooky, galloping critters.

Jo could hunt and dress a deer faster'n wildfire, so she

could probably butcher a cow, too. It couldn't be much different than a deer, only heavier. But she'd gotten attached to their cows, so she didn't want to eat them. They had chickens, and Jo felt no such attachment to them. Between milk and eggs, and a chicken now and then for the pot, a good-sized garden, wild berries, nuts, the roots they dug that Grandpa had called Indian potatoes and such, and the food Jo hunted, they had aplenty.

She gulped down the . . . what had Ma called them? Flapjacks? Strange word. Flap like wings.

Now, how would she get away from here? And how had Dave Warden Boss caught her? Ilsa was better in the woods, but Jo was almighty good. She was shocked that he'd walked right up behind her and grabbed her.

And she thought *she* was as silent as a ghost.

Ma sat down beside her with her own plate and fork in hand.

It was odd having an older woman around. Well, what about this wasn't odd?

"Dave's father and I have brought more cattle up to this highland than this pasture can feed."

Jo didn't know much about that. The cows seemed to be happy.

Ma smiled. "It occurred to me that you know this land, don't you?"

The spark in Jo's chest might be the sin of pride. She'd heard of that one. "I reckon I know this land better than anyone alive, save the animals. Well, and maybe my sister Ilsa."

Jo seemed to be just chirping away like a little bird. Having strangers to talk to was so interesting. Her true besetting sin, Grandpa used to say, was curiosity.

"Do you know where there are other open, grassy fields like this one?"

Jo felt Dave—that's what his Ma called him so she reckoned she would, too—jerk up straight so suddenly it was like he'd sat down on a sharp rock.

Ma swept her hand, still holding the fork, at that ever-growing herd. "If we don't find more grass, these cows will eat all of this and then go hungry."

"It grows back." Jo was surprised Ma hadn't noticed that.

A smile bloomed on Ma's face as if she found Jo's news about grass funny. "It does, but I'm afraid there are too many cows. It can't grow back fast enough. Dave and his pa and several of the hired men have been up here exploring, though clearly they didn't look around nearly enough because they never saw you. The trail up here is a fierce one the cows can barely climb. When they got up here and saw this open meadow, they didn't scout much beyond this area. They didn't find other open meadows. Do you know of any?"

Jo hadn't let up on her eating, but with Ma looking at her all hopeful-like and Dave paying such close attention, she felt a sweep of that pride again. "I do know other places, plenty of 'em, some hard to get to, but they're here."

"Can you guide us there? Show us? We'd be grateful, and in return, well, I can . . ." Ma seemed to be at a loss. Then she focused on Jo's eating. "I can teach you how to make flapjacks and leave plenty of flour and eggs for you."

Jo took another bite of flapjacks. "How much is plenty?"

Ma smiled wide. "You really need me, Jo. Don't you?"

"I take good care of myself, but I think I need you if I'm going to make flapjacks." Jo frowned over the misty memories. "My grandma used to make such as this, though she called them something else."

"So, you'll show us the pastures, and I'll teach you to make flapjacks. I've heard them called hot cakes and pancakes."

"*Pandekage* . . . I think that was it." She mulled over the word. "The *pan* part sounds right. *Pandekage* . . . pancake . . . that's enough like pancakes to be right."

"Would you show us the grassland then?" Ma asked with a sweet voice and yet a strange, intent look in her eyes, as if finding that grass was terribly important.

"I don't like having you take over this highland. Your cows are bound to scare the deer." Not to mention scare Ursula. "But now that you're here, I don't think it's right to let your cows go hungry when there's plenty of grass. Sure, I reckon I'll show you."

Dave stood, swiftly, gracefully, his plate empty and his expression excited. "Can we go now?"

Ma stood more slowly and went back to her cooking. "Not quite yet, Dave. I won't leave here until I see your pa. Surely, he'll be along soon. The cows have to be almost all here—the hired men are. Of course, my husband would insist on bringing up the rear, but he's got to be coming soon."

The cattle numbers had slowed. They were still moving fast, but they weren't bursting out of the woods as often. A few seconds passed between each of them. Snow clung to them, so they must be coming up through a storm that hadn't reached this height. Jo had stood on the top of her mountain many times and seen clouds and rain below her, just as sometimes there were storms up here, and she'd look down from a snow-packed spot to see green grass below. She'd even looked down that trail and wondered what was down there.

Now she knew. People and horses and lots of cows.

"Why is he taking so long?" Ma muttered, and Jo heard the worry and affection in her voice. Her grandparents had fussed at each other sometimes, though not with quite so much affection. Still, she'd heard Grandma's complaints as a way of showing she cared what Grandpa was doing, and it made Jo ache inside and feel lonelier than she ever had.

Was she so interested in people because she was lonely? How could that be when she had her sisters?

Finally a big black stallion vaulted out of the trees. It was moving too fast. Jo saw a man slumped over the horse's neck. The big animal seemed almost to be running away, charging across the valley straight for their camp.

Ma cried out.

Dave started running for the horse. "Whoa. Midnight, whoa."

The horse's head came up and saw Dave. It slowed.

Jo saw red dripping down the man's arm, where it dangled, limp. The man slumped so far forward his head almost reached the horse's neck.

The horse, which seemed to be running wild, slowed more and broke into a slower pace, which juggled the man around. Ma cried out in fear. Dave dashed with speed so fleet it put Jo in mind of a deer.

The horse dropped to a walk. How had the man, who looked unconscious, hung on?

Dave reached him and caught hold. Ma ran toward the man, too. Several of the hired men rushed forward. Dave shouted something about the trail, and four of them veered off and raced toward the place the slumped-over man had entered the high valley.

Worriedly watching, Jo saw Dave doing something with the hand not dangling. Ma led the horse onward toward the fire. As they reached it, a string came loose of the man's hand, where it had been tied to the saddle, and he slumped sideways into Dave's arms.

Dave eased him onto the ground as Ma led the horse a safe distance away. Jo saw all the blood and wondered how the man could still be alive.

Then he moaned and tossed his head. Dave and Ma knelt beside him, and only one possible thing, a terrible thing, came into Jo's head.

A thing she really hated to do.

A thing she really had to do.

She took off running for the woods.

5

T hink I got away clean." Quillon Warden's groggy voice didn't sound that clean. "Long way behind." He gasped for breath. "Saw men coming. Th-they got a bullet into me. Snow's heavy, wind howling down there. R-rode away from the trail and circled back. H-hope my trail is covered."

Dave pulled off Pa's shirt, then his woolen undershirt. His whole side was soaked in blood. Ma brought hot water and began washing the blood away so they could see the wound.

"I told you to get away, Quill." She leaned down and rested her lips on his forehead for a long, shaking moment. "Why'd you have to bring so much? We can rebuild anything as long as we are alive to do it, you old coot."

"Sorry, Izzy girl. I'm here now."

"I've staked men at the top of the trail to keep watch for anyone coming after you, Pa." Dave saw the bullet wound in Pa's belly and felt gutshot himself.

"I'll get bandages." Ma leapt to her feet, took one step toward the mountain of supplies the men had unloaded from the packhorses, and stopped.

"She's gone."

Dave, still on his knees, whirled around. He scowled at the spot where Jo had been. He should've never let loose of her wrist. But he hadn't had much choice.

"Well, she said there was other grass up here. She may not be willing to show it to us. But if it's here, we'll find it." Ma brought bandages back, sounding downright grouchy. As a rule, Ma was a kindhearted woman. But it didn't set right with her to trust someone and have that trust betrayed. Dave didn't feel betrayed because he'd expected her to run off first chance she got.

Strangely, he was a little disappointed though . . . that she'd seen a man shot and used that distraction to run. It didn't speak well of her character. And he was still worried about her. A woman up here alone couldn't survive. Now he was going to have to hunt her down.

She'd sure liked those flapjacks. Maybe he'd take a plate of them and set them out to bait a trap for the half-wild woman.

He turned back to his wounded pa, fearing the worst.

Jo slammed into the house, gasping for breath. Ursula leapt out of her chair where she sat reading.

Jo noticed she gripped the big Bible with both hands, like she was prepared to bash someone with it. Jo wasn't real sure if a person oughta whack someone with the Bible, but Ursula had little fight in her, only fear.

"There are people in the lower meadow. Lots of people. And cattle." Jo gasped for breath from her long desperate run.

"You saw people?" Ursula's eyes went wide. Her grip on

the Bible tightened till her knuckles turned white. Ursula was the image of Grandma, except younger of course. She had white blond hair from Grandma's Danish blood. Blue eyes, and tall. She'd've been a Valkyrie if she'd lived a hundred years ago. A woman warrior. Or so Grandma said of herself and Ursula. Maybe Grandma would've been, but there was nothing warrior-like about Ursula. She'd taken all of Grandma's dire warnings to heart, and people invading their highland home terrified her.

Jo was cut on smaller lines like Ma, the same coloring as Ursula except her hair was more yellow than white, but Ursula was almost a head taller than Jo.

"I talked to them." Jo might've kept silent about it except she couldn't see how to do that and get Ilsa to help.

Ursula held the Bible up to cover her mouth. From behind it she said, "No, Jo, you shouldn't have."

"One of them, he was named Dave, caught me. He sneaked right up on me from behind while I was watching them from the woods."

"Someone sneaked up on you?" There was stunned horror in Ursula's voice, and Jo knew just how she felt. "Are they following you now?"

"No, I escaped." She remembered how Dave had talked, as if . . . as if he was worried about her living out here alone. What was there to worry about in that? She was a lot safer here than down where there were people. "But I have to go back. I came running because one of them is hurt. I need Ilsa."

"What?" Ursula set the Bible down firmly on the table and strode straight at Jo. "No, you can't take her and expose her to them. She'll die. You'll both die."

Jo stepped out the door and yelled, "Ilsa! Ilsa, I need help."

She hoped her sister was close enough to hear. It was a long stretch of minutes. Ursula didn't come out. She was no doubt hiding under the bed.

Then, so suddenly Jo found a smile, Ilsa swung out of the thick trees on a long vine made of woven roots—Ilsa had them strung all over in the treetops. She waited until the rope was low and dropped lightly to the ground.

"What's wrong?" Ilsa was dressed in leather much like Jo. All their fabric and all their clothes had worn out years ago, and they'd made coats and clothes from buckskin. Grandpa had taught them how.

Ilsa had dark hair that danced and curled as if it had a joyful spirit all its own. Black Irish, Grandpa said. Dark hair and shining blue eyes. She'd been so young when Ma and Pa disappeared, and still young when Grandma died. Grandpa had no idea what to do with such a youngster. Ursula took over the care of her and was her mother in most ways. But Ursula had been young, too. She had no idea how to be a mother. So, between her and Jo, they'd let their little sister run wild in the woods until she was more animal than human, but in a beautiful way Jo loved.

And Ilsa had a touch with healing. She'd learned it from Grandpa, who'd learned it from native folks, he'd said. And Grandpa had been ailing the last stretch of his life, so Ilsa had done a lot of doctoring.

Ilsa's eyes slid past Jo. Jo turned to see Ursula in the door, angry, frightened, standing at her full height, and glaring at Jo to beat all.

"Ilsa, someone's hurt."

"Some*one*?" Ilsa blinked those huge, bright eyes. "Those men who were hunting all over up here came back?"

"You knew they'd been up here?" Jo couldn't believe she'd missed them.

"Yes, they came a few times, but they never found the pass into the canyon where we live."

"Well, now there are a whole bunch of men, and a woman, in that big valley close to that steep trail down to the lowlands. One of them is bad hurt. He needs help, Ilsa. All I could think of was you, and your way with healing."

"Men?" Ilsa seemed frozen, and she rarely stood still. "And a woman? It's not Mama and Papa come home is it?"

Ma and Pa had ridden away near twenty years ago. It struck hard at Jo's heart to think Ilsa might still believe they'd return someday.

"No, but they seemed nice. And they need help. We've got to go."

A shy smile bloomed on Ilsa's face, and she whirled and laughed her musical laughter. "I want to see them. I'll come."

She flew in long, graceful strides toward a tree and vanished up into the high limbs.

"No, Ilsa, come back." Ursula rushed forward.

Jo threw herself between Ilsa and Ursula. "We have to help. It's like the 'Prodigal Son,' Ursula. We can't be safe here while someone, even someone we don't know or like, is hurt."

"That's the 'Good Samaritan,' not the 'Prodigal Son.'"

Jo had to admit she got several of the stories mixed up, and it was even more confusing trying to apply them to her life, especially when she barely knew what a son was, let alone a prodigal one.

"Come with us. Come and meet them." Jo rested her right hand on her left wrist and could almost feel Dave hanging on to her. With a little shiver of excitement, she wondered if he'd take her prisoner again. That didn't worry her. She could probably escape as easily as she had this time. And if Ilsa wanted to vanish, she could. It was surprising how hard that girl was to pin down.

"I'll go nowhere near them. They're dangerous." Ursula clamped her arms across her chest as if she were trying to hold herself together.

"They are so interesting. You have to come and meet them. How can you resist?"

Ursula snorted. "Easily enough."

"I've got to go. I can't let Ilsa go in there without me." Jo didn't want to be scolded anymore. And she didn't want to see the fear on Ursula's face and feel it washing all over the cabin, soaking Jo in it.

"We'll be careful." She dashed away, afraid Ursula might grab her and hang on. If she got taken prisoner for the second time in one day—God forgive her—she wanted it to be by Dave.

"Will you look at that." Ma's whisper brought Dave's head around.

He saw another woman, this one nothing like Jo, come running out of the woods. She moved more gracefully than anything he'd ever seen. Running fast as a deer, so light on her feet she didn't seem real, more like a magical creature. She was a little sprite of a thing, her black hair, curly and wild in the wind, flying behind her.

She had a bag of some kind hung around her neck and under one arm. It was large and leather. Just like her clothes.

She had eyes alight with concern, focused on Pa, who lay there awake only part of the time. Dave had a sudden chill of fear, as if some spell was being cast. He had a strong impulse to throw himself between this woman and his father.

The woman reached Dave and halted, worry and a quiet, powerful sense of determination in her eyes.

"I've come to help the man who was hurt." She stood as if she'd wait forever, and impatiently because she wanted to help right now.

Dave knew she could only be one person. "Are you Jo's sister?"

"Yes, she came for me and will be here soon. She knows I have healing hands."

Dave exchanged a worried look with his ma.

Ma had her eyes pinned on the newcomer for long seconds before she nodded. "Come and see. He's . . . he's b- bleeding . . ." Ma's voice broke.

The fairy woman ignored Ma, dodged around Dave, and knelt beside Pa. She muttered words Dave couldn't hear.

"What?" Had she asked for something?

"I pray as I work. God guides my hands as surely as He guided this man to me for healing."

Dave had some serious doubts about God letting Pa be shot just so he could give this woman a chance at doctoring, but maybe he'd been daydreaming when Ma read that part of the Bible to them at night.

The woman eased the bandage aside, then slapped it back in place. She looked at Ma. "I've a potion to ease the pain and slow the bleeding. Get a cup of hot water. My potion needs to steep, and we want him to drink it warm. Now. Quickly."

For a fairy woman, she had a bit of the tyrant about her, and Ma obeyed right quick.

"Tell me what you're doing." Dave didn't know if he could stand by while a complete stranger . . . and he'd have to admit the emphasis there was on *strange* . . . poured who-knew-what down his pa's throat.

The woman knelt close to Pa's head with Dave beside her near Pa's knees. She turned to look Dave in the eye, and the gaze hit him right in the gut. Her eyes were so blue against the dark hair, and there was an untamed quality to her that reminded him of Jo, but there was no other resemblance.

"Jo said she lives up here with her sisters. But I can hardly imagine women living alone up here. You're not safe."

A sweet smile lit up the woman's face. "Where is it safe? Didn't you just come from the deadly outside world? The world that killed my parents? I think I am safe and you live where there is danger and death. And we've done it and survived for years. I've lived with my sisters ever since my Grandpa died."

"How long ago was that?"

"We talk of this while your father bleeds? Is that really your wish?"

Shaking his head, Dave said, "You're right. I'm sorry."

Ma came then with a tin cup nearly full of hot water. "What's your name?"

"Ilsa. Ilsa Nordegren." Ilsa took the cup and pulled some crushed leaves and grass from her bag. She poured it into

46

the water and covered the cup with her hand and shook for a long minute.

Dave wondered how long it'd been since the wild woman had washed her hands.

Ilsa quit shaking, handed the cup to Dave. "Hold this while it steeps. It's hot. Have a care."

Then Ilsa removed the bandage and pulled a wickedly sharp knife from the waistband of her strange leather trousers. She rose from Pa's side and took the knife to the blazing fire and held it to the flames until the blade glowed red.

"My grandpa said this will stop the wound from suppurating," Ilsa explained.

There was a hole in Pa's belly, off to the side, and no exit wound. Dave figured it was going to be up to him to cut that bullet out and hope nothing life-and-death happened during his ham-handed surgery. Ma's hands were shaking too hard to be trusted with the chore.

As Ilsa approached Pa and knelt again, she reached that hot blade right for him, and Dave's hand whipped out and snatched her wrist away. He'd been holding her sister just like this not so long ago.

Ilsa gave him a strange smile. Not annoyed, and Dave knew he'd be annoyed if he was doing something important and someone stopped him. Ilsa was given to smiling at everything, it seemed.

In her eyes was something deep, as if she looked right inside him and willed him to be calm, to be strong.

"I know what I'm doing."

"You have a lot of people get shot up here?"

"No. But they bleed from time to time. And Grandpa taught me the ways of healing."

Dave decided not to ask more questions. Pa was in a bad way. Every man in the West knew that when you were gut-shot, you were done. This wasn't right in the middle of his belly, but it looked bad to Dave . . . and since he was scared to death and had no idea what to do, he decided to let Ilsa have a free hand . . . with him inches away, ready to grab her.

Ilsa, razor-sharp knife in hand, leaned over Pa in such a way she blocked Dave's view of what she was doing. Seconds passed as Dave shifted his position to watch. A metallic scratch set Dave's teeth on edge. Quick as a wink, she handed him a blood-soaked bullet. Then she laid the flat side of the knife against the wound and a terrible burning smell and a hiss made Dave's stomach twist. Ilsa sheathed her knife. Dave noticed it was very thin, so thin it was barely wider than the bullet wound. Next, she pulled something out of that bag, a green pad of something that looked like weeds, and pressed it to the wound.

"It wasn't deep. Leave this packing in place all day." She thrust more of the green something into Dave's hands. "Tonight, before he sleeps, take out the old packing and replace it. For the rest of the day, bind it tight and keep pressure on it to stop the bleeding, though the burn should seal it, and my healing herbs should soothe the pain and prevent suppuration."

Dave studied what he held in his hand. Healing herbs? He recognized moss, but there was more than that. Grass or weeds or leaves . . . who knew?

"Strain the potion and make him drink the liquid." She

thrust a small leather pouch into Dave's hands. "Give him this drink again in a few hours, then again at night, and in the morning. Get him to drink water. I'll be back."

Ilsa was up with that same magical grace. Before Dave realized she wasn't just getting off her knees, she ran straight for the woods, black curls dancing. He leapt up.

"Dave, let her go," Ma shouted. More quietly she said, "I believe her. She'll be back."

Jo emerged from the woods. He was struck that there *was* a resemblance between them. Their coloring was so different he'd've never thought of them as sisters, but they were both slender and graceful. Ilsa was about an inch shorter, but they were both on the short side and cut along the same lithe, delicate lines.

Both so beautiful it almost hurt to look at them, but Ilsa seemed young, almost childlike. Except, did a child operate on a man?

She was nothing like Jo's full-grown womanhood.

The two seemed to be in their own little world, talking and smiling.

Then Ilsa ran off, and Jo came toward him. He noticed she wore a quiver of arrows as well as a bow. The two crossed on her chest.

"Dave, your father's awake."

He didn't want to look away from Jo, but at those words he twirled around to see Pa talking quietly with Ma. He rushed back and knelt at his father's side again.

Ma stood and said, "He seems stable. Weak, but if he doesn't get that wound infected, he'll heal. Ilsa said so and I believe her. Now I need to have a word with the men."

Ma strode to Pa's horse. One of the hands had staked out the horse nearby and left it to graze still saddled and bridled. Ma, stout and of a goodly age, swung up on that horse without any effort. She kicked the horse into a gallop before Dave could ask her what she wanted with the men.

Jo reached Dave's side and dropped down beside Pa. "Ilsa said your papa is on the mend. She said he'd been shot. Grandpa had a gun, so I know what that is. Though I don't use the gun ever. I didn't even wait to see just what was wrong with him before I ran for her."

She'd run, but not away. She'd run for help.

Something huge shifted in Dave's gut, or maybe a bit higher, maybe in his heart.

6

Ilsa is the best healer. Grandpa passed down many things he'd learned from Native folks who knew plants with healing power. And she learned from Grandma, who was the finest at prayer. The combination has kept all of us healthy. We all learned, but Ilsa has a rare gift."

Jo pointed at Dave's mother. "What is Ma doing?"

Dave looked up from Jo and saw a general on the battlefield, only apparently it was a war she was fighting with building a shelter. Though men would still be standing guard over the trail with others minding the still-unsettled herd, a few went to chopping trees. Soon they were dragging in logs to a spot Ma pointed to.

"I think she's determined to get a roof over Pa's head before nightfall."

"She and your men can build a cabin in a single day?"

Dave shrugged. "Maybe a lean-to. In fact, look at her, she's pointing this way. I think she might build a small cabin right here beside Pa. I hope she doesn't try to build it right over our heads. We might be hit with a falling log."

"My cabin is too far to move him, or you could come there."

Dave looked away from his mother. "You're ready now to tell me where you live? And let me meet your sisters?"

"You just met one of them. The other, Ursula, is shy of people. She learned it at Grandma's knee, and she's taken it to heart. As nervous as a rabbit in a wolf's den. If I bring you there, she might leave, hide until you're gone. But if you're planning to live up here, she'll have to get used to you." Jo frowned. "I hope she can do it."

A groan drew Jo's attention to the wounded man. His eyes flickered open, but they seemed dazed. And why not?

Dave asked, "Will you help me bandage the wound? Ilsa told me and Ma to do it, but she's busy."

"Yes, where are your bandages?"

"Stay here with him, and I'll dig them out of the pack. Ma has the healing supplies out so I'll just be a minute." He left her, went straight for a large bag, and began searching.

A hard hand gripped her wrist. She turned to see . . . well, she supposed his name was destined to be Pa, but she hesitated to say it. She most certainly had not been invited to, as she had with Ma.

"You've been shot. We believe you'll be all right, and we're going to bandage the wound now."

Pa Warden held on to her in a way that reminded her of Dave. An iron grip might run in their family. Like Ursula being built like Grandma, and Ilsa having their ma's dark hair.

"Where have you come from? And . . . w-wasn't there another strange woman here a bit ago? I woke up for a moment, or maybe not. Maybe I dreamed—"

Something swept over her, like the washing at the edge

of a pond. This older man with the strong grip. Ma taking charge, bringing order. Dave's kind eyes and his worry for her and his father. It was a family. It all reminded her so much of how it'd been with Grandma and Grandpa. And later with only Grandpa. Well, he'd protected them and kept them fed, but there'd been no softness from that gruff old man. Grandma hadn't been all that soft, either, but she'd brought out a gentler side of Grandpa. That side had been buried with Grandma.

Talking to Dave's pa, and earlier to his ma, seeing how they loved each other. The hope of it, the fullness of it, swept over her until she could barely speak for her throat choking up. But that was nonsense. She was used to this high mountain life. She loved the freedom, and though she wanted a new tin cup, beyond that she wanted no part of the outside world.

She told herself that, but a part of her had to wonder if her thoughts carried truth. This family drew her like little else ever had. A ma and pa. What a wonderful thing that would be. She cleared her throat and brushed aside the strange urge to cry.

Resting her hand over his—the one gripping her—wanting to feel the strength, Jo said, "Th-there was another woman." She had to clear her throat again to go on. "You saw my sister. She has healing ways, and I brought her to help you. We call her our medicine woman. We live up here. You've brought your cattle to our backyard."

Dave's head came up when he heard them talking, and he came back fast. "Pa, you're awake."

There was such love and concern in Dave's voice, Jo felt a burn in her eyes. Tears? She never cried. She suspected the last time had been when Grandma died. By the time

Grandpa went to heaven, she'd learned to control all the nonsense of her tears.

Crouching beside his father and across from Jo, Dave said, "We need to wrap that gunshot wound."

Pa's teeth clenched as he nodded. "Tell me more, young lady. It takes my mind off the pain."

Pa struck Jo as a very tough man. He probably dealt well with pain. She wondered if he was just snooping around in her life like a wolf on the scent. But if it would please him to hear her talk, she'd talk.

"Um . . . we have been living up here all our lives. My grandma especially had a fear of the outside world. She said the lowlands were dangerous with disease and evil men. Grandma told stories of those from the lowlands she'd lost to death, but I can't remember who all. They were old stories. She quit telling them, but only reminded us of the danger. She might have—" Jo's eyes narrowed as she tried to remember, then shrugged. "I haven't heard those stories for years. Then she and Grandpa moved up here, where it was safe."

"There is danger all over, girl. I'm in your highlands right now and carrying a bullet."

Dave passed the strip of cloth under his pa's back, caught it, and drew it over the wound. He repeated this, winding the cloth several times.

Pa let a faint moan escape his lips, then clamped them shut. Jo leaned forward and brushed his hair back. It wasn't solid gray like Grandpa's. If this was Dave's father, then this man would be more of an age with her own father, rather than Grandpa. She angled her head so she could look him in the eye and block his view of Dave's doctoring.

Then she smiled. "I'd as soon say that is proof of the low-land danger, since you brought the bullet with you."

Pa grunted, maybe in annoyance at her answer. Maybe in pain. "The point, girl, is that life can't be lived with no risk. Say, what's your name anyway? I shouldn't keep call-ing you *girl*."

Her smile widened. "Call me Jo. And your name?"

Dave shifted his pa again, working on the bandage.

"I'm Quill Warden." A short, hard gasp was quickly con-cealed. "I own the Circle Dash Ranch straight down this mountain a far piece. My brand is on every cow and horse in this meadow."

Jo looked, and sure enough the nearest cow had a circle on its hip with a downward dash slanted on the bottom right corner.

Dave bandaged. Quill groaned. Dave's brow showed deep furrows of regret.

"Welcome to my home, Quill Warden." Jo forged on, trying to distract Quill. "And I agree that no place can be perfect. My grandpa always said there was nowhere all the way safe this side of heaven. My home is a land of grizzlies and blizzards, cliffs, lightning storms, and mountain lions. But he wanted his family to avoid risk, and he thought up here was best."

"Your home?" Quill's rather bushy eyebrows arched in surprise. "I was up here with my son scouting. How come we never saw you?"

Jo shook her head. "We have a cabin tucked in a canyon with a tight entrance, you missed it. And I'm surprised I never saw you. I usually notice what's going on around my home.

Ilsa said she saw you, just now when I went to get her. She hadn't told us before. Did you stay a long time?"

"We came up three times," Dave said. "But we didn't set up camp, just scouted around."

Jo didn't like knowing that. She would've thought she knew everything that went on atop this mountain.

"How far do you live from here?" Dave ran his sleeve across his brow, tense with worry about his pa. Why would he be? Ilsa had said Quill would be fine. Why wouldn't he trust the word of a medicine woman?

"It's not that far. I ran there to get Ilsa, and I had to talk to Ursula awhile, but Ilsa came straight back. How far is that?"

"Hard to say, and we were looking for open grassland and found this right away. We searched some, but it seemed to be solid forest after this meadow. We knew there was enough lush grass and running water to keep a herd of about two or three hundred head of cattle. We spent most of our time clearing that trail Ma and Pa just rode up. It's meaner'n a rattlesnake."

"We had to knock boulders aside and chisel spots to widen them," Pa said, flinching as he spoke.

Jo glanced at Dave to see him tying off the bandage. Finally done. Jo heaved a sigh of relief.

Dave was so relieved to not be hurting Pa anymore, he sighed until he almost collapsed.

Pa caught his wrist . . . and held on to Jo at the same time. Pa must be feeling pretty good because his grip was like iron.

"It was Wax Mosby, son."

Dave almost toppled off his knees. "You saw him?"

56

"Yep, I didn't see him shooting, and there were two other sidewinders firing. But I was running away from this trail and at the far end of rifle range, and someone skilled hit me. The snow was coming hard, and all I could think was my tracks were going to lead those varmints straight to you and your ma, so I headed away."

Pa's eyes fell shut, and he seemed to gather himself before he could go on.

"I got into the woods, and the snow wasn't gettin' through there yet, so I moved fast to give me enough space that my tracks would soon be covered. I had taken off up a mean slope, because we rode that way first, remember? Trying to find a way up? My tracks were filling in fast. Then I took that trail we found that skirted along the top of the mountain. I followed it until I connected with the trail my cows used. I think I lost 'em."

A chill that had nothing to do with the oncoming snowstorm slid down Dave's spine. "Wax Mosby. There's no one meaner in this whole territory."

Dave noticed Jo patting Pa's hand. Between being shot and finding one of the fastest, most ruthless deadeyes in the West on his trail, Pa probably needed all the comfort he could get.

"It's said he's kin to John Mosby, the one they called the Gray Ghost during the Civil War. And he's like that, slipping around, attacking on the sly, then he vanishes and comes back again from a different direction."

Jo's eyes sharpened. "Vanishes? He's a ghost?"

Dave didn't want to frighten her, but if there was danger coming, she needed to know. "No, not a ghost, he's a very skilled woodsman and tracker. It's also rumored that someone hung the name on him because he operates like Mosby. I don't know if there's any relation."

"And he's a hired gun for Bludge Pike." Pa's hand tightened on Dave's wrist. "How sure are you that you found the only trail up here? I know we hunted, but if there's another way—a way we're not ready to defend against—it's a sure thing Wax will find it."

Dave's eyes met Jo's. "Do you know of trails down the mountainside?"

Jo was silent, her gaze locked on his. "Grandpa talked of one other way down. He said no horse could make it, but a determined man could pull himself up a few cliffs. Of course, I may not know all the ways off the mountaintop."

"Can you show me?" At this rate Dave was going to have to post all his men as sentries, and he wouldn't get any kind of shelter built before winter closed in.

"I've never been on it."

Dave realized he was patting Pa's hand just like Jo. Maybe Dave needed comfort almost as much as Pa.

"We can go. And it's by a grassland larger than this. You wanted to find more grass." Then Jo's brow lowered. "What Gray Ghost fights in a war? What war?"

Dave shook his head. "When was the last time you heard any news from the outside world?"

Jo frowned. "News? What do you mean? Things are new down there?"

Dave almost smiled. "No, I mean when was the last time you went down the mountain and spoke to another person?"

"I've never gone down the mountain."

"Not once in your whole life?"

"No, and no one's ever come up. Grandma said folks were dangerous down below. That's how my parents died. Grandma warned Mama and Papa long and hard before they left. And they never came back, so she had the right of it. Grandpa went down for supplies, and each time he came back up, he'd camp away from the house for a time, until he was sure he brought no fever with him."

"What if he had gotten sick, who would've doctored him?"

Jo shrugged. "As far as I know he never got sick. Maybe he was careful and stayed well away from feverish folks when he went for supplies. Then Grandma died. Grandpa went on as before, going down for supplies, and left Ursula, Ilsa, and me up here alone. He'd camp away from us just as Grandma wanted, even though she wasn't here to fuss, then he'd come in with the supplies. He did that until the day his joints got to aching too bad to go down. And he'd been teaching us to survive here so we wouldn't need supplies from down below. He brought seed for corn and wheat and taught us how to grow it. We learned what things would grow up here on a mountaintop and how to keep a garden. Toward the end he got . . . confused. He talked to Ursula like she was Grandma. He sometimes didn't remember any of our names, and he spent most days either rocking by the fire or staying in his bed. When he died, it was fearsome to be alone. And sad. We missed him. But we managed. We remembered his teachings, and we remembered the rules he'd set down. The ones we'd already been taught by Grandma. We never went down."

Jo's head came up, and she asked, "Did you bring enough food for everyone here?"

Dave shook his head. "No, we'll have to go—"

Jo moved so suddenly Dave was struck dumb. He watched her whirl to face the nearby woods. She moved with such grace it was nearly a dance, and she moved to the music of the wild. In a single motion, she swept her bow off one shoulder. Her strange clothing floated and fluttered like leaves in the autumn woods. Her muscles rippled with a strength that was shocking in such a fine-boned woman.

In one continuous motion, she drew an arrow from her quiver and sent it flying. She whipped out another and shot, then a third. It was all done in an instant, without hesitation. She was thinking, seeing some threat, acting on it, all faster than Dave could even see what was happening.

Than a loud squeal from the woods drew everyone's attention. The cowhands, Ma, even the horses looked.

A wild boar burst out of the woods with a single arrow in its flank. Jo let fly a fourth arrow and a fifth.

The hog fell dead at the far end of the clearing.

The noise stopped around her. The chopping, the hauling, quiet voices.

"You hit a running boar from fifty yards. He was at least that far away by the time you let the last arrow fly." Dave could still see her whirling, shooting, faster than lightning but so graceful it was like each second unfolded like a perfect picture that he knew he'd always remember. With her bow and arrows, she was so much better than he was with a gun, it pinched his feelings a bit. But being bested didn't pinch hard enough to make him deny what a skilled hunter she was. He would like to watch her move like that for the rest of his life.

He'd never used a bow and arrow, but he might try to learn. He'd enjoy having her teach him.

7

Jo turned back to Dave to see him shake his head.

"You've provided supper for all of us in the twinkling of an eye."

"It'll last longer'n just supper." Jo pointed to the spot she'd originally aimed at. "There are two more I got with my first shots, there in the woods."

"Three?" Pa said. "You got two more in the woods? I can't even see past the trees."

"I heard them and smelled them, knew they were wandering close, knew they were heading away from us. There were five in all, but two were little, spring piglets I reckon. Not a lot of good eatin' on them. Best to let them grow for another season or two. And I had to move fast to get the third one, but it was wounded, weren't no help for it. I had to get him."

"Two more down? And two got away?" Dave looked dazed. "I can't even see them. How do you know you got them?"

"I've got sharp eyes and ears like a nervous jackrabbit."

Jo smiled at Dave, then turned to Pa. "We'll cook pork over a spit, but we'll make sure there's a soup full of tender bits for you. It's easier on your belly."

Jo hung her bow back over her shoulder. She did it so easily that he was sure she never let it get far from her hands.

"I've got to see to the butchering and hope my arrows are in good shape. Saves me making new ones."

She rose to her feet to get to work just as Ma came walking up. "Jo, that's fine shooting."

"I've been feeding my family since before Grandpa died. I reckon that's more'n ten years now. I've learned to hit what I aim at."

As she walked away, she heard a hissed conversation behind her and wondered what the Warden family was on about. Well, if they wanted her to know, they would speak up. She strode toward the boar that had made a run for it.

Dave caught up to her. "I'll dress out the hogs. You stay and talk to Pa. He seems to be taken with you."

Narrowing her eyes, she stopped and crossed her arms. "Taken? Your father has taken something from me? I can't think what. I have my quiver and bows."

Dave smiled, and she forgot every other thought in her head so she could watch that smile.

"It's a saying from the lowland. No, we don't want to take anything. *Taken with*, it means Pa likes you. He thinks you're a fine woman."

"I'll go back then. You'll be awhile with three boars. I'm mighty fast at the butchering, but if you want me to stay with your pa, I will. Maybe you should ask some of these men you brought along to help you."

She turned to go back to her wounded new friend and heard Dave laughing quietly behind her.

"And Dave, have a care with my arrows. It's a lot of work to make new ones."

Now she was sure she heard laughter. She turned to see what was so funny, but he'd headed on toward the closest boars, the two she'd brought down instantly. Two of his men were walking toward him, probably to help with the butchering.

Needing three arrows for that third hog was just plain shameful.

Dave kept moving, laughing a little harder now. She had no idea why, but honestly, she probably didn't want to know.

Ilsa came down out of the trees to help.

Jo had seen her perched up on a branch when she shot the hogs. Ilsa had a way of fading into the leaves. . . . Though most of the leaves had fallen, so now she faded into the branches.

Ilsa watched and learned and finally decided she was needed, so she came down from the tree and tended Quill with her usual almost-miraculous hands.

There were stories of healing in one of their Bibles, and Jo had often wondered if Ilsa had the gift of healing. She was as kind to animals as she was to people. Good grief, she was even gentle with plants. She was a wonder with weaving whip-thin tree branches, woody vines, and sturdy tree roots into ropes she could swing on. And everything she touched healed and thrived.

So much of Grandpa's care had fallen to her when he was ailing. Heaven knew, even at such a young age as Ilsa had been then, she'd had endless practice at doctoring.

Now that Ilsa was here, Jo turned to helping Ma, who was making fried pork for dinner. Jo felt a spark of pride that she'd helped provide the meal, something she did for her family.

Ma had several skillets. She said she'd brought everything from the bunkhouse. Jo didn't know what that was, but she could only guess it was a house where they stored a lot of pans.

Together, they cooked a mountain of meat for the hands and potatoes that were different from the Indian potatoes that grew up here, but very tasty.

Jo ate while Ilsa checked the bandage. She didn't change it. She seemed satisfied with how Quill was doing. She talked quietly with Quill and sent up prayers to heaven as she worked. Jo should leave with Ilsa when she headed for home. Jo didn't *want* to, but she should.

The sun set on the short fall day, and quietly, snow sifted down as the moon rose.

The cowboys finished knocking together a shelter as the night turned cool. Pa was gently moved into the small building by Dave and one of his hired men. The little building was about the size of the milk cow's stall in their little barn and had no fireplace. But it had room enough for Ma and Quill to sleep side by side.

Getting her husband under cover for the night had been Ma's first priority, so the men had stopped everything else.

Then they made a strange building of cloth. Jo heard it called a tent, and they hauled their things inside. Maybe even these tough cowboys had no love for sleeping in the snow.

Jo's curiosity over how they'd build a house had kept her nearby, though that wasn't as important as Quill. Talking to him really seemed to help him. The man was in pain and struggling not to show it . . . which probably made the pain even worse.

And it wasn't as important as Ma. Jo reveled under her kind words and gentle hands. She hadn't realized quite how much she'd missed by not having a mother. And it made her ache for the loss of even her grandma's gruff scolding.

Add to that, she was fascinated by Dave's deep voice and strong arms, the way he worked hard and talked with the other men. She hung on every word.

Then there was Ma's good cooking.

Altogether, Jo hadn't been able to leave. It was well after dark, and now she had to go home.

As Ilsa stood, Jo rose with her. The clothes she'd made so carefully to conceal herself in the woodlands danced and fluttered in the cool fall breeze. She swayed with exhaustion as she realized she'd stayed out all night last night, been very busy all day, and was now nearly falling asleep on her feet.

Dave was at her side instantly and caught her arm to steady her. Had she really looked like she was near collapse?

"I'll ride home with you."

Ilsa arched a brow. In the firelight, Jo could clearly see her confusion. "Why would you do that?"

"Because it's not safe in the woods."

Ilsa looked at Jo.

Jo shrugged and asked, "What danger is there?"

Dave didn't seem to understand the question. "It's night in a deep woods in the wilderness, and you're two women alone."

Which was no answer.

"I've been known to wander the woods at night," Jo said. Many, many nights. Most nights. "I like it. Many animals are night critters. If I want to see them and learn their ways, I have to be out at night."

"It's not safe. Just because you haven't gotten hurt so far doesn't mean you should do it." Dave's voice rose with every word.

"I do it all the time. And here I stand, unharmed. Yes, there might be dangerous animals, but mostly they run away from me." She wished they wouldn't. "I have to be very quiet and sly to get close to a lion or a grizzly. I've gotten near enough to touch them, but when I do, they always run."

Dave's hand clamped hard on the top of his hat as if it were threatening to blow away. "You touched a grizzly?"

He came closer, and he was already very close. "That's dangerous. You can't get that close."

"I just said I *have* gotten that close. No harm has come to me." It was probably men she shouldn't get close to.

Out of the corner of her eye she saw Ilsa drift away, slide into the woods. Here was Dave trying to protect them both, and now, because of his kindhearted fussing, Jo would be walking home alone instead of in company with someone. Ilsa vanished, became part of the forest. Jo almost caught her breath with envy. Ilsa had such grace that her movements rarely caught the eye. She moved with such silence that once she vanished, it was nearly impossible to find her. Jo and her sisters had played hide-and-seek in the woods all their lives. Ilsa had mastered both hiding and seeking. Jo had, too, but she didn't have Ilsa's skill. Ursula wasn't nearly as good as Ilsa and Jo, but she was still very good.

"I have to go. Do not come with me. Ilsa is already gone, but I'll catch up to her quickly. If there is any danger, we'll handle it, though I can't imagine what danger there could be. I've lived in these woodlands all my life. They are my haven and pose no risk."

Dave seemed frozen with doubt. She turned and walked away quickly, hoping he didn't thaw and come after her. Then he'd have to walk back through the woods to get here to his camp. And she'd probably have to follow him to make sure he didn't get lost in unfamiliar land, and if he caught her following, he might think he needed to walk back to her cabin with her. And then she'd need to follow him again.

Honestly, she was very tired. She just didn't have the energy for it.

As she drifted . . . no, wafted after Ilsa, she called behind her, "I'll be back."

He let her go, and she was a bit surprised. Now she'd go home and face Ursula, who would be half-mad making up things to fret about.

Maybe all that worry would make Ursula as tired as Jo, and they could set aside any squabbling. Jo hoped so, because dangerous as it was, she was not giving up this chance to see other people and learn about them.

Ursula would be terrified for her, for all of them. But Jo would do it anyway.

She was going to show Dave the highland meadow. It was well hidden.

How upset could Ursula be anyway? What in the world could she say? Nothing. And that was final. There was nothing Ursula could say that would stop her.

8

"If you spend time with those lowland invaders, you'll die." Ursula's arms flew wide, and she slapped the wall behind her hard. She'd been stepping away as she listened to Jo's tale of the interesting new people that had come to their mountain.

Honestly, the threat of death should have stopped her, but Jo wasn't even a bit discouraged.

"And you'll bring death home so Ilsa and I will die. Is your curiosity worth the lives of our whole family?"

Jo knew her sister was scared, but she was just going to have to get over that. "Now, Ursula—"

Her big sister charged right up until their faces almost touched. Ursula was a lot taller than Jo. She could really loom over a person. Jo's mind scrambled thinking of what would calm Ursula down. Not much.

"You have to stay away from them. Do you want to die? Grandma and Grandpa wanted us to live. And now our home is being invaded, and those invaders will bring death."

"Ursula, please." Jo rested both hands on Ursula's upper arms, holding firmly, hoping the grip would reach through her sister's fears. "We can't stop them from coming. We have no way to do it."

Ilsa sat at the table, not part of this argument. Withdrawn, apart from the whole world as usual, but watching.

"This mountain belongs to *us*." Ursula ripped loose from Jo's grasp but didn't back away.

"We don't use that grassland. Dave's cows are hungry. It's not right nor Christian to turn them away or to act hateful toward them."

"We've lived all these years by doing as Grandma said." Ursula had been just old enough when Grandma died to take all her teachings as if they were commandments.

Commandments written in stone.

Commandments written in stone by the fiery finger of God.

Jo and Ilsa had been a little too young to be quite so fervent—or maybe it was just in their nature to not let fear hold sway over them.

Ursula was like Grandma in build, temperament, and looks. And she'd mothered them, which gave her some control over her little sisters. That had chafed as Jo grew into an adult woman, but she'd never had such a conflict with Ursula that Jo had bothered to shake off the reins of having a mother three years older than her. And it had been no burden to let Ursula be the head of the family. Grandma was a fierce woman who loved them very much. Ursula was gentler and less inclined toward anger. Her need to stay up here came from fear burned into her by her grandparents. For the first time, Jo thought of Grandma and realized it was fear that had driven her, too. Strange that it had never before occurred to Jo that Grandma was afraid. It had always seemed that she simply had stern rules to live by and passed them on. Jo hadn't spent any time wondering why.

"You only have to look at all the people up here from the Warden ranch to know not everyone who lives down below dies."

"Too many do. Far too many, the risks—"

"Stop." Jo grabbed her again and shook her. "You can't live your life afraid of everything. Or maybe *you* can, but I don't want to be alone all my life. God didn't create us to cut ourselves off from everyone. Grandma's teachings are nonsense."

Ursula slapped her hard across the face.

Jo stumbled backward with a cry of pain.

"Ursula, no!" Ilsa jumped to her feet so fast her chair toppled over.

Jo's hand went to her cheek. Her eyes met Ursula's. She could see her big sister was as shocked as Jo.

Ursula covered her mouth with both hands and gave a muffled cry.

"What are you doing?" Jo hadn't been slapped since Grandma died.

Ursula whirled away.

Jo's cheek started to burn. Ursula had struck with all her strength. Jo would be bruised tomorrow.

"I'm sorry." Ursula's voice broke. She ran for the corner of the room, her hands over her face as if she were the one who'd been slapped. Her breathing was loud and gasping. She might be crying.

"I'm sorry. Forgive me. I am . . . I am . . ." Ursula spoke into her hands. Jo, busy with pain, couldn't hear all she said.

Then Jo's shock twisted to anger. She charged across the

room and grabbed Ursula, yanked her around so they faced each other. Ursula was taller, but right now Jo was a giant in her fury.

"You are *not* going to make me into a coward just because you are one." Jo and her sisters bickered sometimes, but not like this. "You've never hit me before, and you are *never* going to hit me again." Jo held Ursula's arm tight enough that Ursula flinched. That ended the worst of Jo's rage and stopped her from hitting back . . . barely stopped her, because she wanted to attack.

"I am not a child to be ordered by someone and punished if I disobey. I know you're afraid, but Grandpa went to the lowlands all the time and never died."

"Ma and Pa, though—"

"Stop." Jo shook Ursula hard, and it seemed like Ursula, whatever rage made her lash out, was now willing to let Jo push her. Her head dropped, her shoulders slumped, as if she were collapsing in on herself.

"All those people who have invaded our mountaintop are from the lowlands, and they are fine." Jo put all her anger into her words—well, not counting the shaking. "Healthy. They have lived all their lives in that dangerous place. Grandma's fear, with Grandpa backing her, isn't real, Ursula. You've got to *think*. The fear you have has no *thinking* behind it. People from down there are living and surviving and able to talk to others. I am sure there are dangers, but I'm tired of being cut off from the whole world. Grandma and Grandpa wanted us to live this way, but God cannot agree with that. He can't have made a world of deadly danger, then let the three Nordegren girls have the only safe place. That is the thinking of a half-wit."

Ursula's head came up. Again that flash of anger. They all considered her to be the smartest, the leader. She didn't much like being called a half-wit. Well, fine! Jo didn't much like being slapped.

"You know our parents died—"

"No, stop!" Jo cut her off. "I'm not going to—"

"You had your say." Ursula broke in, as angry now as Jo.

"You hit me. I am yelling to stop myself from hitting back. This isn't about taking turns."

"You will make your own decisions then, Josephine." Ursula's hand swept between them. Not a slap, but Jo jumped back.

"Do as you wish with no thought of the danger to all of us. It will be as with Grandpa. You go to them and stay with them as long as you want, and then, when they leave, you stay away from us for two weeks. When you're sure it's safe, come back. And if you sicken and die from their diseases or are harmed by their guns—"

Ilsa must have told Ursula about Quill's bullet wound. Jo hadn't spoken of it.

"—then you let them tend you until you are well. Only then will you be welcomed back here."

Jo jabbed Ursula in the chest. "This cabin is no more yours than it is mine. I'll come and go as I please. You have no power to refuse me my own home. Now enough. I didn't sleep last night, and I won't sleep tonight until you leave off your hollering at me. Good night."

Jo turned and stormed into her room. The cabin had three bedrooms. One for her grandparents, one for her parents, and one for the three girls. Now each girl had her own. Jo slammed the door so hard she heard something topple in the other room. She even knew what it was. A pretty gathering of stones and woven grass made by Ilsa, sitting on a small table on the wall beside Jo's door. Well, Jo wasn't going out to put the thing back in place. If she went back out, she'd have more angry words to say. And enough had been said between her and Ursula tonight. Too much, in fact.

Jo got ready for bed. She'd be up and gone in the morning before she had to talk to Ursula again. And she'd lead the Warden family to grazing enough for their herd. And she'd eat their delicious food and talk more with Ma and Quill and, yes, with Dave. The thought of him was what made her strong enough to ignore Ursula's dire fears.

But she couldn't just leave her sisters. Her mind wandered to all she did around here. She provided the bulk of the food with her hunting. What would her sisters do without her?

And what if she did get sick? Could she really bring death to all of them? And Ursula wasn't thinking of Ilsa, who had also spent the day with the lowlanders. Or maybe Ursula didn't know. Ilsa must have talked about Quill being shot, but maybe Ursula believed Ilsa had learned about that from Jo.

Would Ilsa sneak? She was a sly one. Or would she face Ursula and defy her and be cast out, too?

Ursula and Ilsa were Jo's whole world, and had been since Grandpa died. Did a woman give up her whole world because a new one caught her interest? Did Jo have to turn her back on her sisters or possibly leave them to suffer hunger because of her besetting sin of curiosity?

Worry gnawed through Jo's anger, and the night stretched long and sleepless before her.

—o○o—

Months Earlier
New York City

Mitch Warden caught the reflection of a rifle in the window. He dropped to the ground just as a bullet shattered the glass in the elegant mansion behind him.

Another bullet fired and kicked up splinters from the spindly tree he dove behind. Gas lamps barely cut through the gloom.

The tree he picked was too thin, and the bullets tore at the bark. Mitch rolled, crawled on his belly, crouched, and leapt, dodging and moving the way he'd learned in the war, keeping the tree between him and his attacker.

The rifle gouged the dirt inches from his head. His attacker had sharp eyes in this deeply shadowed ground.

A set of steps that fronted the house lay just ahead, offering the only shelter. Staying low, he ran for it. The rifleman kept up his firing. Mitch threw himself forward and hit his right shoulder on the side of the steps so hard he was afraid the bone snapped. He crawled under them, worrying about his shoulder. He hoped he hadn't damaged it. But with or without the use of it, he'd find a way to survive this.

Five shots, six, seven—a repeating rifle, and a good one. The second he reached the meager shelter, he drew and came up firing long and hard into the park across the street. It was a far distance for a pistol, but Mitch's gun was a good one, too. And Mitch knew how to use it all too well.

He didn't need to aim. He'd done all his figuring while he ran. A cry from across the street ended the attack.

Mitch sprinted straight for the gunman. The recklessness that had made him rich rode him hard now.

No one bothered Mitch Pierce Warden without paying a hard price.

And being shot at was going to cost his attacker dearly.

He dove through a hedge. Thorns tore at his skin. His right shoulder took the abuse poorly.

Then he was on the man—who didn't fight back. He lay bleeding, barely conscious.

Mitch kicked away the bushwhacker's rifle that had fallen by the man's side.

He frisked the man and found two holstered guns, a third up his sleeve, a knife in his boot, and another in a scabbard under his shirt. He stripped the weapons, throwing them hard enough they sank into the hedge. Then he dragged a small pouch out of his assailant's pocket.

Money was as familiar to Mitch as his own face, and a quick toss told him this was full of twenty-dollar golden eagles. Probably right around a thousand's worth. The same amount he'd found on the other man who'd tried to kill him.

Mitch caught the man by the front of his shirt and jerked him forward. "Who sent you?" Mitch knew this was a hired gun. It wasn't the first murder attempt. But it had to be the last. Whoever was hiring murder was paying for top men. Both attacks had come too close. And Mitch was being very careful.

"You tell me, and I'll get you to a doctor. Otherwise, you die right here." Mitch slipped the money into his pocket. He wasn't giving it back and golden eagles weren't that common. He might be able to trace it.

Besides, he figured he'd earned it by surviving the attack.

"I'm as good as dead anyway," the man whispered. "I live

by my weapons, and there are plenty who'll want a notch in their gun by killing me. And my right hand is shot to pieces. My right hand and plenty more."

"But you've got a chance to live. Most men would be willing to take that chance."

The man whispered a name, and Mitch, a cold-blooded man who didn't trust many and called even fewer friends, found he could still be shocked.

In fact, he was so shocked he wasn't sure he believed it. Anyone who knew him and wanted to cause trouble might mention this name.

A shrill whistle told Mitch help was coming. This neighborhood had a good night watch, and gunfire would bring them running.

"I'll send for a doctor."

The man nodded and said, "I can see you doubt me, but that's who hired me. You're too good a man to be back-shot by a low-down snake. Others will come. Heed my words."

"I'll be right back." Mitch jumped up and fought his way through the hedge again just as help arrived. He quickly identified himself and told the security guard what had happened. This neighborhood was too wealthy to trust their safety to the police, so private sentries were always on patrol.

The guard said, "I'll get shackles on him, then run for a doctor myself."

Mitch nodded, then stopped when his head spun. Had he hit his head along with his shoulder? "He's right through here."

The hedge was harder to get through now, his third time. He ought to have busted a trail through by now. Was there an easier path through here? He wouldn't know until daylight—and by then he'd be home.

"He's gone." Mitch scanned the area thinking the man might've tried to get away and collapsed nearby. He spotted every weapon he'd tossed aside. The man was hurt bad if he didn't have the strength to pick up even one of his guns.

"He was barely conscious. I didn't think he had the strength to run."

It made ice flow through his veins to think of this man out there, maybe still coming.

"If he's shot up as bad as you said, he may have found the strength to run off, but he'll never survive. It saves me having him locked up."

Mitch had been to war. He'd seen some mighty shot-up people survive.

The man was nowhere to be seen. Another sentry arrived, then a third. They gathered the guns, heard Mitch's story, then walked him home. His house was right next door to where he'd been waylaid. He needed to bandage a few scrapes and soak a few bruises, get off his feet so his head would clear, and start making plans to stay alive. One guard stayed behind to try to follow the trail of blood—mighty hard in the dark.

Mitch lived in one of New York City's finest neighborhoods. The city had been good to him. His house was well lit with enough lanterns on the posts out front to drive all the shadows away. As he pulled his key out of his pocket, his arm hurt, and he wondered again if he might've broken it. But no, he'd been using his right hand all along. He started up the steps, but a wave of dizziness sent him staggering backward.

The sentry caught him, and his shoulder was suddenly on fire. The sentry held him up and banged on his door at the same time.

The door swung open, and his butler gasped. And his butler was a man who never showed a lick of emotion.

A light from his front entry fell across Mitch, and he saw his right sleeve soaked in red.

"Mr. Pierce," the sentry said, "I think you've been shot."

I'm not going to start making survival plans as soon as I hoped.

It was his last thought before his knees gave out and darkness pulled him under.

9

October 1873
Hope Mountain

Dave fell asleep the minute he lay down. He hadn't slept a wink the night before, and it'd been a long, stressful day.

His eyes blinked open in the gray light of dawn. He'd slept through the night. He'd meant to take a turn sitting by Pa. He'd told Ma to wake him if he didn't come in. Had she been unable to leave Pa's side? She'd be exhausted today.

Shocked that he'd never stirred all night, Dave looked up. The sun had only begun to push back the night. The tent flap was open, and he saw that the small building was silent. Rushing in now might wake both his parents when they needed sleep.

And he should've ridden out to check cattle a time or two.

Feeling guilty, he tried to think of what to do first. That's when he heard the heavy blanket used for a door to their little shed rustle. He turned in time to see someone slip in. How had someone gotten this close? He'd posted a watch on the trail, but maybe his men had fallen asleep. The whole crew, him and his cowhands and the men who'd ridden up from below, had been up most of the night the night before. Had the man who'd shot Pa slipped past everyone and—

"Shh, it's Ilsa."

Dave sat up straight, barely stopping a yelp of fear. He didn't think he'd made a sound, but he felt his cheeks heat up. Good grief, he was blushing. He felt like a fool for letting Ilsa and Jo sneak up on him. He hoped they couldn't see much in the dark.

"She'll have awakened your pa and ma by now," Jo whispered. "But there's no room in there for you."

Dave waited a minute for his heart to stop trying to pound its way out of his chest. He remembered catching her after she'd stolen that tin cup.

He'd known someone was about. Things had been moved around at night, and he was watching. It was a good thing because if he hadn't been, he'd've never found her.

Oh, he was good, mighty good in the woods. But the way she moved, she was more shadow than woman. He'd found her hiding in the forest, but only because he knew where she had to be did he manage to get his hands on her.

He could tell he'd shocked her then. Well, good. Maybe she'd think he was such a fine tracker that she wouldn't bother to hide from him.

He sure hoped that's how it went, because he'd never catch her if she knew how lucky he'd been.

"I managed to sneak up on you, huh?" Jo chuckled quietly. The men slept all around him, except for those out riding herd.

Which made him realize what woke him up. She was still shaking his shoulder, so gently it was like being rocked in a cradle.

If it wasn't for that, he'd've fired every one of his men. As it was, he'd have to fire himself, too, so he decided to just forget it.

Then she quit shaking him, and he really missed her touch.

"Follow." Jo stood, silent as a breath of wind, and walked out of the tent without waking his slumbering cowhands.

He followed, hoping he was half as quiet. He couldn't hear anything from inside the building, either. Could Ilsa be so quiet and gentle she checked over a patient without waking him?

Strange bunch these Nordegren women. Strange, wild bunch.

"I have a fine place where we can drive your cattle. There's a natural canyon wall that'll hold 'em on three sides . . . I think. I've never gone all around it, but it looks like there's no other way out. It has a narrow entrance that will be easy to block. If you want to go up there and see it, I'll take you. If the meadow suits you, we'll come back and get the cows."

The campfire jumped and drew Dave's attention. One of his men was up and stoking the fire, building it up. The soft clop of hooves told him a rider came in from checking the herd.

The soft cry of a mourning dove said the sun was coming, and he realized the gray had lightened. No outcry from the cabin. Pa had lived through the night. Dave felt the sting of tears at the thought because he'd been so sure Pa would be fine. But that first look, that bullet to the gut. Only now

Dave admitted how scared he'd been. But Pa would make it. The cows would have grass. And a beautiful wild woman had just asked him to go riding.

He swiped his eyes with the back of his hand and dug deep to control the foolish inclination to cry with relief. Then he smiled. It was a good mountain morning.

"Let me talk to Ma, and we'll see what Ilsa says about Pa. If he's holding up, we'll head out."

Jo nodded. "If you're right about how fast your herd will eat down this grass, you might not have much time. And when the snow comes heavy up here, everything'll get a whole lot harder."

"I'm more worried about Wax Mosby than I am about snow," Dave said quietly. "You said there is another way up here."

"Grandpa only spoke of it, so I'm not sure where it is, but I know it's a mighty mean trail. The one you took is the pick of the litter. It's the way Grandpa always went."

"If there is a way in, I want to see it." Dave watched the sky go from a pale blush to bright blue. The sun finally came with power. "I'll talk to Ma, and if things are all right, we'll go."

10

J o stayed.

It suited her to watch the camp wake up. To watch Dave walk to the little shed they'd built and go inside.

She remembered thinking Ilsa was doing this last night, staying back, watching. Now Jo realized she did it, too, and she'd been doing it all her life.

She watched.

She watched wild animals.

She watched her sisters.

And for the last few days, she'd watched Dave and his men. Her curiosity wasn't what made her hang back and watch. That didn't explain it. No, it was just her natural way to wait, think, study.

Now here she stood watching. Why did she do that? She wondered if it was normal. But how could any of her life really be normal when she'd spent it up here with only her sisters for company?

With a sinking heart, she had to wonder if living such an

isolated life had made her into a strange version of normal. Or was she the truest kind of person? Had her life, lived so alone, made her the purest form of herself?

As she waited, she adjusted the quiver of arrows she always carried, strapped so they hung across her back with a leather strap over her head, under her arm, and across her front. Then her bow went on top of the quiver, the arc of wood at her back while the string crossed the opposite way of her quiver, making an *X* right over her heart.

Dave came back right away. Whatever he heard must've reassured him. Then he went to a line of horses picketed to graze and threw saddles on two of them. She heard him murmur something to the men. All of them were now up and moving around.

Dave led both horses over to her. In the light of the new day, with no forest to cast shadows, Dave's eyes went to her cheek, and he frowned.

"How's your pa?"

Nodding, Dave said, "He's doing good. Ilsa was changing the packing on his wound. She said he has no fever, and that's a real good sign. I meant to spell Ma last night, but she said she fell asleep beside Pa, and they both slept straight through until Ilsa came in. I told my folks we were going to saddle up and go scouting for pasture, and they didn't try and get me to stay."

"Saddle up? D-Dave"—Jo hadn't meant to stutter—"I-I haven't been on a horse in years."

Dave gave her a rueful smile. "Well, this is a steady mare. If you want to ride, I think she'll suit you. If you don't, then I'd understand if you just want to hike around."

"No, the pastures I want to show you are at the far end of our home. We'd be all day walking there, so let's ride."

Dave helped her mount up, and it was an undignified business that left her unsettled because he'd touched her, and except for him taking her prisoner yesterday, she hadn't been touched by a man since Grandpa died, and he wasn't one to give a little girl a hug.

Yesterday had unsettled her, too.

She showed no sign of settling anytime soon.

Jo turned her thoughts away from such nonsense, grateful he'd helped lift her on the horse.

"What direction?" Dave asked.

Jo risked releasing her grip on the saddle horn with one hand and pointed toward the woods he'd caught her in. "We go that way, and there's a trail we can get the horses through, but how do I make it go?"

Dave chuckled. He reached over and took the reins from Jo, which were just something else to hang on to, so it gave her more than she wanted to do. He started out.

"I'm leading the horses, but you're the one who knows where to go. I think I know the trail you're talking about, but if I head wrong, speak up."

"You are heading wrong." He was going too far toward the trail the cows had come up yesterday. "Go straight ahead, now that way, around that clump of aspens."

"There's no trail."

Jo didn't know what to say to that. There was a trail, and when he saw it, he'd know. It didn't show, not from here.

Dave followed her pointing and rounded the aspen. He whistled quietly. "I've never noticed this."

"We get elk up here a lot, and they use this because it's unusually wide for a forest trail, bigger than what a deer would leave."

They couldn't ride side by side. Dave guided his horse ahead, still hanging on to her reins, leading her horse through the dappled forest trail.

With Dave in charge of the horse, Jo could almost enjoy the feel of the big critter moving along, carrying her. Trees of every kind arched overhead like a ceiling.

She remembered Grandma talking about churches she'd been in, and Jo had always wondered if the stained-glass windows were as pretty as her forest in the fall.

The gold color of the aspens and cottonwoods were splashed with orange bittersweet berries and red leaves from the sumac. There were pine trees with the lush needles and pinecones hanging low on their evergreen branches. A gust of wind scattered a bit of snow, not heavy, and there wasn't a cloud in the sky, but the weather was changing up here. There was no time to waste guiding Dave to the high meadow.

It was a long ride, and the morning was half-gone when they came out into a clearing at the base of a stony wall of rock. "There it is."

"This clearing isn't big enough to—"

"Not here." Jo pointed again. She'd like to lead, but she didn't have the nerve to take her reins back. The horse would probably just stop.

Skeptical, Dave glanced back a couple of times, but he rode on right toward the mountainside.

They came up to the rock wall.

"Turn to the right, and ride alongside the wall. There's a gap that doesn't show from this direction."

Dave did exactly as he was told.

It touched something in Jo that, despite his doubts, he was listening to her. Trusting her.

Dave knew better than to distrust Jo.

He'd seen plenty of odd things in the mountains, a gap that was hidden from the eye among them. But he sure wanted to scoff.

Then the solid wall of rock opened to his left. The rocks were sheer, forty feet high, but there were enough uneven and discolored spots that what looked like just another stripe of color was really the wall stopping with another wall right behind it and space between them. He turned and looked at the trail, bordered on both sides by sky-high walls. He kept moving, riding right in. It looked like it ended ahead, but by now Dave was sure it wouldn't. He got near the end, and it curved off to his right and took a sharp upward slant. His horse seemed calm as it walked onward and upward.

The ground was uneven, not worn down by years of heavy travel, but a herd of elk could come this way easily enough and so could his Thoroughbred and cattle. Getting them started up this narrow canyon mouth might be tricky, but once they got one cow going, the rest would follow. The trail rose more sharply, but it was wider and better traveled than the trail they'd taken the cattle up from their ranch.

The sky overhead was a narrow line, then he gained the top of the rock walls and a valley swooped down below him.

Dave wanted to draw his horse and look at this beautiful, vast grassland, just stop and savor the view. But his horse kept going, and Dave saw it was also a sharp descent, so he let the horse have its head while he looked at the swaying grass. There was a pond on the far end of what had to be hundreds of acres.

And no sign that another man had ever set foot here.

Well, Jo knew it was here, so she'd come. Probably her sisters, too. Even her grandpa. But no one had stayed, and Dave was suddenly jealous. He was going to have to let Pa have this for the winter. And Pa was going to want to keep it.

Dave had always regretted his brother, Mitch, going off to the city, though he claimed to love it there. But what if Mitch would come home? This valley was big enough to support another family. What if he'd live here, side by side with Dave?

He loved his big brother something fierce, and missing him was like a sore on his soul. It never went away. And with trouble down at the ranch, they could really use another strong man at home.

11

A Few Days Earlier
Colorado

Mitch knew this land like he knew his own face. And he was a man who had for years owned an excellent mirror, so that was saying something.

The land outside the train flashed past as the sun set. The view eased into his bones.

Home.

A shrill whistle said they were stopping, and Mitch knew just where. The train had few travelers, and he'd spoken to none of them and done all he could to draw no attention, including moving from one passenger car to the next every few hours. There were four cars besides the engine and caboose. He hoped if anyone noticed he was missing, they'd assume he'd just moved.

He stepped out of the train when it stopped at a water tank in the middle of nowhere. No one paid him much mind when he unloaded his horses. And he'd paid the conductor good money to not notice, and the stock car was the last one before the caboose. Mitch just saddled up, loaded all he had carried along on his packhorse, and rode back the way the train had come until he'd rounded a curve so no one could see him. Once the train chugged away, he turned to go west. A long way west.

He'd packed wisely, a bedroll and filled saddlebags.

And though it hadn't been his plan, he'd brought every bit of his wealth, all in the form of gold.

Now, finally, he was on the last stretch. A journey he'd begun planning the second time someone almost killed him.

He'd spent two months quietly getting his affairs in order, letting his arm heal, and doing some investigating. The would-be murderer had spoken the truth. Now Mitch knew his enemy.

He couldn't find proof that would bring someone who'd hired murder to justice, so he gave in to the longing that had been growing in him to go home.

During those two months, he'd very quietly sold all he owned. He'd hired eager, competent managers so the new owners would be successful . . . and his enemies would be harmed.

With no one knowing he'd turned all he owned to cash, he announced a trip to Europe. He was very careful not to do it with much fanfare, but enough so the news would reach the ears of his enemies and lead them astray. A man named Mitch Pierce—the name Mitch had gone by in New York City—had boarded a ship heading for England.

Then a man named something else had gone west on a train heading for Chicago.

He changed trains and his name in Chicago and tarried

long enough to see if he could pick up someone trailing him. He hadn't been followed. Then he'd moved on to St. Louis and a new name and then on to Omaha. He was there when the Panic hit. Banks failed, starting in New York City and tumbling across the country like falling dominoes. Millionaires like Jay Cooke and Henry Clews went bankrupt. These were men Mitch knew, powerful men who were too deep in debt from building railroads and factories.

He'd tarried in Omaha and read all he could find about the economic crisis. The ruthless businessman in him wanted to go back to New York. With the gold he carried, he could pick up whole buildings, whole railroads, for a fraction of their worth. If he did it right, he could come out of the Panic as one of the richest men in America.

But then, when the next panic came, it might be him filing for bankruptcy.

No, instead, he held on to his money. The Panic didn't appear to be ending any time soon, and he got word that his old business partner, Pete Howell, the man who wanted him dead, had lost everything just as Mitch had arranged. And that was before the business world collapsed. Then he heard that Katrina's father had lost everything. Katrina was the woman Mitch had thought he could love—or at least marry. She'd helped Pete pay for the assassin. Learning that was a betrayal that made Mitch furious. But he realized it hadn't broken his heart.

That he'd misjudged both Pete and Katrina was a goad that convinced him more than even the hired gunmen that he needed to go home.

Mitch carried a fourth name along with him to Denver.

In Denver he'd packed for the frontier and bought two

good horses—one for a pack animal. He'd planned to find a bank and have the gold locked away, but with the Panic, Mitch didn't trust any of them not to fail.

He'd carted the gold along and taken the train as far as he could south out of Denver, heading for a place no one wanted to kill him.

His fancy city clothes had been left behind, traded for rugged broadcloth shirts, denim jeans, sturdy boots, and a buffalo-hide coat—and from the moment he'd ridden away from that train, he went back to his real name.

It was full dark, but he knew the land well enough to find a game trail taking him toward the mountain where his family ranched. It was a winding path, but it went the right way, mostly west, climbing into the foothills of the Rockies.

He'd lived away from the Circle Dash a long time now. Over ten years since he'd gotten wounded in his first Civil War battle and been told his fighting days were over. Ashamed to not fight, he'd found a way to serve by helping out an officer.

He discovered a knack for organizing and planning, and a flare for ruthlessness. He'd done some spying and rose to the attention of a general. At the end of the war he'd stayed in the East. Suspicious and private by nature, he'd called himself Mitch Pierce when he did his sneaking around during the war. Once the war was over, he stuck with that name. He'd never been the friendly type.

First, he worked for a steel mill, then he owned one. It'd taken the guts of a riverboat gambler, but Mitch had risked a whole lot of money he didn't have and struck it rich in the boom after the Civil War.

He owned one mill, then two, then five, then a bank and

a row of New York City buildings. He'd invested in railroads and plenty more. There were some who whispered his name along with Vanderbilt, Carnegie, and Astor. He could've been one of those robber barons. He found that a talent for risk taking and ruthlessness was a good fit for that world.

And then someone tried to kill him.

Mitch had killed the man and found a thousand dollars in gold on him and a note that said it was taken in payment to commit murder.

Then the second attempt. He'd wounded a hired killer so badly the man would never shoot again.

And for a man with a reputation as a fast draw, not being able to shoot was a death sentence. Others would come after him, hunting a reputation. They'd pick him off like a wolf pack sniffing out a three-legged bighorn sheep. Mitch had investigated and found the killer had vanished. Mitch suspected the man was dead.

That felt like Mitch had as good as killed him, and Mitch didn't like the way that set on his soul.

There'd be more attempts, and to stay alive, Mitch would have to kill again. His dislike of the man he'd become in the city, and knowing his future would include fighting for his life and very likely killing those who'd been hired to murder, forced his hand.

He wanted home. So, he laid careful plans and made his move. Now here he was—a man alone. No one knew where he was or who he was.

He enjoyed the feeling of that as he rode along.

The wind had a bite, and he smelled snow in the air.

He also smelled sagebrush and pine needles. He heard

rustling in the woods and caught the shiny reflection of a pair of eyes. He judged it to be an elk.

It made him smile, and he whistled "Nearer, My God, to Thee," a favorite song of his ma's. And as he rode through the night and the next day, he felt nearer to God than he had in a long time. That shamed him. He hadn't attended church back east. He hadn't cultivated friendships with people who were at peace with God.

Just another good reason to come home. He knew he couldn't physically get nearer to his Heavenly Father, he had to do it in his soul. He spent the long ride in prayer and song, and longed for the ranch and his parents and little brother, Dave, as peace wrapped around him like the loving arms of God.

He avoided people—not hard to do in this area. In truth, though he rode for hours, he hadn't seen a single soul. He crossed a trail well-traveled enough it must lead to a town, but he didn't go in. He planned to arrive at home without anyone knowing he'd come. The Circle Dash was so far from a town, it was likely no one would pay much mind to the return of the older Warden son.

Word would get out Mitch Warden was home, but no one would connect him with Mitch Pierce, the New York City industrialist who had quietly vanished.

The next night he was nearly falling asleep on horseback. Giving in to exhaustion, he scouted the area for a long time to make sure he was alone, then he built a small blazing-hot fire, no bigger than his Stetson.

He ate jerked beef and drank water from a spring that held the cold of oncoming winter. He carried apples in his saddlebags and hard biscuits and a tin of cookies. It struck him as the finest meal he'd had in ages.

He woke up the next morning with only one more long day ahead. Tonight, he'd sleep in his own bed at his pa's house, eat food cooked by his ma, and see his little brother after ten long years.

But by midday snow was falling, and it got heavy enough, and the wind sharp enough, that he gave up on reaching home.

He cut across a trail that he knew led into Bucksnort, still a long ride from his folks' place. He didn't like going in there because he didn't want to be recognized. But he'd been a long time gone, and he looked little like the boy he'd been at sixteen, the kid who'd run off to war.

The thought of a hot meal and a real bed out of the snow lured him in.

He didn't like to admit it, but facts were facts. He'd gotten soft.

When he reached the town, he saw little had changed. It was a small, dusty frontier town, well . . . dusty with snow. There was a single block of businesses facing each other across a narrow dirt street. A few cabins behind the short row of ramshackle businesses had lantern light. Tinny music came from the saloon.

Beyond that, there was no life, no motion. Mitch rode in slow and easy. Always a cautious man, he tied his horses in back of the saloon. It was farther if he had to run, but no one would see him coming until he stepped inside. No sense giving men who were the worse for liquor time to think before they saw him.

He wasn't a drinker. He was a man too determined to always be at his sharpest to let whiskey dull his thoughts.

But the saloon was where people were, so he'd get out of the cold, and maybe they had a meal, though it was late. He'd find out if the old boardinghouse was still in business.

He walked along the side of the saloon, and as he approached a shuttered window, he heard muttered conversation and caught the name Quill Warden. Pa.

He stopped dead in his tracks.

"He hit old Quill Warden. Couldn't find the body, but they got him sure enough." One voice rose above the rest. "Wax is a deadeye."

"Smilin' Bob claims he got the shot on Warden, not Wax."

"Bob's a braggart. But come to that, I didn't see who did the shootin'. Deal the cards."

Mitch's heartbeat slowed. His breathing went calm and cold. It'd always been like this when there was trouble. Cool under fire, his pa called it. His pa, Quill Warden.

He wanted to go in there and rip answers out of the talker's throat.

Instead, he stayed calm and listened.

"I don't know where the rest of the family went. Into the highlands west of their place, I reckon."

"I'll open. Quit yer jabberin' and play or get out," a gruff voice interrupted.

Rough laughter followed, and they started talking about their poker game.

If they said more, Mitch didn't hear it. He was galloping for home.

—o◯o—

Dave's horse arrived at the bottom of the canyon and stopped, reaching for a mouthful of grass. He let his brown stallion have his head, which gave Dave a chance to sit and soak the beauty in.

Jo came up beside him, and her horse went to grazing with a crunch.

The wind swept across the grass as if it were being brushed along by the hand of God. The trees swayed in the gentle breeze. The wind wasn't as sharp up here; the walls wee serving as a windbreak.

He was surrounded by a bowl, with a perfect blue sky arched overhead. Movement at the far end of the valley drew his eye, and he watched a small herd of elk bound away. Checking for what he knew had to be there, he saw a majestic bull standing halfway up the far side of the canyon. Always on guard, even though Dave guessed the old beast with his massive horns didn't expect to see a man and woman come riding into his kingdom.

Dave watched as the cows, their half-grown spring calves at their sides, vanished on bounding feet, then the bull elk moved off his craggy perch to follow his family.

That old guy was in for a surprise. He was no longer going to have this beautiful kingdom to himself. He was going to have to share with a big old herd of cattle. And still there would be grass enough for all.

The elk herd headed away, and Dave wondered where they were going. What was on past this canyon? Could there be more grass, more beauty?

Dave broke out of what was nearly a trance as he absorbed the sights and sounds, the crisp air and soothing winds of this place. He saw an eagle's nest that was so huge it had to be ancient. The stalks of grass swayed and danced on the wind until Dave almost heard music. It was hard to turn away from the breathtaking view, but all the questions that clamored to be answered helped him turn to look at Jo.

"Do you know if that trail we just came up fills in over the winter? Is this place cut off?"

"I've been up this trail in the winter a few times, and it was open." Jo was silent a moment. "I've come just to see it. Sit back there where the trail opened up on this canyon. I've always known that elk herd wintered up here, and if I needed to, I could find meat here because of them. But I never needed to hunt in here. In fact, riding down this slope is the farthest I've ever come, even when I've been in the mood to wander far afield."

"Far afield except you never leave Hope Mountain."

"Is that what you call it, this mountain we're on? My grandpa called it Lost Peak Mountain."

He was silent awhile. "When I was a kid, my brother and I tried every way we knew how to find a trail up here, one we could ride a horse on. We were so far apart in age, and he left when I was still mighty young. A few summers, though, we did a lot of climbing and got up that trailhead a few times, but it is such a long, hard climb that we never explored it. We couldn't be gone overnight, and the way that trail was, it was already a long day up and down—but I knew that one meadow was there. I always remembered it. I always wanted to find a way up here. I never told my folks, though, not until just this year when I wanted to start a ranch of my own. Ma'd skin us if she knew we climbed up here when we were kids."

Jo smiled. "You couldn't come up, and I couldn't go down. I've never even ridden through the entrance to this canyon."

"Why?"

"I have no idea, but I always stayed out. Grandpa did tell me there's another valley, higher up. But I've never searched for it." Jo added, speaking in a near-reverent whisper, "I'd like to see it sometime."

Dave was thinking about just how far they were getting from a town if the whole family settled up here. But he wanted it. He wanted to own it. The land office would sell it cheap because it would look like wasteland on their map. But considering the situation down in the lowlands, it'd be worth their lives to go buy it. Even if they risked it, went down and bought it, then lived to get back here, the purchase was public record, and anyone hunting them would know right where they'd gone.

But maybe if they slipped down, bought it, and got back up before the snow closed the trail down to the lowlands, they'd be safe until spring.

He gazed with what he was sorely afraid was pure greed. He'd rarely seen such a likely place for a ranch. And he'd be switched if it'd be owned by anyone but him. Pa would want it, but he was going to have to stay right where he was down at the Circle Dash—once it was safe again.

This land was going to be Dave's.

Then, because he was drinking it all in and staring so hard, he saw something that made him squint. "What's that?" He pointed to what looked like a tumble of limbs and branches almost swallowed up by a copse of trees to the right, not that far away.

Jo turned and studied the spot he'd indicated. Finally, with a little gasp of pleasure, she said, "I think that's a cabin. It's built a lot like ours, only smaller. And it looks as if it's made by Grandpa's hand. I wonder if that's where he lived until we were sure he didn't bring a sickness home from his trips to town. He never said where he stayed, and I reckon he did that deliberately."

"My grandma could sure fuss at a man, and Grandpa would sometimes leave when she was flying out at him, say he was going hunting or trapping. He'd be gone a long spell. Sometimes so long it scared me a little, wondering if he might be gone for good like my parents."

"There's a cabin up here, already built." Dave couldn't believe the luck. It looked strange, but if it kept the snow off his head, he could start living there tonight.

"Looks like. I've never seen it before. Let's ride over."

Dave nodded, then said, "I'll teach you how to ride as we go. Your mare is calm from taking a long walk, and she's shown no signs of feistiness. If we drive the cattle up here, I won't be able to lead your horse. So, if you want to come, you'd better learn a few riding tricks."

He turned to see her hands tighten on the saddle horn until her knuckles were white. Fighting back a smile, he said, "First, let go."

He lifted his hands in front of her. "It's not like the horse is real slippery, now is it? Have you come even close to falling off?"

Shaking her head a bit, she said, "No."

Dave waited. He wanted to rush back down to the camp and get the cows driven up, but he really did wish she could ride a horse.

Slowly her hands relaxed. She rested them on the front of the saddle, close enough to grab the horn in an emergency.

"Now take the reins." He handed them over, careful not to make any sudden moves.

She clutched them but didn't do any yanking around that could upset the horse.

"Your mare is used to being ridden with a group of other horses, so I'm going to head for your grandpa's cabin, and I'll be surprised if she doesn't just come right along. Just stay easy in the saddle and ride along."

Jo nodded, not looking all that excited, more like grimly determined.

Dave set out at a walk so slow and easy it'd rock a baby to sleep. The mare fell in beside his stallion, and they were over at the strange-looking house in a few minutes.

"You stay up there and let me tie up the horses, then I'll show you how to get down."

He was soon at her side. "Hold on to the saddle horn now. Put your weight in this stirrup. Sort of stand up on your left leg and swing your right leg slow and easy over the horse's back, then let that swinging leg go on down all the way to the ground."

Jo did it. She did it so well, Dave grinned at her as he helped her dislodge the foot still in the stirrup.

"You make a likely cowpoke, Jo. Now let's go see what's in that house over there."

12

Jo was trembling. It surprised her because she had rock-solid nerves in the normal way of things.

She took one step toward the cabin, and Dave's hand came to rest on her back. "We don't have to go in if you don't want."

Jo turned to him. She really had no experience with men. With people, come to that. Just her sisters and animals. And as always, she was curious.

"What made you say that? What did I do that made you wonder if I didn't want to go in?"

Dave met her gaze. His expression was so kind. "You lost all the color in your face. Pale as milk."

His eyes went to her cheek again. He reached up and drew one finger, gentle as a breeze across her cheek. "You've got a bruise. I thought so before, but when you went so pale it really stood out. I-I didn't hurt you, did I? When I caught you in the woods?"

Jo was ashamed of what Ursula had done and didn't want to cast her sister in a bad light.

"Pale as milk, really?"

Something flickered in Dave's eyes that said he wanted an answer about the bruise, but he didn't demand one. "Yes, and you seemed unsteady like you might . . . oh, not collapse, you seem a little too tough for that, but turn and run maybe. Why don't you want to go in?"

"You mean my face actually changed colors?"

"Yes, haven't you ever seen your sisters get pale when they're sick?" His fingertips caressed the bruise again.

"My sisters and I don't get sick. You have to catch a sickness from other people, so how would we?"

"Um . . . I suppose you can't catch a sickness, but you might run a fever with an infected scratch?"

"That happened a few times. Ilsa doctored us. Grandpa taught her so much, and he was sick toward the end. Not from going out among people, because he hadn't gone out for a long time. But he said old age was catching up to him. He started to forget things. He said he was a—a—what did he say? Doddering old fool. I remember that. Sometimes he thought Ursula was Grandma. He was confused the last stretch of his life. Ilsa had herbs and potions he'd taught her, and that was one thing he remembered. He enjoyed talking about all kinds of healing tricks with her. He called her his little medicine woman. But you said I got white. Pale. That happened to me?"

"It did."

"Hmm." Jo turned to face the cabin and lifted her chin. "I'm trembling and scared because it's a part of Grandpa's life I know nothing about, and I thought I knew him very well. But now I realize how often he was gone. He ran traplines and went to town to trade. And the fights with Grandma, of course. Sometimes hc'd be gone awhile, but I can't really remember how often or how long.

"He only went down the mountain to trade once in a long while after Grandma died. And he continued the rule of staying away for two weeks after he got back. What if he'd died up here? We might never have known what became of him. He'd have just vanished like our parents did." Jo's head whipped around to look at Dave. "You don't suppose something like that happened to our parents, do you? They got sick and were ordered by my grandma to stay away, and they were off somewhere, camping, waiting, and they d-died alone. Home closed to them."

Dave slid an arm across her shoulders. "I'm sorry life held so much fear for you. And it still does for Ursula. None of you have ever gone down, have you?"

"No. When Grandpa died, we were scared. We had no way to buy supplies. But he knew we'd live on past him, and he prepared us for that day. He taught us to live off the land. We'd learned much of it at Grandma's knee, too. She'd grow wheat and corn, then grind it into flour of sorts."

"I can't believe corn and wheat grow up here so high."

"Grandma said it's hard to grow anything in such a short summer. But the canyon we live in is very sheltered. And there's a hot spring coming out of one area. It seems to keep the land around it warm, because Grandma said in that one stretch, she could grow a nice garden, and if she planted very early, she could get a crop of corn and wheat. She taught us how to care for our garden and milk a cow. How to tend the chickens."

"So, you raise everything you eat?"

"I'm the hunter in the family. I bring in the meat. Elk and deer now and then, and wild boar. But we eat smaller game a lot. Rabbit and grouse, young bighorn sheep are good, and mountain goat. And I know where to get honey and Indian potatoes. There are nuts and berries and greens, oh, so many things. It's a rich land, and Grandpa taught me all about it, and he showed us all how to find the healing herbs Ilsa uses so well. And we learned to store up plenty for the winter, because it's a harsh time."

"I'd like to see your home, Jo."

"It's tucked away in a canyon with a narrow entrance, almost as hidden as this one. Not a huge meadow, but big enough for us. It's beyond a crack in the canyon walls, so you would have been lucky to find us when you were scouting." Jo's eyes met his, and she felt her brow lower with worry. "I'd like to show you my home, but Ursula would hate it."

Jo touched her cheek, and she saw Dave notice, his eyes sharpening.

"Does that bruise have something to do with me, Jo?"

"No, it only has to do with my very frightened older sister."

"I won't stand by while someone hurts you."

That made her smile, and her cheek stung a bit. "Let's hope you don't have to fight my big sister."

Not one second of humor flashed across Dave's face.

"I have to think about it first," Jo said. "I could take you there, and we could slip around and look. Or wait until Ursula goes off. But if we were found out . . . it's like the story we talked about from the Good Book. If I lie and Ursula finds out, someday I may need her to believe me, and she will remember my lies."

Dave blinked at her. Silent for too long. Then he asked, "What Bible story is that again?"

"The one about crying out for help when it's not needed. 'The Boy Who Cried Wolf.'"

He nodded silently for a time, then said, "Maybe you should talk with Ma about this. For now, let's see what's in this house. I might just move right into it."

"Oh," Jo froze. "I was thinking I would move into it. Ursula doesn't want me in the house while you're here. She's afraid . . . well, it's nonsense, but she really is afraid we'll all die."

"Did you tell her about Wax Mosby shooting Pa? Did that frighten her? I'd certainly understand that."

"No, well, yes, I suppose that would upset her, too, but she's afraid you'll bring a disease or bring some other kind of harm. Grandpa was fierce about us staying on—you called it Hope Mountain?"

Dave nodded.

"The last year or two . . . or maybe three of Grandpa's life, he wasn't thinking clearly. Not a day went by when he didn't warn us to stay up here. Toward the end, he must have said it a hundred times a day. That the lowlands were full of danger and deadly sickness, sin, and evil men. He was frantic that we would break that one golden rule."

"Uh, you don't think staying to the mountaintops is the Golden Rule, do you? Is that in your Bible?"

"'All things whatsoever ye would that men should do to you, do ye even so to them.' Grandma said that was the golden rule, but she said it was easier to say, 'Treat folks like you wish they'd treat you. Only don't wait for them to be kind and honest. Be kind and honest first.'"

Dave knocked on his head gently.

"What are you doing?"

"I'm trying to figure out where in the Bible there's a story about a boy who cries wolf."

"It's right in there. It's in the smaller of the Good Books."

Dave ran his hand right up into his hair and nearly knocked his hat off. Then he scrubbed the top of his head and said, "I'd like to see both of your Good Books sometime. Maybe we can sneak and do that while Ursula's not looking. For now, let's go look at the cabin."

"I'm going to have a talk with your mother." Jo turned and headed for the cabin. "You're too old now for it to be anyone's job but your own, but sure and away your ma shirked with her Bible teaching when you were young."

Dave came after her quietly. Too ashamed of the truth to speak in his own defense, no doubt. Well, he oughta be.

She got to the cabin door, and a warm place right in her chest swelled. The cabin had been swallowed up by the woods. She wondered if the trees that had grown in close were holding up the house these days. But there was still a roof and a door that stood upright and was tightly closed.

"Grandpa's house. I feel like I'm opening a part of his life I never knew about. I wonder if Grandma even knew this place was here." She had to lift on the door to drag it open. It swung inward. Swinging in was the usual way when the snow came feet at a time. Sometimes there just was no way to swing outward.

The smell was first. It was musty and stale, but it was

Grandpa. "This door hasn't been opened, I'd reckon, since Grandpa came home the last time."

Dave came up behind her, and she realized she'd stopped in the doorway. She had to force the next step, but she took it and went in farther to find a cabin that was larger than the one Jo lived in . . . at least larger than their main room was. Grandpa had added three bedrooms to their home. This one didn't have any other rooms. To the right was a four-poster bed, on the left wall was a kitchen—though there was no fireplace. A small table divided the room. There were things everywhere, all buried under years and years of dust.

Jo gasped as she looked at a cabin far more beautiful than hers.

"Do you have bedcovers like these?"

"No, absolutely not." She went to flip up the corner of a quilt faded almost to white. Dust puffed into the air, but the bottom was clean and made of bright blue and red cotton with countless pretty stitches, making swirls and flowers. The bed had corner posts and overhead a stretch of white lace that formed a canopy. "Grandpa never sewed. He had to've bought this pretty thing."

"Look at the plates and utensils." Dave drew her attention to the kitchen side of the cabin.

"We have tin plates and cups at home." Jo walked the few feet to a beautifully made chest about waist-high with open shelves. On top was a huge glass bowl and sitting in the bowl was a pitcher. It was white with bright flowers decorating the fine, thin glass. Pretty cups and plates sat on the shelves, and in one carefully carved wooden box with no lid, she could see forks and knives and spoons. All with delicately carved handles.

"And our spoons and forks are plain. Why would Grandpa have these things up here? Why didn't he tell us all this was up here before he died? We could have used these things."

"You said he was confused. Could he have lost his memory of this somehow?"

"That must be it. He'd have told us about these things." Jo had to believe he would.

"How did he haul it up here? He couldn't have ridden his horse because that trail is impassable. Didn't you say you have cows? How did he get cows up here when I had to work hard on that trail to get mine up?"

Jo frowned. "We always had cows. I have no memory of him bringing them here, but then I was born up here, and everything was as it is now."

"I think"—Dave's eyes seemed to look through the walls into some distant place he could only see in his mind—"I think there must've been an avalanche. There was one stretch of that trail that I had to climb up clinging to ledges with my fingertips. If your grandpa lowered his furs using a rope, he could get down. And if he left the rope, he could use it to climb back up. He could tie things off and hoist them up with the rope. But he couldn't carry much, not hefting it on his back."

"So he brought things up, a few at a time? He carried them on his back all the way from where he bought them?"

"Unless he had a packhorse stashed in the lowlands. Our ranch is close to the base of the trail. Not right next to it, but close enough your grandpa had to know we were there."

Dave shook his head. "I wonder if Pa knew him or if your grandpa slipped past our place on foot every time he went to town. Someone had to know him if he went into Bucksnort, the closest town, to trade. And it's a far piece on horseback. If your grandpa was on foot, with a heavy pack, he'd be days getting there."

Dave reached into the top drawer and pulled out a leather bag. It was black with a little drawstring at one end. Dave tried to unknot the string and it snapped. The whole bag was brittle with age. He tugged to open it and the bag split, and coins rained down onto the floor.

Jo squeaked in surprise. Dave grabbed at the little coin purse and stopped the money from falling.

"These are twenty-dollar gold pieces." Dave picked one up as Jo bent down and collected the coins that had fallen.

"What is that? What is a gold piece? The Bible speaks of gold."

"It's money. These are made of a valuable metal, and people in the lowlands would trade you fabric and food for one of these coins."

"Money." Jo frowned and searched her memory. "Money is the root of all evil." That's all she could remember about money.

"No, the love of money is the root of all evil. You can have it and use it, and if you don't love it over loving God and loving other people, it's okay to use it. It's handy. I could take one cow to town, and someone there who needed a cow would give me one of these." He held up the coin. "Then I'd take it to the store and buy things I needed. Or"—Dave pointed at the big bowl and pitcher—"things I wanted."

"And there are a lot of them." Jo straightened, one hand clutched around coins from the floor. With the other, she pinched a gold coin between her thumb and index finger and held it up to eye level.

She studied the coin, then her eyes shifted their focus so she looked right at Dave. "Why would Grandpa do this? Why would he live with all these fine things and not bring them home to us?"

Dave shook his head and looked around again. "He never brought anything fine and pretty home? Just flour and sugar?"

"Oh, not sugar. Grandma thought it was a sign of weakness to want things from town. She only wanted Grandpa to get a few things, the bare necessities. Only things we couldn't find for ourselves."

Dave picked up a small canister. "Did he then . . ." Dave was watching her so closely she wondered at her expression. "Did he like these things and want them, and he knew your grandma would be unhappy if he brought them home?"

A faint memory tickled Jo's thoughts. "He'd bring us candy." Jo searched her memory. "No, he'd *sneak* us candy. I remember once, but it was so long ago . . . he gave us each a peppermint stick, and Grandma threw a terrible fuss over it. She tried to take it away and Grandpa—"

Jo looked into the past and felt that strange burning in her eyes. "He made a joke of it, but now I know it wasn't a joke. He sort of grabbed Grandma and was holding her while she tried to get the candy. Grandpa laughed and yelled, 'Run, eat fast!'"

Jo covered her mouth as she thought of Grandma's fury.

She'd been fighting mad. Grandma had always had a temper. "My sisters'n me ran outside laughing like wild critters. We hid in the woods to eat the candy. When we came back, Grandpa was getting his coat on to go outside. He told us, very sternly, we were never to eat candy again. We might die.

"He was very solemn. Grandma sort of humphed like she did a lot, then went back to work, Grandpa opened a flap on a pocket of his coat and showed us three more sticks of candy. Then he held his finger to his lips and went out to do chores.

"We all knew after that, we'd get candy when Grandpa came back from town, but never in front of Grandma. One stick of hard candy each, every time he went to town. 'Our secret,' he'd say. 'If Grandma finds out, there'll be no more of it. She doesn't want me spoiling you with things from the lowlands.'"

"Why is it such an old memory?" Dave asked. "He must've done it every time he traded."

"Yes, but he stopped when Grandma died. It was like he took on all her worst fears after her death. He almost never went to town, and when he did, he'd never bring candy. We weren't babies anymore by then anyway. Only babies need candy."

"Your grandma liked things simple."

"I reckon that's a nice way to say it. She was scared of everything, and she got mad when something scared her."

"And your grandpa must've liked a few fancy things. Since she wouldn't let him have them down at your cabin, he hid them up here." Dave shrugged one shoulder. "I suppose it's not a bad way to keep the peace."

"Building your own cabin, then lying and sneaking for

your whole life? That's not a bad way to keep the peace? It seems terrible to me. But we all learned to do it because Grandma wouldn't listen to any sass. I remember saying to her one time, something like, 'It can't be deadly for everyone down off the mountain or there wouldn't be any people left alive and there wouldn't be any towns for Grandpa to go trading.'"

"And did she scold?"

"She slapped me." Jo rested one hand flat on her cheek, felt the tenderness, and thought of Ursula last night. Ursula had been there years ago and witnessed Grandma's anger. Her big sister was turning into Grandma.

"It was a hard and fast rule to never talk back to Grandma and to never talk about leaving the mountaintop. I knew better than to say anything." Jo shook her head. "But glory be, my grandma had gotten half-mad with all her fears. I just had to say something to put a little bit of reason into our lives."

Dave had slowly moved nearer as she talked, as if her words drew him.

"Grandma could hand out a lickin', but she wasn't one to slap us on the face in the normal run of things. In fact, that's the only time I can ever remember her doing it. A'course, I was careful not to sass her again, especially not about going down the mountain."

Dave rested one hand on her face, bringing her out of her dark thoughts. She tried to forget the strange sadness the story woke in her. She looked up and saw kindness, compassion, and something else, something that drew her as the cold weather drew the birds south.

Silence stretched between them, thick with pleasure and a

kind of closeness Jo had never felt before. In fact, she'd never known it existed. Dave's eyes flickered downward, and she could feel that quick glance like heat on her lips. She licked her lips to cool them. Dave's eyes narrowed, and he seemed closer than before.

She forced herself to go on. "I kept my thoughts to myself. But nothing could stop me from being curious." She knew just how curious she was right now about the look in Dave's eyes, and how it felt to be so close. She smiled, then stepped away from his touch, surprised at how much effort that took. "Enough of old memories."

Dave's hand slowly dropped. "We shouldn't be here alone together." There was a roughness in his voice that seemed to rub against her in some mysterious way.

He cleared his throat. "We'd best get back. I can get a herd of cows moved up here yet today. The cabin has no windows and only this one door. No fireplace. He made it so nice. Why did he skip that?" Dave sounded annoyed, and Jo turned to look at him, wondering why.

"He probably cooked outside over a campfire. I think he stayed closer to home in the winter. We needed him to cut wood and fight the drifts to do chores."

"If someone else lives here, they'll need the heat, so we've got to build a chimney."

Jo looked around. Yep, she'd need it to be warm if Ursula still wasn't over her fit when the snow fell. That was going to be a lot of work, and she had no idea how to build a chimney. But it sounded like Dave might be planning to help her.

Dave gestured at the door. "Let's drive some cattle up here."

13

Mitch skirted the edges of the ranch, looking for signs. He found plenty. None of it from his family.

He had his ma's last letter, and he had a good idea where they'd gone, just no idea how to get there.

He and his brother had run wild in these hills as youngsters, and Dave always had his eye on Hope Mountain. They'd climbed the mountain and found some likely grazing land, but they'd never found a way up fit for cows.

He remembered from the saloon, one man had said, *"I don't know where the rest of the family went. Into the highlands west of their place, I reckon."*

The highlands, Hope Mountain for sure, and that was a good place to retreat to with gunmen on their tails, but where had the cows gone? All Mitch could think was either Dave and Pa had found a way up, or they'd blasted a trail. Either way, under two feet of snow, Mitch wasn't going to be able to find the path, which meant he'd have to make his own.

And the snow kept falling.

The side of a mountain was nowhere he wanted to be.

"He hit old Quill Warden. Couldn't find the body . . ."

The words that man in the saloon said came as close to knocking Mitch down as any ever spoken.

And Wax Mosby. Mitch paid attention to any news from around his Western home. Wax Mosby was a known man and a dangerous one.

Mitch knew an old corral his family kept away from the house by a warm spring that ran year-round. He turned his horses loose in it, not wanting their tracks all over. Because he knew this land well, he found a hidden crack in the base of the mountain only he and Dave knew and stashed his supplies, including his gold, in there. Then on foot, he scouted the ranch, quietly of course. He did everything quietly. There was no sign of life in the cabin or the bunkhouse.

He quit his hunting as the sun rose in the east. Mitch was worn clean out.

Resigned to the hard way of finding someone to welcome him home, he strode toward the first path to Hope Mountain that came to mind. He slung his rifle across his back, his saddlebags with a canteen and some jerky over one shoulder, his six-gun holstered on his hip, and headed out. Or better to say, headed *up*.

As he climbed, the snow changed from soft, powdery stuff to needles of ice. The path, treacherous in the summer, was a nightmare under sleet.

Why had he been so all-fired eager to leave New York City? A few folks shooting at him was stacking up to be pure fun compared to this.

As the cows climbed through the narrow, upward canyon mouth, Dave, with Jo at his side, reached the top of the rocky trail where it curved over the canyon wall and headed down into the bowl of the valley.

He found a wide spot, got off to the side, and watched his cattle march down into the lush grass. He saw the dried stems, hay made without him cutting a swath, brush against their bellies. A couple of spring calves kicked up their heels and dashed to the far end of the canyon. The cattle moved slowly, spreading out, ripping mouths full of grass, heading for the pond on the far end of the meadow.

Jo sat calmly beside him, studying the playing calves with a pretty smile on her pink lips and a flash of humor in her sparkling blue eyes. Still wearing her odd clothes that hid her so well in the autumn forest. Her fine blond hair was in a knot on the back of her head, but plenty of it escaped, and she paid it no mind.

He noticed her rest her hand on her mare's shoulder and pet the old girl. Jo had found a new friend.

"I should ride in the direction those calves are going. They might find a way out of here, and we'd have a time of it rounding them up." He smiled at Jo, who'd been such a steady and constant companion. "You want to head over there with me? It'll take an hour at least, over and back. But I think I'd better go."

Alberto rode up as Dave finished speaking. "I know you want a look at that cabin you were talking about, getting it set up to live in. I'll ride a circuit around the canyon and look for bolt-holes."

"Take Jimmy Joe with you."

Alberto gave Dave a narrow-eyed look. "That youngster talks until it's like to make my ears bleed." Alberto twisted in the saddle and hollered. "Jimmy Joe!"

"Thanks, Alberto. Fire off a bullet if you want someone to come a-runnin'."

"Good advice for everyone. Keep your eyes open, Dave. We don't know if Wax Mosby had any other way up here."

"Let's ride on to the cabin." Dave noticed that Jo was getting pretty good at riding. Of course, staying in control of the gentle horse he'd given her was about as tricky as staying in a rocking chair.

They walked the horses. The herd wasn't a fast-moving bunch, no herd was, so Jo's riding had been nothing but a walk. Dave decided to leave trotting and galloping for another day.

They reached the cabin, and Dave swung down, then hovered near Jo, holding the reins as she dismounted.

"You're getting good at that." He held on to the reins as he studied the cabin and contemplated sleeping here tonight.

"I'm going to sleep here tonight." Jo strode toward the cabin.

Dave stumbled and rammed his shoulder into the cabin wall. Too bad the outside of the cabin was hidden by limbs and underbrush and whatever else Jo's grandpa had piled up. Some of it was sharp, and he heard his shirt rip.

"In fact, I might just move in permanently."

"You can't move in here." Dave growled as he rubbed the scrape on his shoulder through the newly torn hole. He was gonna need a new shirt. "I'm moving in here."

Jo whirled. "You? Why? You don't have to live right next to your cows, do you?"

"Why would you move in? You've got a cabin."

"Your parents need you. Your ma is tending your pa in the cold, and that leaves her with a lot of work and too few hands."

"You can't live up here alone."

"Just like you said I can't live up here with my sisters the day you grabbed me in the woods and dragged me out and kept me prisoner for hours?"

"Oh, it wasn't hours," Dave said in disgust. One hour at the most. "You've got a cabin. I don't."

Jo leaned close, glaring. "Are you planning to steal my other home from me, too?"

Dave straightened. "Hey, that's not a bad idea."

Jo kicked him in the shin.

"Those moccasin things don't hurt much."

She glowered and crossed her arms. Turning, she pressed her back to the door. Almost as if she were blocking his way in, which she sure as certain was. "Maybe you'd let my folks sleep at your place."

"Ursula would kill me. Or she'd die of fright. She might find a way to do both. My sister is getting crazier all the time."

"But you do have a cabin, right? And well-built like this one? Your grandpa knows tight construction. This cabin is made to keep out the winter winds."

"Our cabin is tight, but there's no room."

"You said it had bedrooms."

Jo's jaw tightened, and he got the idea she really did not want to say something. Which made him ask, "How many bedrooms?"

Her jaw worked funny, it made her look mighty stubborn. Finally, she said, "Three. Three bedrooms. But no *empty* rooms."

That sent Dave's brows arching almost to his hairline. "Three bedrooms for three people? I always shared a bedroom with my big brother, until he moved off to a city. Do you each sleep in your own room?"

"Yes." She ground the words out like it was killing her to admit it. "There was one for Grandma and Grandpa, one for my ma and pa, and one for us girls. Now we each have our own. We all get along a whole lot better if we've got a closed door between us."

"Then you can leave your crazy sister in one." He paused for a second. Ilsa was pretty strange. Jo might have two crazy sisters. But only the one seemed foaming-at-the-mouth mad. "You and Ilsa can share, and Ma and Pa can take over one until Pa's feeling better, and we get a good cabin up for him."

"Your folks can't stay there."

"Sure they can. You can make room for them for a few weeks, can't you?"

"No."

"That seems mighty unfriendly. Why can't they stay?"

"Because Ursula wouldn't allow it."

"She's one sister of three. She doesn't get to tell you what you can do with your own house."

She looked straight at her toes. "You'd think so, wouldn't you?"

Dave leaned close. "We could lie in wait, then sneak in and take the place over. By gum, we could lock *her* out."

Jo looked at him in dead silence for a long moment. Then a smile broke over her solemn face, and a chuckle leaked past her clamped jaw, and she relaxed and laughed. "We could take her, couldn't we?" Jo's shoulders squared, and her eyes flashed with good humor and determination.

Dave's expression turned serious. "The truth is, Jo, this snow is falling faster every minute. The little lean-to we built yesterday isn't fit for the winter, especially not when Pa is so badly hurt. Letting us move into a cabin that's already built and warm might be the difference between life and death for my pa. Please let us stay."

14

"Why am I climbing this stupid mountain?"

A rocky ledge, coated in ice, crumbled under Mitch's hand. For a gut-twisting moment, he dangled out over thin air with fifty feet to fall. One hand with a grip, his feet swinging free.

He clawed at the mountain, got both hands back to work, and scrambled to find footing.

As he climbed, he muttered words so rude that, even without a single cuss word, Ma would probably get out the bar of soap.

Ah, he couldn't wait to see her.

He moved on, fighting for each bit of progress.

His hand landed on something not coated in ice. Then he found another clear spot. Then his feet were above the slippery ledges. A few yards on, he found a place wide enough to sit. There'd been no easy, wide ledge like this when he and Dave had climbed before.

Where was he? Lost? Climbing toward some sheer section

of the mountain that would trap him so he couldn't go up or down?

Or maybe there'd been a rockslide, and the rocks broke in such a way to leave this ledge. He had no idea where he was going to end up.

Exhausted, he sat and caught his breath. He needed to rest for a minute and think.

He still had his saddlebags and guns. He dragged his canteen out and drank water so cold it made his teeth ache. He drew the leather gloves off his stiff-with-cold fingers and finagled around until he could tuck his hands under his arms, inside his shirt.

As he sat there, warming up, out of the sleet but not by any measure out of the cold, he realized he'd gotten above the worst of the storm. And looking down, he saw his home.

Pa had built a nice spread.

Thinking of Pa sent a shudder through him that had nothing to do with the oncoming winter.

He knew exactly why he was climbing this stupid mountain. To find out about Pa.

Was it possible? Could that strong man be dead?

Quill Warden would be a hard man to kill.

But strong wouldn't stop a bullet. It'd help a man dodge them, but if one landed, no amount of brain, muscles, or strength would stop it.

Mitch considered himself strong, and he had a scar from the bullet that'd creased his right shoulder.

Mitch studied the land below, wondering if he could see things better from up here.

There was no sign of a downed man. But in the deep snow, there wouldn't be.

"Couldn't find the body, but they got him sure enough."

Mitch heard those words from the saloon over and over again. *"Couldn't find the body . . ."*

Mitch needed to find the outlaw who had done this and make him pay. Wax Mosby. Shaking his head, Mitch knew the Warden family was tangling with terrible enemies.

What had they said? Budge . . . no, Bludge. One man had said, *"The Circle Dash is on the far west end of Bludge's range."*

Mitch had no idea who Bludge was, but if he hired his killing done by the likes of Wax Mosby, then Bludge was a killer himself.

Hired guns sure enough weren't just in the Wild West.

Mitch thought with cold satisfaction of that day shortly after he'd headed west, when his old business partner would've awakened to find creditors at his door. Pete Howell, a man who'd reminded Mitch of himself. Only Howell hadn't been an ambitious, reckless kid. He'd been a viper. And Mitch had arranged for him to take a hard fall.

Then Mitch looked down the mountain and hoped he didn't have a hard fall in his future.

While he sat there catching his breath and thawing his fingers, he saw three men ride up to Pa's house. They dismounted and headed for the cabin.

Friend or foe?

Mitch wasn't going to take a chance on introducing himself. As the third man reached the door to enter, he scanned the area, and he did it well, a cautious man.

The man's eyes searched in the woods. Even from this distance Mitch recognized a skillful man.

Slowly, the eyes scanned every inch, then climbed the cliff Mitch was on, and stopped.

Without being able to see the man, not even really seeing the details of his face beyond a dark beard that didn't sway at all in the wind, Mitch knew he was looking right into this man's eyes. A man who could have already killed Mitch's father.

Mitch didn't move, didn't even breathe. Maybe the man couldn't see any more detail than Mitch could. Maybe Mitch even looked like a dark crevasse in the rocks.

Would he start shooting? Would he call out his men and come climbing after Mitch?

Like the stirring of a sleeping hound, the man slowly began raising his finger. It rose an inch at a time. Higher, still higher.

Then it stopped, aimed right at Mitch's heart, and he wasn't pointing his finger so much as he was mimicking an aimed gun.

The man smiled. White teeth flashed, parting the motionless beard. Then he turned and went in the house, and no one came out. No alarm was sent up.

Mitch sorted through things he'd picked up here and there, information that he stored in his head as surely as Ma put away root vegetables for the winter.

The strangely dark, unmoving beard.

It was waxed. Wax Mosby was known to have a strong inclination to wax his mustache and beard. No one knew why, but there were some who said he was very proud of his beard and he tended it carefully.

Wax wasn't going to come after him. At least not right now.

But if he did—when he did—Mitch had just shown Wax Mosby the trail to his parents' hideout.

Mitch ran his palm over his face and realized he hadn't shaved since he set out from New York City. That'd been months ago, with the time he lingered along his journey to make sure no one was on his trail.

But now, if Wax Mosby wanted to follow, he knew the trail Mitch was on. Mitch turned and went back to climbing.

Wax Mosby stepped into the house. His mind working, flipping through possibilities.

Who was that up on the side of a mountain in a blizzard?

"We got the place, Wax. We done it." Smiling Bob, named that because of the ugly scar on his face that pulled up one corner of his mouth in a twisted kind of smile, laughed.

Wax wanted to shut his mouth and do it permanently. "Bludge said these folks were nesters, taking over his land. But look at this place."

Wax made a wild gesture at the ranch house they stood in. Solid, settled, old. Furniture handmade. Cushions and curtains. Dishes that matched, and glass stuff, not like the tin most folks had. "A woman lives here. Look at that desk, there are papers in all the cubby holes. That didn't fill up in a few months."

"Maybe new folks moved into a place that'd been deserted." Smiling Bob didn't believe it, but he didn't mind who he had to kill to earn his pay.

"And kept the letters from the folks who were here before?"

"Maybe Bludge bought out the old owners, and nesters found it and moved in. Maybe the old folks left things behind to travel light. Maybe the newcomers didn't bother to go through what they found."

Wax strode to the desk and pulled out a handful of letters. One from someone named Mitch, with a date that was ten years old and addressed to this place. "The man you shot was Quill Warden. And he's been here for years. They're not nesters, and they're clear and away off Bludge's spread. He's not driving off settlers, he's making a land grab."

"You want to talk that way about the boss, you say it to his face," Canada Phelps growled.

Wax met his eyes. Canada was a hothead, but he wasn't stupid. He wouldn't start shooting because he wasn't fast enough. Wax was the fastest gun in five states.

Phelps and Smiling Bob together weren't fast enough. That didn't mean Wax wanted a shootout. A gun could hang up or misfire. He didn't start shooting if he could help it. That'd earned him the reputation of a cold, clear-thinking man.

He'd found out just how skilled he was with a firearm when his ma and little sisters were killed and he hunted down the killers. Then he found out he could chase outlaws and earn rewards. Then he found out how well people would pay for his skill. But he didn't kill for hire. He fought for the brand. Some might not see the difference, but Wax knew there was one.

"I do work for Bludge, and I will say this isn't right—I'll say it to his face. You two can stay here and attack innocent ranchers if you want, but there's plenty of honest work on Bludge's ranch. I'm heading back." And he'd leave that man on the cliff alone. That had been so strange a chill went down Wax's spine.

It was as if an angel was perched up there watching, judging, avenging.

Was that a real man trying to climb up, get clear of the trouble here? Or was it a descending angel coming to rain fire down on the heads of unjust men?

Shaking off the fanciful notion, Wax knew it was mighty interesting to see someone all the way up there. Wax liked high ground, and whether that climber was going up or down, it figured there must be something up there.

"Nah, don't get all out of sorts, Wax." Smiling Bob headed for the door. "We're done here. I'm not going on the prowl to find cows and cowpokes in this weather. We'll ride back with you."

Wax didn't lead the way out, neither did he lag behind. He didn't want these two to get ahead enough to take up a shooting position, and he sure as certain didn't want them following where they could back-shoot him.

It was then Wax was hit hard by something he already knew . . . but he was young enough to not really believe it until right now.

He was going to die.

And he was going to die hard and bloody and soon.

Someone faster was bound to come along, and Wax, in his reckless youth, had already used up as many lives as a cat.

Bludge was paying him top wages, and the folks they'd driven off were nesters who were on Bludgeon Pike's land. Wax had seen the deeds.

And they were made to move along without harming them.

But all the success they'd had must've gone to Bludge's head because now he was taking from someone who had been here and was settled, and considering the way all the people and cattle had vanished, they were tough, knowing, and wary. They wouldn't be likely to just move along.

No, they'd go to high ground, and they'd wait and watch.

And Bludge would want a fight. And he'd want Wax in the thick of that fight while Bludge sat safely behind his desk.

Wax was going to find Bludge and have a long hard talk with him. He didn't want to quit. He was going to need the money Bludge was paying to start a new life, and he'd have to change his name and shave off his beard.

Wax ran his hand over his heavily waxed beard. It came to a point below his chin and his moustache curled up. He'd always liked wearing it that way. It'd have to go.

Maybe he'd go back to his real name, too, Jacob Mosby, and find a new state, one he wasn't known in. He'd heard California was nice.

He plotted his future. He had to change or die.

"Yes." Jo jerked her chin with determination. "Your parents can stay with us. That's my house, too, and I have just as much say as Ursula. And your ma and pa are fine people. It'd be good for Ursula to spend some time with new people. She's about over the edge to a full-blown lunatic. But there might be time to pull her back. Your ma can help me save her."

Dave smiled. Then gunfire split the air.

The horses he held jerked on the reins.

Dave saw Jo's fear, but he had no time to study it. He thrust her reins into her hands and yelled, "Hold on to your horse."

Then he swung up, glanced back, and jabbed a finger right at her nose. "You stay here."

He spurred his horse, but it wasn't necessary. The critter was game, and they were flying across the yard.

Jo's horse jumped and whirled toward Dave, racing away. She almost dropped the reins and was dragged a few feet. Afraid the horse was getting away, she remembered how she'd gotten on before and mounted up . . . and the horse took off.

Jo wasn't exactly disobeying orders. The horse just tore after Dave, and Jo went along for the ride.

Dave veered, and when Jo got to his turning point, she found a game trail, left by the elk probably. The footing was good, and Jo mostly just clung to the saddle horn with the reins twisted between her fingers.

Ahead of her, Dave rushed around a clump of trees. The gunshots came from that direction. Jo was really sorry she was taking this ride because, whatever trouble was up ahead, she was just going to be in the way, at least until she got this horse to stop. Then maybe she could help with her bow and arrows.

Her mare followed on Dave's heels, and once around the trees, she found Dave on foot. Her horse quit its mad dash and pulled up beside Dave's mount. Jo was clinging tightly to the saddle horn, or she'd've gone over the horse's head.

Dave was on foot running toward one of his hired hands. Jimmy Joe, she thought.

"Up here, I've got a man cornered," Alberto shouted.

Dave stopped to crouch beside Jimmy Joe.

Jo swung off the horse and rushed for Jimmy Joe. She wasn't the healer Ilsa was, but she could do plenty to help. She slid down to her knees beside Dave. "Go help Alberto."

"Jimmy's out cold," Dave said. "Bleeding from the head. Can't tell if it's a gunshot nor how bad it is."

Jo whipped her bow off her shoulder, then notched an arrow and aimed toward the boulder Alberto had pointed at.

Dave ran his gaze over her, primed to fight, and seemed startled. Then he gave her a furious look that set her back a little. More of Dave's men came thundering in.

Dave leapt to his feet and charged up the steep slope for Alberto with such flat-out rage that Jo realized Dave wasn't furious at her, it was whoever had shot Jimmy Joe.

Dave's men rushed on past her up the hill.

The men were between her and the boulder she'd aimed at. She didn't dare let an arrow fly, though she considered it. She could aim just right, and the arrow would curve over the boulder and hit someone behind it.

She might decide later to get into the fight. For now, Jo hung her bow in place and returned the arrow to its quiver, then turned her attention to Jimmy Joe and saw a rock right beside his head. She wiped at the blood and decided that might be what caused the wound, not a bullet.

"How bad is it, Miss Jo? Will I live?" Jimmy Joe sounded dazed, very young, and very scared. Well, he thought he was dying, that'd shake most anybody.

"No gunshot wounds. It looks like you bashed your head, but you're awake and talking, so that's a good sign."

With feeble tugs, Jimmy Joe took off his neckerchief. "Use this as a bandage."

"Thank you." She took the bandanna, then pulled her knife out of her boot.

Jimmy Joe's eyes got wide, then they rolled back in his head, and he fell asleep. Strangest thing Jo had ever seen.

One of Dave's men came back. "No more room up there, and it seems to be just one man. What can I do to help, Miss Jo?"

"I need to tie a bandage here, and when he wakes from this nap he's taking, we'll let him hop onto his horse and ride back down to where Dave's folks are. Ilsa ties a better bandage then I do, and she'll be there."

"But will he live?"

Jo looked up into the eyes of another very young man. This one with red hair and so many freckles his face was nearly the color of a bittersweet berry.

"He's your friend?"

"Yep, Jimmy Joe and I rode west together after the war."

Jo shook her head. "War? Was that necessary?"

The man stared at her, one red brow arched. "Yep, had to fight it out. Keep the union together."

"Union? Like a union suit? My grandpa wore such as that I believe. You fought a war to keep long underwear together?"

There was an extended silence, then the man said, "Word is you've been up here for a mighty long stretch, Miss Jo."

"That's true."

"You missed some things. But for now, how is J.J.?"

"Your friend will be fine." She split the bandanna in two. One half she folded into a pad to press against the wound, the other half she tied around his head to hold the pad in place.

The gunfire had ended, and a shout . . . no . . . more like a scream came from overhead. Then something else that made no sense in a gun battle. Laughter.

"Throw out your gun. I give you fair warning, you're on Warden land, and we won't give it up without a fight. I've got five men against one. You can't beat us."

There was a long silence. Dave looked to his cowpokes. They were a steady, salty crew, mostly Civil War veterans.

"Warden land?" From behind a pile of boulders the attacker said in a strained voice, "Pa, is that you?"

That voice. Dave shook his head hard, trying to make himself believe it. "Mitch? No, it's Dave."

"I'm coming out." Slowly, an arm first. Then, when no one shot his arm off, a shoulder, then finally Mitch Warden.

Dave's eyes burned, and for a terrifying moment he thought he might cry. Instead, he screamed the way he'd heard Apaches do it.

He dropped his rifle and launched himself from behind cover and ran at his big brother. As he ran, he shouted, "I am so glad I didn't shoot you. Ma would never let me hear the end of it."

He was teasing, but to think he might've shot his brother. It was enough to make the steadiest men shake in their boots. Enough to make his eyes burn again.

Mitch emerged fully from the rock and came running. "Dave? No, you were a sprout when I left. I can't believe it's you."

They collided, and Dave hugged Mitch with all the longing that had eaten at him in the years since he'd left.

136

Then he picked his big brother up—not so much bigger these days—and thumped his back, trying to put all his welcome into that pounded fist.

Finally, he got control of himself and stepped back. Mitch rubbed a wrist over his forehead like he was wiping away sweat. Not much chance of sweating up here in a snowstorm. Nope, Mitch was fighting for control same as Dave.

They looked at each other and smiled.

Dave yelled over his shoulder, "My brother's come for a visit. And he . . ." Dave was suddenly struck dumb. He looked past Mitch's shoulder. "How did you get up here?"

"Climbed."

"You climbed and ended up coming from that direction?" Dave thought of all the climbing and exploring they'd done as kids. No trail had ever led them here.

Mitch suddenly went rigid beside Dave. "Wait, forget the climbing. I heard Pa was shot. Where is he, we need to—"

"He's going to make it." Dave cut him off before he could get more worked up. Then he quickly caught Mitch up on all that had happened.

"So you ran?"

That stung. Dave was quickly remembering how his big brother could push.

"Not me. I bought a ranch up in these highlands and moved up here. Then here came Pa yesterday with all his cows, horses, and hands, and Ma, too. I reckon that means it's Pa who ran. Go brace him about being a coward, that'll be a good way to say howdy after you've been away for ten years. That is your point, isn't it?"

Mitch shook his head and waved one hand. He backed

up and dropped to the ground, leaning back on a man-high boulder. "No, no, sorry. I'm just on edge. Running don't suit me, but I know it doesn't suit Pa, either. He had his reasons, and if I'd been there, I'd've made the same choices he did."

Dave decided not to punch his brother minutes after seeing him for the first time in over ten years.

"I haven't slept for a day and a half," Mitch went on. "I haven't eaten much, and I just climbed a mountain in a blizzard." Mitch looked around. "Snowing here, but no blizzard. I could tell I climbed above the storm. I'm sorry I said anything, Dave. You can have one punch. I won't say a word about it. If you knock me cold, just toss me over a horse and haul me down to see the folks."

Had he made a fist? Dave hadn't noticed, but maybe Mitch had.

"Did you shoot Jimmy Joe?"

Mitch's eyes had fallen shut. Now he opened them and looked down the slope to where Jo knelt by J.J. "I don't think so. I fired a couple of times in the air hoping to back off whoever was shooting at me. I didn't know who was coming. Is he all right?"

Dave turned and saw J.J. sit up, supported by Jo. She looked up the hill.

"How is he?" Dave called down.

"He hit his head, no bullet wounds," Jo hollered back.

Looking back at his collapsed brother, Dave asked, "Have you got the strength to get up and ride? I'd like to head for Ma and Pa."

Nodding silently, Mitch gathered his strength. Dave went to him and extended a hand. Mitch, the big brother, looked up, smiled, and caught Dave's forearm just as Dave caught his.

They were face-to-face—of course they had been before, too, but they'd been busy hugging. Now eyeball-to-eyeball, Dave looked down a ways at his brother.

"Whoa, I didn't notice how tall you'd gotten." Mitch wasn't a real tall man, same as Pa, an inch or two under six feet. Or three.

"I was still a kid when you left. I had some growing left to do, I reckon." Dave topped six feet by an inch or two. Or three.

"And you still had the voice of a kid. That's why I guessed it was Pa, though you don't sound like him. I wanted it to be him so bad, though. When you said Warden land—" Mitch's voice broke and he quit talking.

Dave slapped him on the back. "I'm gonna have to stop calling you big brother."

They smiled at each other. They'd always been so different.

Dave was dark and blue-eyed like Ma, easygoing for the most part. Quick with a smile and ready to throw his back into any chore.

Mitch was more like Pa, blond with brown eyes, built plenty sturdy, strong and hardworking, not afraid of nuthin', and he could be cold-blooded when he needed to be. And so smart that Dave had always admired him and wondered at him at the same time.

Best friends even with the years between them. Together again. They started down the hill.

"It's good to have you home, Mitch."

"Good to be here. I had some trouble back east, and I

decided to get out. Give up city life. I've been missing you and our folks and the ranch for years now. When someone tried to kill me, I headed home."

"Sounds like Pa heading for Hope Mountain when murderers roamed in packs."

"It's just like that. Live to fight another day." Mitch and Dave kept on down the slope. "So who's the woman? She yours?"

Dave slapped him on the back hard enough he stumbled forward a few feet.

Mitch grinned. "I guess that means yes."

"I've wished you were here a hundred times, Mitch. Maybe a thousand. And never more than right now. I need another strong man at my side, to fight with me and Pa. We've hired good, loyal men, who've been with us for years, and they're a salty bunch. But we've got trouble, and it's going to be all we can handle. Having you here puts heart into me. Welcome home."

15

Jo got to ride on the back of Dave's horse.

They rigged a thing they called a travois for Jimmy Joe, which was unlike anything Jo had ever seen before. She planned to make one of her own to haul deer and elk meat home. It'd have to be smaller, though, since she didn't have a horse and would have to drag it herself.

"You say you lived in a city?" She was having trouble figuring out just what a city was. Of course, she knew of cities and towns. Grandpa had gone to town to trade his furs. And there were stories in the Bible about cities. Jerusalem, Bethlehem, Sodom . . . Gomorrah.

"Yep, New York City, biggest town the country has, way back east."

"Back east of what?" She knew north, south, east, and west. The sun rose in the east and set in the west.

Mitch gave her a confused look.

Dave said, "Ma and Pa will kill the fatted calf for you, big brother."

Jo sat up straighter and looked around Dave to see Mitch. "So you're the prodigal son?" Nodding, she added, "Ursula might say I'm the prodigal sister."

Mitch scratched his head as if her words made him itch. "The prodigal son took half his pa's money and got into all sorts of trouble, then he ran for home when his foolishness got to be too much for him. Pa gave me a horse, a rifle, some supplies, and a little cash money when I went off to war. After the war, I made good money and brought it back with me. I don't consider myself a man who wasted money nor lived a life full of sin."

"Except for the trouble that drove you here," Dave said.

"Yes, except for that."

Mitch had a hard way of talking, faster than Dave.

The three of them led the way with most of the cowhands following. They stopped at Grandpa's cabin and left an addled Jimmy Joe, Alberto, and five other cowhands behind. The rest rode with them back to the camp where they'd built the tiny cabin to shelter Pa.

They got back so fast they didn't have time for talking. Ilsa stepped out of the cabin just as they came into the clearing. Jo saw her take one look at the newcomer and vanish into the woods. She did it so quick and quiet that Jo didn't think anyone had noticed she was even there.

Let Ilsa run from a stranger.

Let Ursula scare herself to death with Grandma's dire warnings.

Jo liked them.

Curious as always, she intended to listen and learn. She wanted to hear more about a city. Maybe Grandpa had gone down to the New York City Mitch was talking of, but Jo wasn't sure, and she wanted to hear everything.

"Ma? Pa?" Mitch swung down from his horse. "I'm home!"

Ma shoved aside the blanket covering the door, stepped out, and looked at him in stunned disbelief. Then her disbelief was replaced by joy. "Mitch!"

She rushed for him.

"Mitch?" Pa yelled from inside the cabin.

Ma hit hard enough to knock him over, but Mitch fell against Dave, who caught him and stopped them from going down. Then Mitch hung on tight.

"Ma, I haven't had a decent hug from a beautiful woman since I left home." His eyes burned again. He was turning into a weakling. But it felt so nice to be held and loved.

Pa yelled something else, and Mitch remembered Pa had been shot. Mitch was wild to see what kind of shape he was in.

He didn't want to let go of his ma, so he scooped her up off her feet and carried her right along to the shanty. He stepped inside and almost stomped on Pa's feet. But he'd seen the size of the place and figured there wouldn't be much room.

Mitch knelt on Pa's right side. Since Ma was still clinging, Mitch smiled at his very-much-alive father, then pulled his left hand out from under Ma's knees, reaching it out. He couldn't shake properly, nor give Pa a hug, which Mitch would've liked to do, but with his hands full of his weeping mother, this was the best he could do for now.

Pa clasped his hand. Their gazes met, and the biggest smile

Mitch had ever seen on a gunshot man bloomed on Pa's face. Mitch figured he had one to match. Mitch was nearly stunned by how good it was to see everyone. Why had he stayed away so long?

"You look good, Pa. Dave said you're healing well."

"My son. Mitch. My son. My son." Pa's voice broke. He swallowed hard and went on. "We've missed you so much."

Pa was as much as saying that Mitch's coming home was way more important than his being shot. Mitch had to swallow hard himself.

"I missed you, too. For the last few years I've been figuring to quit the East, but I've done well there, and it was hard to find the right time to go." Someone shooting at him helped him decide now was good, but there'd be time for that story later.

Ma collected herself enough to sit on the ground beside Mitch. It took plenty of guts, but Mitch reached down and gave his father a gentle hug. He and Pa had never hugged much. Mitch remembered one really good hug. The day he'd caught Mitch running off to war at fifteen.

Pa had stopped him, and Mitch had been furious. He'd said, "I'll try again. I'll go. I want in this fight, and even if you stop me now, you can't really stop me."

Pa stopped him for most of a year. Then just after his sixteenth birthday, Pa gave Mitch a horse, a gun, a saddlebag full of bullets, and some twenty-dollar gold pieces so he could afford to eat well on his way to finding the war. Then he'd sent his son off with a hug and a prayer.

Now they hugged again. It was like bookends to all the missing years. This hug was far more joy than pain. After a minute, Pa slapped his back hard enough to knock a man over, but it was about the best feeling Mitch ever had.

"I've got fifty questions, son. I'm still mighty weak, so I'd better not start in asking. Instead, I'll just let you tell me all about what's going on. And then we'll cook up a plan to get my ranch back."

Dave came to the open door of the shanty.

Smiling up from where he sat on the ground beside Pa and Ma, Mitch scooted over, dragged Ma close, and said, "Come in, baby brother, and sit. We've all got stories to tell."

Dave came in pulling that strange woman behind him. Jo. What kind of name was that for a woman? Dave closed the blanket-door and sat. Jo sat beside him. That's when Mitch noticed the strange, fluttery clothes—she wore trousers.

"Mitch, you go first," Dave said. "We're settled in, so you can talk all night."

Jo had never heard so much talking in her life.

She tried to remember every word of it. Ma had hung on it, too, all through Mitch's story of a betraying partner and two murder attempts and selling a steel mill—whatever that was.

Then they'd gotten to the cattle and the outlaws, Wax Mosby and Bludgeon Pike. Jo knew all that, so when Ma said she'd start cooking, Jo went with her. The door covering was left pushed aside, and the fire was close enough they heard most of what was said.

Before Mitch had come home, Ma had already put six chickens to roasting with potatoes and other things with wonderful smells tucked all around them. She'd made a rising of bread and two apple pies. Jo could barely believe the wonder of this food.

Mitch's stories of New York City were so interesting and confusing. It seemed more like the fairy tales Grandma used to tell about horses that could fly and women who were half human, half fish.

"There's Ilsa," Jo said quietly to Ma. She pointed up in a tree where Ilsa lurked and watched. Braver than Ursula at least.

"I was so busy hugging my son, it was quite a while before I noticed she was gone."

"I think a stranger confused her a little."

"Why? All the cowhands are strangers. She's seen so many new faces in the last few days it's a wonder she noticed one more."

It was a wonder.

"I'll go talk to her. She probably wants to check Quill's wound and doesn't want to go into that little cabin with it so crowded."

"Tell her there's plenty for dinner."

Jo ran over to Ilsa, who was scampering down the tree trunk. She looked between Jo and the little cabin.

"Someone new. But not one of the cattle drivers." Ilsa liked to understand things first and then act. Standing back to watch, like Jo. And Ursula was the worst of the three. Honestly, it was a wonder any of them ever talked.

"Dave has a brother who was off living in a big city. He's home now, and they've been making a bigger fuss over him than we used to when Grandpa would get home from one of his long journeys." Jo remembered the cabin and told Ilsa about it.

Ilsa blinked her shining blue eyes. "I know the trail you're talking about, but I've never been up there."

Jo told Ilsa all about Grandpa's cabin and how it must be the place where he lived when Grandma insisted he stay away from them.

"I only remember just the fewest things about Grandma. I was three when she died. But I remember Grandpa being gone, and I remember treats. Why didn't we ever go into that valley?" Ilsa asked. "We both have explored almost everywhere, and we knew about that trail."

Jo was silent. Something niggled in her memory. "I don't know. But for some reason I always knew I wasn't to go in there. I can't remember Grandpa forbidding me to, not exactly, but he must have said something. I wonder if Ursula remembers anything about it."

With a shake of her head, Jo said, "Nothing we can remember will change the past. Come and meet Mitch and see what all Ma has made for supper. Apple pie and bread made with a real special kind of flour."

Ilsa's little nose wrinkled as she sniffed the air, then pleasure flashed in her eyes. "Pie. I've heard you talk of such, but I've never had any."

As they neared the cabin, Jo whispered, "Dave wants me to take his parents to our cabin and let them live there."

Ilsa gasped. "Ursula will never allow it."

"It's our house, too, so Ursula can't allow and not allow."

"But she won't . . . endure it. She'll leave."

"Where can she go? She can't live through the winter away from the cabin."

"She might try."

147

Jo looked at Ilsa. Jo was so used to thinking of her as little, but Ilsa was a woman fully grown, and, in her own way, very wise. Yet Jo never looked to her little sister for advice. It was time to admit her little sister had grown up.

"Do you really think so?" Jo waited. Wondered.

Ilsa now took a turn being quiet while they both considered it.

Finally, into the silence, Jo said, "We can't leave Quill out here in this cold. The little cabin was shelter for a night, but it's got no fireplace, and to warm it with the campfire you have to leave the door open. A fine solution on a cool night, but ridiculous when the bitter winds and blowing snow get here."

They both looked up at the snow that'd been coming down, light but steady, all day.

Ilsa said softly, "It's here already."

They walked closer to the tiny cabin. Ma had gone back inside, and they heard talk and laughter from within.

"What will we say to Ursula?" Jo eased the bow around her neck and under her arm so it didn't rub, then she did the same to the quiver. It was a motion she did many times a day to make sure the two weren't hung up somehow, in case she needed them fast. "How can we convince her?"

Ilsa shook her head. "I doubt we can. I think it's best if we just bring the Wardens home with us. Tonight, we'll just load Quill up and off we'll go. One of us will get there ahead so she won't be able to latch the door."

Jo grinned. "I think that should be you."

Ilsa rolled her eyes. "Ursula might well run if she can't keep them out."

"Ursula thinks she's the mother and we're the kids."

"There might've been some reason for that when Grandpa was alive and I was so young. A lot of the raising fell to her."

"I helped raise you, too." Jo gave her a good-natured shove.

The smile faded from Ilsa's face. Her bright blue eyes shone with what might be tears. Then her little sister threw her arms around Jo. Muffled against her neck, Ilsa said, "Yes, you did. And I thank you for that."

Jo decided the Nordegrens could be a hugging family like the Wardens, so she squeezed Ilsa tightly. "We all made it through by being full-grown when we were still youngsters. You needed a lot of help at first, but you have been doing your share and more for years. And I thank you for that."

"We're a team, and Ursula is a big part of that team. We've got to help her accept these folks. Showing up at the door and just charging in with them is going to be so hard for her."

"Can you think of what to say that will make it easier?"

Ilsa stood away from Jo and looked at the Warden family. Jo could almost hear Ilsa's brain working. Finally, she said, "Nope, I think charging in is about our only choice. We'll hope she gets over her fear and stays with us. And if not, she'll get over it and come home when the weather gets too cold."

16

Jo didn't tell the Wardens to be quiet. Besides Dave, she didn't want them to know they were slipping up on Ursula.

But she didn't linger outside talking. She headed briskly for the door.

She swung it inward, relieved it wasn't latched. Dave rode right up to the cabin, pulling his father behind his horse.

Jo didn't even look in. She wasn't going to start shouting at Ursula, and if Ursula wanted a fight, well, she thought . . . hoped . . . prayed . . . her big sister would have trouble behaving so badly in front of outsiders.

Dave and Mitch got on either side of Quill while Ma held Dave's horse. Jo admired how well they worked together.

"Jo, what is—" Ursula squealed and backed away as Dave and Mitch eased sideways to get through the door with their pa.

Ursula hit the wall right beside their fireplace and only then stumbled to a stop. There was no way out unless she jumped through their single, small window with the tight shutter.

Jo wouldn't be surprised.

Ma came in following after Quill. She watched Quill anx-
iously, so she never noticed Ursula. But Jo saw Dave looking
around, at the cabin, at Ursula, taking in every detail all while
never being careless with his father.

He must've never told his parents what a big problem coming here was.

"Bring him into my room." Ilsa emerged from her bedroom and swung the door wide. She'd clearly been hiding
so she wouldn't give herself away to Ursula. "I've got my
things all moved aside."

"Ilsa, you too?"

Jo closed the door to the outside to keep the cold out and
her sister in. She took one long look at the gentleness the
two rugged men showed to their father. Then she turned,
determined to be gentle with Ursula.

Jo's heart twisted when she saw her sister pressed against
the far wall, her hands clamped together at her waist so tightly
all her knuckles were white. Ursula's eyes were wide and
locked on the crowd of people. Yes, four extra people in the
house was a huge crowd by the Nordegren sisters' standards.

Ursula's breathing sped up. Her eyes were full circles locked
on the Wardens. Jo saw the color drain from Ursula's face.
Pale as milk.

Jo hurried to her side, afraid she was going to either collapse or start screaming and running.

"Ursula, Quill was shot." Jo talked fast, hoping to get it all
said before Ursula bolted.

"There's always danger when other people are around,"
Ursula whispered as if she were reciting a commandment,
"terrible, deadly danger."

"They were running from danger, it's true, there were men attacking Quill's ranch at the bottom of the mountain. They were forced to come up here where Dave had moved. Now Quill is wounded, and they have no cabin with heat. He won't survive outside. What else could I do but offer them shelter?"

"What else?" Ursula quit staring and turned like a trapped wildcat. She was no longer pale; instead, her face flushed with anger, ready to attack.

"This is from the Bible, Ursula." Jo jumped in to say more. "I—that is, *we* are the Good Samaritans."

Jo reached up, moving slowly so she didn't startle her agitated sister. She rested one hand on Ursula's face, remembering Ilsa's hug and the Wardens and their hugging. Touch, how often did any of them touch? It was so wonderful. Like water after a long spell of thirst. Maybe Ursula would sense some of that wonder.

"I know you don't want the outside world to harm us, but we are called by God to take Quill in and care for him. And if you fear that, you have to face that fear."

Ursula was much taller than Jo, built bigger all around, though still slender, like Grandma. And Ursula had been the boss, the parent of this family, but right now Jo was teaching her.

"If taking Quill in means danger, we will face that danger together. We are strong women, Ursula. In everything else, except the outside world, you are the strongest, bravest woman I know. You can do this. You can obey God's call to love your neighbor as yourself."

"God also tells us to beware of a wolf in sheep's clothing. We do not know these people."

"The Bible doesn't say that."

Jo whirled around to face Dave. Ursula grabbed Jo's shoulders. Ursula might have ducked, but she was several inches taller than Jo and that left her with little shelter.

"Of course it does." Jo shook her head. What poor knowledge he had of the Scriptures. And now was no time to bring it up anyway. Ursula knew her Bible very well, and she wouldn't take someone criticizing—

"Sinner!" Ursula jabbed her finger straight at Dave's chest as true as an arrow in flight. It came right out alongside Jo's cheek. "How dare you come into my house and tell me my beliefs are wrong? How dare you go against one of the Good Books?"

Dave looked from Ursula to that finger she was using almost like a weapon to Jo. Without turning his back on them, Dave called out, "Ma, get in here."

Since his mother was probably in there fighting for Quill's life . . . well, maybe not quite that, but still the trip had been hard on him . . . Jo doubted she'd respond.

"What is it?" Ma came out looking alarmed.

Jo had to admit there'd been a tone in Dave's voice that would put wings on a mother's feet.

Dave said, "This is Ursula, Jo and Ilsa's big sister."

Ursula still stood, pointing, accusing. Though she had quit talking for a second.

Jo doubted that would last.

"She thinks the story of 'The Wolf in Sheep's Clothing' is from the Bible."

"Oh." Ma frowned at Dave. "It is. It's from Matthew. Um . . . I can't remember the chapter and verse but it says, 'Beware of false prophets, which come to you in sheep's cloth-ing, but inwardly they are ravening wolves.'"

"That story is there," Ursula said, "but there is also the one from the smaller of the two Bibles. A certain wolf could not get enough to eat because of the watchfulness of the shep-herds. But one night he found a sheepskin that had been cast aside and forgotten. The next day, dressed in the skin, the wolf—"

"No, that's not the Bible verse." Ma glanced back at the room, a furrow of worry creasing her forehead. Mitch and Ilsa were with Pa, and Ma trusted them both, but it was clear she wanted to be in there helping. "The story you're telling is based on the Bible verse. But what you're quoting is not biblical."

"Heretic." Ursula's finger shifted.

Dave muttered, "They think the story of 'The Boy Who Cried Wolf' is in the Bible, too."

Jo pitied him. Ursula seethed.

Ma's brow arched. "Where did you find it in the Bible, can you show me?"

Jo was impressed with the reasonable tone. Being called a heretic couldn't be any fun.

"I'll get it." Jo rushed to the little table in the front-right corner of the room and picked up the Good Books and brought them to Ma.

Ma took them both, set the smaller of the two black books aside, and held out the big one, then glanced at Jo. "Where is it?"

Ursula marched over to the smaller book and hugged it to her chest. "It's in here."

This time Ma arched both brows. She could honestly say quite a lot with her eyebrows. "That's not the Bible, this is." She held up the big book.

"We have both Bibles," Ursula said with tight anger, as if on the verge of driving Ma out of the temple for selling doves. Then Ursula's chin came up. "If you don't know both of them, that is your own failing. I'm sure not everyone can afford two books. But we were blessed with both of them, and we know every word."

Very quietly, as if afraid she'd startle a madwoman, Ma said, "Can I see it?"

Ursula froze.

Jo said quietly, "It's right they should know the Bible, all of it. Both books. It would be a sin to keep God's Word from them."

Ursula, with motions made jerky by her unwillingness, slowly extended the little volume. Ma just as cautiously reached out. She took it.

Ursula didn't let go.

Ma waited.

She waited some more.

Then, with a yank, Ma got the book away from Ursula and looked down at it.

Dave leaned in to look at the printing on the cover. He shook his head with tiny, violent motions. "What is this?"

Ma thumbed it open, turned a page, turned another, finally after much study, she said, "This isn't written in English."

Dave leaned close. "I don't recognize a single word." He looked up at Jo. "Can you read this? Do you speak this language?"

"Yes, of course."

"What language is it?"

"It's . . . it's . . . what do you mean?" Jo reached for the book and thumbed through the pages. "Here is 'The Boy Who Cried Wolf.'"

She began, "'A shepherd boy tended his master's sheep near a dark forest, not far from—'"

"Wait a minute." Dave came to stand by her side. He jabbed a finger at a single word in the middle of the page. "What's that word right there say?"

Swallowing hard, Jo squinted at the book, then shook her head and thrust the book at her much older and wiser big sister. "You tell him."

Ursula took the book with a disgusted sniff. Since Jo had handed her the open book, Ursula took it and started on the same story. "'A shepherd boy tended his master's sheep near—'"

"Stop." Dave pointed at a different word, lower on the page. "Tell me what that one word is. I sure can't read it."

Ursula hesitated, then snapped the book closed. Dave barely got his finger out in time.

Hugging the book to her chest, Ursula said, "You mock the Holy Scripture."

"Ma." Dave sounded so annoyed, Jo almost smiled. He was glaring at Ursula, standing right in front of both of them. Ma came up to his side and looked between Jo and her sister for a while.

Finally, Ma came up with the other Good Book in hand and opened it to the very beginning. "Read this."

Jo knew it exactly. "In the beginning—"

"No." Dave interrupted her reading and pointed to a single word. "What's that word say right there?"

Jo moved through the Scripture in her head until she was to the word he pointed to. "Evening."

"I saw you talking your way up to it." Dave sounded about as aggravated as a man could be. What was wrong with him?

"Hush, son." Ma came up beside him and caught his arm. Dave gave her a sharp glance, and Jo noticed Ma's fingers were really dug in. Might even be painful. Whatever it felt like, it hushed him up.

"We need to think about this." Ma was deeply silent as she looked at the book, frowning.

Then she said at last, "Ursula, you don't want us here, that much is clear. We're sorry to invade your home this way. I've already set our cowhands to building a suitable cabin immediately, and they'll work fast, but I think my husband's life might depend on having warmth and shelter for the next few days. Will you allow us to stay?"

Jo was sorry Ma had put it like that, because it wasn't wise to give Ursula a choice.

Ma went on. "I have good supplies, we brought up almost all our food stores from the ranch house we abandoned in the lowlands. We have enough for the whole winter. We're bringing you more work, but I can help. We can use my flour, my potatoes. I've got apples, and we can make pie."

Ma's voice took on a strange tone, almost like she was . . . tempting them. And who was it that was the Great Tempter? And yet Jo couldn't quite picture Ma with horns and a pitchfork.

"I know you feed yourself without such supplies. It's clear

you've survived well for years. Maybe you could teach me about the food you find up here and how you prepare it."

"I had her apple pie last night, Ursula. It's a wonder." Jo would've let Ma have the house for more apple pie. So maybe there was some temptation going on. Satan and apple pie didn't seem to go together. Although Satan and fruit did. Jo shook away the confusing notion.

"And I'll leave enough flour, lard, apples, and sugar with you when we go, so you can make plenty of it."

Jo leaned close to Ursula, who stood rigid with fear. It showed itself as anger, but Jo knew it for what it was. Ursula, still hugging the smaller of the Good Books, watched Ma.

Jo thought she saw just a hint of longing under the anger and fear . . . and that took some imagination to see, but Jo had plenty of that. And it wasn't longing for apple pie, it was longing for an older woman to talk to. It'd been so long since Grandma died. So much longer since they'd lost Ma. Jo thought maybe Ursula had missed their own ma just as Jo did.

"They've been up here several days, Ursula. I know it hasn't been two weeks, like Grandma asked of Grandpa, but it has been days." Six days for Dave and his men. Two for Quill and Ma and their cowhands. One day for Mitch. Jo didn't want to load Ursula down with details. "And none of them have any illness. So, we won't get sick from them."

It hadn't really been long enough—not by Grandma's standard—certainly not long enough in Mitch's case—but Jo didn't want to debate how long it took for someone to come down with a disease. Surely Grandma was being overly cautious. "And if the Wardens being up here draws outlaws, we won't have to worry about that until spring. And we'll have to worry about that in the spring no matter where they sleep while they're here."

Ursula flinched and clutched the book tighter.

Jo whispered, "It's time to be brave, Ursula."

That earned her a furious glare.

"It's time to be the Good Samaritan. They aren't the wolves in sheep's clothing. They're real sheep, nice as can be." Jo wasn't exactly sure the Wardens were sheep, but sometimes a woman got to talking and her mouth led her in strange directions.

Anyway, better to encourage Ursula to think of them as sheep instead of wolves. Probably best if she thought of them as people, but—Jo shook her head.

Turning to Ma, she said, "Last night's apple pie was as good as anything I've ever eaten. Will you really make us another one?"

"I would love to." Ma smiled. It touched something in Jo. Something that had been sleeping for a long time. A part of her that had missed a mama she couldn't even remember, except for a few wispy moments. When Dave had touched her, Jo had realized she thirsted for physical touch. Now she knew she thirsted for a ma, too, and maybe everybody did. Why wouldn't they? It seemed normal and good to like Ma Warden so much. . . . It wasn't about temptation, it was about loneliness and love.

Jo gently elbowed Ursula, who seemed to be sitting balanced between yes and no. The elbow knocked her to the yes side.

"You can stay. And I'd like a bite of pie, too. And I'd like to learn to bake one. Maybe we can work to-to-together on it."

Ursula was a loner, even among the three of them. She didn't do "together" very well. It might be fun to watch her try.

A shout came from the bedroom. Quill, in pain.

"Watch what you're doing," Mitch thundered.

"I can't pack this wound right without it pinching a little." Ilsa's voice bit like a rattler. Jo looked at Ursula, who looked back, alarmed. Where had that voice come from in their little fairy princess of a sister?

"Pinching? He about came off the bed."

"Mitch Warden, you get out here." Ma had herself a voice, too.

Jo wasn't sure if she could snap people to attention like Ma or roar like Mitch. But if Ilsa could do it, then Jo could. Although honestly, she hoped no need came up to yell at anyone. She was a peaceful woman.

Then she snuck a look at Ursula, clutching the book Jo now realized she really couldn't read. A strange notion because she thought she knew how.

And who would tell such a story as a boy crying wolf if not some kind of prophet or even Jesus himself? It was too wise to just be some idle story. Why, there was even a moral at the end about honesty that was right out of the Ten Commandments. Frowning, she listened to Ilsa hiss like some kind of demented rattlesnake. Ma yelled again, and Mitch came out snarling.

Strange, he'd mostly been hugging people up until now. This was an unfortunate side of him.

Ma jabbed a finger at Dave. "You go in and help Ilsa." Then that sturdy weapon turned to point at Mitch. "You go see what needs doing outside. Unload the supplies we brought. Put our horses up. Do any outside chores, and don't come back in until you've calmed down."

Then Ma's bottom lip quivered, and she launched herself into Mitch's arms again. "I'm sorry. You've barely been home a day. I'm sorry to scold. I won't do it again. You just sit down, and we'll get you a meal, and—"

"No, now calm down, Ma. I don't think our doctor lady knows what she's doing, strange medicines and whatnot. But I don't know any better, either. I reckon it's just been a long journey, and I'm overly worried for Pa. I will go put the horses up and get the supplies brought in. I would be mighty pleased if you'd make a pot of coffee." He'd never removed his coat, so he gave his ma a loud smacking kiss on the cheek, tugged his hat in an odd way, then left.

Jo turned to see tears coursing down Ma's face. She went to her. "What can I do to help? I don't want you to cry."

Ma produced the fussiest looking piece of cloth from the wrist of her sleeve and used it to wipe her eyes, then blew her nose.

"I'm just so happy to see my son. I've got this huge joy just packed inside, and it's coming out in wild ways. Tears and hugs and even temper, I'm afraid. As if a simple smile of happiness just isn't big enough to express all I feel. Does that make sense?" Ma dabbed at her eyes again.

"Not even the littlest bit of sense, Ma."

A chuckle escaped with a few more tears. "No, well, it hardly makes sense to me. I'm just fumbling around trying to apologize for all my rudeness, and explain it to you and to myself at the same time."

Ma tucked the cloth away. "I've got control of myself now."

Mitch came in right then carrying sacks loaded with supplies. One of the cowpokes brought in another. They both left and returned with as much of a load a second time.

"That's a good start," Mitch said. "I'll be in with more later, but I've brought most of the food. You can find what you need for a meal."

He reached for the door and paused. "Jo, do you have chickens to feed and cows to milk, chores like that? I can see to them."

"Oh yes, that would be fine." Jo carried a bucket to him in one hand and a bowl for the eggs in another. When she got close she whispered, "I don't think I should leave Ursula alone until she's calmed down some."

Mitch whispered back, "Try to calm both of your sisters down. The one working on Pa is a caution, too."

Jo quickly explained what Mitch needed to know for the chores, including the hidden cave where the chickens roosted and the side canyon where their cattle grazed, tucked away from view of the cabin.

Dave stepped out of the room where Ilsa tended Quill.

Mitch said, "You shouldn't leave Ilsa alone with Pa."

Dave stared at his brother in a mighty confused way, then turned and went back to Quill's bedside.

The second the door clicked shut with Mitch leaving, Dave came back. "I can't figure what he didn't like about the way Ilsa was treating Pa. His wound is tender, but I watched her, and she's doing it same as usual, and Pa wasn't fussing. He was embarrassed he let out that one shout."

Ma rested one hand on his shoulder. "Don't get on about it,

David. I think Mitch is just feeling like he should have been here before. Now that he is, he's trying to make up for his absence by being overly protective of your father. It's a shame he scolded Ilsa, but I think his heart is in the right place."

Ma turned to her cooking and began mixing and chopping, rolling and measuring, with speed and skill.

Jo watched in wonder as Ma turned apples into peeled and sliced curves, then threw things into a bowl and mixed with her hand until she produced a white ball that she put on a floured spot on the table and flattened into a circle, her hands moving so fast Jo couldn't catch all the details.

Jo noticed Ursula watching, too, but with a slightly less friendly expression. In fact, Ursula looked for all the world like someone had taken her place.

Dave helped Ma, and Jo listened to them visit about simple things like food and the weather and how happy they were to see Mitch.

Jo got the feeling both of them were talking lightly and moving carefully to give Ursula time to calm down and maybe start to believe they meant her no harm.

Jo wondered if she should press her back to the door to prevent Ursula from making an escape attempt. There was still the window, too, but Jo could only be in one place.

When the Wardens were giving all their attention to the kitchen chores, Jo eased up by Ursula and tugged on her arm. She got Ursula moving and didn't stop until she'd drawn her into an empty bedroom. Ursula's own room, where it looked like all three Nordegren sisters would be sleeping tonight.

Jo closed the door, shutting themselves away from the Wardens. Whispering, Jo asked, "Can we read?"

Ursula jerked as if Jo had jabbed her with a pin. She opened her mouth, anger flashing in her eyes, then said . . . nothing. She looked down at the book she held clutched in her arms, she relaxed her hold, then slowly, as if afraid something might jump out at her, she went straight to the story of "The Boy Who Cried Wolf." There was a drawing at the top of the first page of a wolf, and Jo realized she'd always known which story it was by the picture. All the stories began with a simple drawing.

Staring at the words, Ursula began slowly. "A shepherd boy tended his master's sheep near a dark forest, not far from—" She clamped her mouth shut and stared at the words. Finally she closed the book with reverent silence and looked up, her eyes brimming with tears. "I can only read it in the exact right order. Your fr-friend is right. I can't pick out a word on its own and read it. But I know the whole story—isn't that reading?"

Rather than answer the question, Jo clutched Ursula's arm. "I know all Grandma said about how dangerous the outside world is."

Ursula trembled violently. Jo slid an arm across her back and pulled her into a hug. "Think of how much they need help. They don't even know about this whole other Bible. We can teach them. And Ursula, think of how much they could help us. The food will be so welcome. Mitch is doing the chores for us right now. And what if—" Jo leaned close, to enlist Ursula's cooperation before any of the Wardens could hear—"what if they could teach us to read?"

Ursula looked up and a single tear rolled down her cheek. "You know there are long stretches of the big Bible that we pass over. I'd decided it was because they weren't important. Remember how Grandma would skip whole books? She'd call them history lessons not heavenly lessons, remember? Maybe we shouldn't be skipping them. They can help us, and we can help them." Jo leaned closer. "The Wardens are wrong about there being one Good Book. We can teach them more than they can teach us. It's an act of Christian love to share our other Good Book."

"B-but how can we share it if we can't read it, and they can't read it?" Ursula clamped her lips shut as if she knew she'd just accepted that the Wardens were staying.

Jo's spirit soared, but she controlled the excitement, instead, frowning down at the open book. "Grandma spoke these Bible stories in English. So even if the Wardens can't teach us to read this, we can tell them the stories. If they don't learn what's in both Good Books, can their souls be saved?"

Ursula looked at the door, looked *through* the door as if studying the Wardens' souls.

"We have to help them, Ursula. They are the lions caught in a trap of ignorance. We will be the mice that nibble them loose."

Ursula reluctantly looked down at the Good Book. "It's as if God sent them here so we could teach them and they could teach us." She hugged the book to herself then, and though it trembled, her chin came up and determination flashed in her eyes. "It's our Christian duty to let them stay."

Jo threw her arms around her big sister, too pleased to hide it.

"If they become dangerous," Ursula said sternly, "we have

166

to flee. We have to. I won't let our family die. Grandma taught me too well."

"Let's hope we don't have to flee at least until spring." Jo heaved a sigh of relief and said, "So you're all right if I tell them they can stay?"

Ursula's mouth turned down into a deep frown, her brows lowered, and creases appeared on her forehead. Everything about her seemed to speak of defeat and fear.

"God didn't ask the Good Samaritan to give his life." Jo pushed Ursula to get past her doubts. "But Jesus had to. It's the Christian thing to do, even if it endangers us. 'Greater love hath no man than this, that a man lay down his life for his friends.'"

Ursula's brow arched and she scowled. "They're not *my* friends."

"'Love does no ill to his neighbor.'"

"'A fool is reckless.'"

"'Let not your heart be troubled.'" Jo could keep this up all day.

"'A prudent man foreseeth the evil, and hideth himself.'" Ursula could too.

Jo wanted to quit now that Ursula was going to let the Wardens stay and go help Ma. So she pulled out her strongest verse.

"The greatest commandment: 'Thou shalt love the Lord thy God.'" Jo met Ursula's gaze. "'And the second is like unto it, Thou shalt love thy neighbor as thyself.' The greatest and second greatest, Ursula, no verse you quote can be above these."

Jo wanted to shake her sister. They weren't going to die

just because they had company come over, for heaven's sake. But she didn't want to make any sudden moves around Ursula, not when she'd given her consent, however reluctantly, to letting the Wardens stay.

"Let's go tell them. And tonight, after the meal, maybe we can try and help them understand about the second Good Book."

"The poor things," Ursula whispered.

Nodding, Jo led the way out of the bedroom.

17

Wax waited until he was summoned.

It didn't suit him to wait on any man. But he wanted his pay from Bludge, and it was gettin' so he could barely look at his boss. Wax was in no hurry to see him.

He sat in a cabin usually given to the ramrod, the second-in-command after the ranch foreman. But Wax didn't like sharing, and the ramrod had moved on with the cold weather.

He liked to live in an orderly place. As neat as his waxed beard and moustache. And in a bunkhouse full of cowhands there was always a mess. He also liked privacy to clean his guns and sharpen his knives because he didn't like anyone knowing where he kept his hideout weapons.

A couple of the guns he wore right out front where anyone could see them. His two Colt Peacemakers, holstered on each hip. His Winchester was always either hanging from a strap over his shoulder or stuck in his saddle. But he had Russian two-shot pepperboxes up both sleeves and a Smith and Wesson rimfire six-shot in a special holster under his shirt. The same with the knives. One was in a scabbard on his belt, easy to see, but he had four more concealed here and there.

He cleaned the guns, sharpened the knives, and put all his firepower and cutting power back where they belonged. He even slept with most of them. Then he waited for Bludge to demand a report. He was mighty demanding, as were most men who hired their fighting done.

A hard fist hit the door. "Boss wants to see you."

The footsteps faded away fast. No one liked to look him in the eye when they were hollering out orders.

No one except Bludge.

Wax judged the rest of the men to be wiser than the boss, and that was never a good thing.

Jo and Ursula came out of the bedroom where they'd been whispering over that strange foreign book.

The sisters made a picture. The three were so different from each other. Jo was the prettiest with pale yellow hair and eyes so light blue they were almost gray. Those eyes flashed like fire when she was aiming and shooting with that bow and arrow. Jo was a little thing with fine bones.

Next to her, Ursula had hair more white than yellow, but Ursula was a good five or six inches taller. And she was a full-grown woman with generous curves and visible strength in her arms. As different as two blue-eyed blondes could be.

Ilsa wasn't beside them, but she wasn't a woman to be forgotten. She was an inch or so shorter than Jo, and so dainty she looked like she might be able to fly. Masses of dark hair and bright blue eyes full of mystery and dreams. But when it came to doctoring, Ilsa was confident and quick. All that mystery faded to knowledge and practical thoughts.

Of the three, Ursula was by far the most hostile. Right now, trouble flashed in her eyes. Dave saw only two ways for this to end. Either she left or his whole family did. He hunted around in his brain for something to say to Ursula to pick a third way and all stay together.

He figured he would've had less trouble reasoning with fractious longhorns.

What could he say? What would make her accept them and trust them? Well, *trust them* might be a little much to ask. But what could they say that'd keep everyone inside out of the cold?

Be honest? Ask about the reason for her fears? Talk of things . . . like . . . his pa taking a bullet to the belly? An oncoming snowstorm that would trap her with strangers for months? Ask her what in the world made her think there were two Bibles?

Nope, honesty was a bad plan, nothing in the truth to make her calm down.

"Ursula, we brought flour with us. And Ma's making bread. What do you use to make bread if you don't have flour?" That's it. Ask her about her life. She could teach them.

Ursula's eyes narrowed, and she clutched that strange book tighter. What was in it? He'd have to let one of the Nordegren women read it later, and by *read* he meant quote it from memory while turning the pages. Could they possibly have the whole Bible memorized in the same way? It wasn't possible that they could read English but not realize this book wasn't in English.

"I know some healing. Near as much as Ilsa. Let me go see how your father abides." Ursula headed straight for Ilsa's room, now remade into a hospital.

Dave opened his mouth, then closed it and watched Ursula walk right past him without once glancing his way. She went into Pa's room with Ilsa, and he knew a little of how Mitch felt with a strange woman tending Pa. He didn't put any crazy behavior past Ursula, but he thought Ilsa would protect her patient, so he let Ursula go.

The minute she was out of sight, he rushed to Jo's side and whispered, "What did you say in there?"

Jo touched one finger to her lips and whispered back, "You can stay. Try and not be dangerous in any way, please."

Dave nodded. As long as neither Bludge nor Wax got up here, he felt safe making that promise.

"Jo, come over here, please," Ma said. "You can help me peel these potatoes and shape the loaves. I've already made the pie crust. If you're interested, tomorrow I'll teach you how."

Jo's eyes lit up. Dave decided *pie* was the word he'd adopt as the one thing that would get Jo to do most anything.

Then Jo doing most anything caused his mind to skid like a longhorn on a frozen pond. Things flashed through his mind and shocked him right down to his socks. He veered his mind away from "most anything."

Maybe the pie would calm Ursula down. It'd had that effect on him and Mitch when they were boys.

Dave came up beside Jo. "When Mitch and I were boys, Ma used to holler for dinner, and we'd come tumbling in the room, racing, wrestling, laughing. Mitch was a lot older, so he usually won the races, but I was a scrapper and made him work for it. There we'd be, yelling and shoving, and Ma would set the dessert—be it pie or cobbler or cake—right smack in the middle of the table. Then she'd look the both of us right in the eye, and say, 'Settle down or the pie doesn't stay on the table, and you'll be going without dessert for a week.'"

Ma laughed fondly. "That is what I said word for word most every meal of your lives. It worked like magic."

"Ma is a fine cook and never put a bad meal on the table. I'd do anything for her dessert, whether as a boy or now as a man." He dropped his voice so only Jo could hear. "I hope Ma has such a fine touch for dealing with Ursula."

Jo nodded, looking worried.

Then he asked in a normal voice, "What *do* you use for flour up here?"

Jo smiled at him, and he thought of "most anything" again and was tempted to bang his head against the wall just to give him a big old lump on his head to occupy his thoughts.

Maybe some pie centered on the table and a couple of sharp words from Ma would calm him down.

"We grow corn and make johnnycakes mostly. We also grow a small field of wheat, but it's not plentiful and not for every day. We have a grinder that chops both corn and wheat. It's much coarser than your flour, but it's good. We used to have yeast—Grandpa would bring cakes of it home from his trading trips—but most of the time we used something Grandma called sourdough. We've been using that for years. It raises bread nicely, though I remember yeast bread fondly."

Jo washed her hands and went up beside Ma, who was working on the counter near the dry sink. Ma smiled at her. "Sourdough. I've used that before, but not since we began keeping yeast on hand. I'd say you can teach me a few things, too."

Ma went on, "Why don't you tell me some of the stories from your second Good Book. The one you started, 'The Boy Who Cried Wolf,' is one I've heard of, though not for years."

Mitch came in just in time to hear Ma ask to be told an old fable. Dave hoped his big brother could keep his mouth shut long enough for them to help these poor deluded women understand they were mixed up. Parable, fable, honestly, they were alike just enough a child could get confused. But adding to the Bible was a huge sin. The Nordegren women needed the Wardens to straighten them out so they had a hope of getting into heaven.

Ma looked over her shoulder at Mitch, and her eyes glowed with joy. It reminded Dave that she'd always liked Mitch best. And it appeared that was still the truth. He wondered which critter in their herd was qualified to stand in for the fatted calf, 'cause Ma looked ready to kill it and roast it.

Jo was right. This *was* the story of the "Prodigal Son." And maybe Mitch had left all his troubles back east. But what if he'd brought them along when he came home? That made him a whole lot like a wolf in sheep's clothing.

But if Dave started fussing about Mitch's troubles and then it turned out nothing was wrong . . . that would make Dave the boy who cried wolf.

He shouldn't be upset with Mitch, but he hadn't liked how close he'd been standing to Jo earlier. It made Dave think of things out of his reach, and that was nothing but a fox giving up on grapes and declaring them to look sour.

"What happened out there, Wax?" Bludge nearly stabbed Wax to death with his cold-as-sleet blue eyes. He sat behind a massive desk in an office that was near in size to the ramrod's whole house.

Bludge rocked back on a chair that swiveled and rolled. A skinny, short man in a big chair behind a big desk. And he'd bought it and had it hauled in just this year, like everything else around this place.

It was all new. Wax had known it from the beginning, but he hadn't given it much thought. The whole Pike Ranch was raw, barely built. The barn, the corrals, the bunkhouse, foreman's cabin, ramrod's cabin, and this huge ranch house. None of the wood had weathered, nothing sagged. There weren't paths worn from years of riding in and out.

There was all of that at the Warden place.

Wax was a noticing kind of man, and he'd wondered at Pike's claims of being set on by nesters. He'd talked like an old-timer, well set in the area. Wax had just thought the man was building a bigger, better homeplace, probably had a small cabin tucked back somewhere. Wax had checked with the land office in Bucksnort, and Bludge owned a mighty big stretch of property. Wax hadn't thought to ask for how long.

It set right to drive men off of land owned by someone else. And Wax had a way. Folks talked of his eyes. He struck fear into folks, and most of them moved on peacefully.

Wax wasn't going to shoot a man down, but if his cabin

burned and gunmen rode in hard, guns blazing, but no bullets landing, those folks headed on west, and they did it fast. To Wax that was fair enough. They couldn't live on land someone else owned.

But Wax had been at this job now since the beginning of summer, and they'd been going farther and farther afield. Bludge controlled forty thousand acres, and he wasn't close to satisfied.

They'd driven off nesters that Wax wondered about.

The money was good, and he'd seen Bludge's deeds, but he hadn't seen them lately, and he couldn't remember the exact borders. Bludge had also split up his gunmen, and in groups that went their own way, without Wax, there'd been a few deaths. Fair fights, they said.

Wax had begun to get very tired of this job.

He needed a stake, and he'd already made plans to stick out the month, take his pay, pick his moment, and quietly ride away. Start a new life.

He needed this month's pay for his plans to work.

Then a couple of days ago Bludge had pointed to a nester on his land, and Wax had ridden out.

He'd found a well-set-up ranch, years old. With all the signs of being there long before Bludge. Wax wasn't sure about deeds and such, but the Wardens were a long way from nesters.

"We cleared them out, boss."

"I want to get someone settled in their cabin permanently. Watch over the cattle left behind. Those cows are on my land, and I'm claiming them. It equals the rent they should've been paying me."

"Are you going to rent out chunks of your land?" Wax knew the answer and should keep his mouth shut.

"Not on your life." Bludge laughed like a donkey brayed, and it set Wax's teeth on edge.

He bit his teeth together to keep from giving information to his boss that would only upset things.

Things like there were precious few cattle at the Circle Dash spread.

There were signs that Warden had a big herd. Maybe a thousand head, judging from the pasture size and the fencing and the number of horses, all of them gone, but plenty of signs of how many had been there.

Something else he didn't mention was that man high up on a cliff where there was no trail. No reason for a man to be up there unless he was trying to stay close, and that didn't bode well for Bludge's fight with the Wardens to be over.

"Winter's coming down on our heads, Wax."

"How are the winters here? How deep does the snow get? How cold are the winds? I spent winters not that much south of here and things are pretty mild."

"We—we—uh . . . it's hard to say. It can get mighty deep, and the weather bitter cold, and it can be mild, too. Unpredictable. We're higher up, of course, than the land south of here."

Wax was struck by Bludge's vague answer. Everyone knew what to expect from the winter where they lived.

Bludge didn't know.

He hadn't lived here long at all. Was it possible he'd just come in this spring with a herd, bought up a lot of land, built these buildings, and started hiring gunmen to drive off nesters? Or were they nesters at all? Maybe they were homesteaders with an honest claim. But Wax had seen deeds.

Wax was braced to refuse to spend the winter with a couple of back-shooters from Bludge's crew.

"Wax, I want you to hold the Warden place alone. Treat it like a line shack. You'll have to move fast before the snow gets any deeper. I don't expect trouble there, but I might have it closer to home and want plenty of men around this place."

"It's already so deep it'll be a fight to get back there unless this lets up."

"Can you do it?" Bludge said it in a way that called Wax a weakling, maybe a coward. Since he was neither of those things, Wax didn't let it bother him overly—if you didn't count wanting to knock Bludge's teeth down his throat, and Wax didn't count it because he didn't do it.

"I'll need supplies and a couple of packhorses." Wax was careful not to sound eager, but getting out of here, alone, for the winter, well, it suited him. The Wardens had a tight, well-set-up cabin. He might make it through the whole winter without having to quit this job. It was only October, and if things snowed in like they looked to be going to, Wax might earn a whole winter's pay before he quit in the spring, and do precious little, what with their being few cows to tend. And without having to scare off any more nesters.

"Sure, get what you need. We're done with most of the nester trouble for the year. Things get pretty sleepy around here in the winter." Bludge had a look on his face Wax didn't like.

Running his fingers over his stiffly waxed moustache and the goatee that came to a point below his chin, Wax wondered why Bludge would send his toughest gunman away like this. Was he still expecting trouble from the Wardens? Did he know they were a hardy bunch and wouldn't give up that ranch without a fight?

Wax didn't doubt it. But they were snowed away, or would be soon. Any trouble wouldn't come until spring.

He thought again of the man he'd seen high up on the side of that cliff and knew he was one of them. Things weren't going to be simple. But Wax expected a quiet winter and to be gone as soon as he picked up his pay in the spring. He'd head for California and a new life with a new name. His own name.

"I'll head right out if that's all right, boss. The snow's let up some for now, but if I wait even until morning, I might not make it."

"Go." There was nothing about Bludge's tone to like. But Wax didn't mind going, so he jerked his chin in agreement and backed most of the way to the door, trying to look like it wasn't because he didn't care to turn his back on the boss.

Then he wheeled and went out, ready to get away from all of them. Hoping he hadn't already left too late. Hoping he wasn't heading to the worst possible place to spend the winter.

18

As they gathered at the table, Ursula began their usual prayer with her singing.

"Praise God, from whom all blessings flow."

Ilsa and Jo never sang along. Ursula's voice was too beautiful. They both preferred to listen.

"Praise Him, all creatures here below."

Ma set the pie in the middle of the table just as Dave said she always did before a meal, then turned to listen to the song.

Ursula sang with her eyes closed as was proper for a prayer. But Jo, who usually did, too, watched the Wardens to see how they'd act.

"Praise Him above, ye heavenly host."

Mitch and Dave straightened and watched as Ursula sang. Both of them seemed frozen in place. And it was a beautiful song, so Jo understood.

"Praise Father, Son, and Holy Ghost."

Ursula's voice faded, and she kept her head bowed. Jo bowed hers, eyes closed, late but still in time to pray in her heart for things to go well. For Ursula to let go of her fear. For Quill to get well. She always prayed for her parents. They were dead, it had to be true. Yet, Jo had always asked God to care for them wherever they were.

Jo opened her eyes in time to see Ursula raise her head. Everyone in the room watched her in silence.

Ma spoke first. "You have the most beautiful singing voice I've ever heard, Ursula. You have blessed us with 'The Doxology.'"

Frowning, Ursula said, "Blessed you with the what?"

"That song. I know it well. It's a very common way to pray before a meal. It's got a title: 'The Doxology.'"

"I've never heard its title before," Jo said. She glanced at the table, loaded with steaming-hot food. The delicious smell made her mouth water. "Can we eat?"

With a smile, Ma said, "Of course."

The meal was the best Jo had ever had, even better than the food Ma had cooked before. But it was awkward because Ursula took her plate and stood in a corner.

Jo was surprised to feel embarrassment for her big sister. She hadn't spent much time worrying over what anyone thought of her. It had just been her sisters, and they were all used to each other. But Ursula's behavior was odd and shameful. So rude, so ignorant. All her fears were nonsense and unchristian. Facing other people was hard for Ursula, but it had to be done.

Once the meal was finished, including a pie so delicious it almost brought tears to Jo's eyes, and before Ursula could escape to her room, Jo said baldly, "We don't know how to read."

Ilsa had missed all of this with her doctoring. Now they sat, six of them at a table for four. There'd only been four chairs, but Mitch had settled into a rocking chair he pulled close, and of course Ursula stood. Quill had stayed in bed, so she didn't count him.

"We do too know how to read," Ilsa said, sounding surprised and a little insulted. "Why do you say that? We can read both Good Books all the way through. We've done it many times."

"There aren't two Good Books," Mitch snapped.

Ma swatted him on the back of the head. "Hush. Just you hush."

Mitch looked up at her, one brow arched. Jo could see the man had a whole lot he wanted to say, but to his credit, he minded his mother.

Dave said quietly, "You have the stories *memorized*. That's a handy thing, but you just know them in English and say them, probably from hearing them read . . . uh told . . . to you over and over. You didn't even know it's written in a foreign language."

"It's written in what?" Ilsa asked. "What does 'foreign language' mean?"

"It's a language other than the one we speak."

Furrowed brow, a slightly tilted head, Ilsa was the image of a confused woman. "You mean some people don't speak English? And we couldn't understand what they were saying? Why don't all people speak the same?"

"I reckon we know both Bibles that way, too, then. We read from one of them most every night." Jo thought of how she'd been out watching the Wardens before they'd seen her, then she'd been with the family as much as she could. She hadn't read the Bibles in days. Of course, now it appeared that she hadn't ever read the Bibles.

Hastily, Ma said, "That's a wonderful and impressive thing if you have so much of the Scripture memorized."

Nice as Ma was, Jo was left feeling mighty stupid.

Ma went to pick up the Bible and opened it, lovingly, gently turning to a place quite a ways from the front. They always started at the front and read their way through. Each of them taking a turn. Each of them read one chapter every night. They'd been reading Psalms lately. It was strange to see Ma pick it up and open it in such a disorderly way. They'd marked the book with a slip of paper that had always been in it. Now Ma just picked any old spot.

But then if Ma could truly read, she could start in anywhere. Jo was still a little suspicious about whether or not the Wardens were right. After all, Jo had been reading for years.

Ma sat at the narrow end of the table, with Dave at the other narrow end. Jo and Ilsa faced each other. Ursula stood near the door to her room, but she didn't leave.

Mitch rocked near Ma's left elbow.

"Well, will you look at this."

Jo leaned to see what had caught Ma's eye.

It was a strange section she had always flipped past. Several pages had handwriting on them. It had seemed disrespectful for someone to write in the Bible like that.

"What is it?"

Ma drew one finger down the page slowly, studying. Her finger stopped right near the bottom of the writing. "Here are your names and the dates you were born."

Ma looked up. "This says, Josephine Sigrid Nordegren. It has the day you were born. You're twenty-four years old."

Smiling, Ma said, "Ilsa is nineteen."

"Is my name more than just Ilsa?" There was a strange, frightened look on Ilsa's face, and Jo understood it. It was odd to think they hadn't known their whole names.

"Yes, it's Greta. Ilsa Greta Nordegren. You must be Swedish. I think those are Swedish names."

"Danish," Ursula said. "Now that you say Swedish, I remember Grandpa teasing Grandma about being a Swede. She'd get huffy in a way that was funny, an old joke between them, and say she was not a Swede, she was a Dane and Danes were far better than Swedes."

"And you're Ursula Susan. Susan is your mother's name. The date she married your father is listed here."

Nodding, Ursula said, "I always knew I bore my ma's name, and I knew my sisters' middle names, too. I remember my ma telling me what she'd named each of us."

Ma ran her hand up the page. "There is no date written in for the death of your grandparents, nor your parents."

"I never saw anyone write in the Bible." Jo watched Ma's hand caress the fragile paper. "Maybe it was Grandma who wrote these things down, and how could she write in a death for our parents when we had no idea what happened to them? Then when Grandma died, I suppose Grandpa never thought to write it down."

"Your Grandmother lost five children."

"What?" Ursula gasped. "She had children besides our pa?"

"Yes, here are two daughters during her first marriage."

"*First* marriage?" Jo almost hollered. "She was married before Grandpa?"

Ma tapped on the Bible at a group of names. "Yes, your grandpa was her second—no, I think he's her third husband."

"What?" Ilsa squeaked.

Ma ran her hand up, then down, then up again, reading silently. Finally, she said, "Her first died at the same time as her daughters, all of cholera back east. It says Baltimore. And there was a son, Josef, who is listed as born but no death date. Then your grandma remarried and had a child in North Platte, Nebraska, so that must've been the year they came west, because the Oregon Trail follows the Platte River west."

"Not Josef." Jo pronounced the *J* like the letter of her first name. "Yo-sef."

Nodding, Ma said, "I have heard that. It's probably the Danish way to pronounce it. But it's spelled *J-o-s-e-f*. It's spelled much like the beginning of your name, Jo. I'm sure you were named after your father."

The twist in her heart was warm and hard. Tears burned in her eyes, though they didn't fall. "I've always known it as Yo-sef. It never—I never thought—" She swallowed hard. "I'm named after my father?"

So many places Jo had never heard of. Grandma had been to all of them.

"The child born in North Platte died—" Ma's voice faded. "What is it?"

"The child died of typhoid when he was two weeks old." Ma looked up, her eyes sad. "Then another child born a year later died, and so did her second husband. Then she lists a marriage date to your grandpa—it says only Colorado, no town listed. I have no idea how she got from the wagon train to Colorado. But look at the slashing handwriting. It looks like it was written in a fury. The paper is torn in spots. She still has a living child that dates back to her first marriage. Then another child born to your grandpa—that son died when he was ten of . . . it just says fever. Maybe that's when they moved this far away from town, or if they were already here, maybe they went to town and caught it there."

"Unless Grandpa came back with a sickness." Jo wondered about that remote little cabin and Grandpa's long absences every time he went to town. Had that been built after Grandpa brought something deadly home?

"We can't tell the circumstances from what your grandma has written down. There aren't details about how the disease came to her home. There's a note of a death. William Anderson, fever. He's the only child your grandma and grandpa had together." Ma drew her finger up the page and suddenly Jo was mad to learn how to read. She wanted to understand this.

"Why wasn't William Anderson named Nordegren?"

Ma's finger moved again. From the corner of her eye, Jo saw Ursula come closer. Mitch stopped rocking and leaned in.

Ma glanced up and saw everyone watching. She hesitated. "Do you—do you girls want to hear all this? I didn't start this to upset you. It is a common practice to write down important dates—births, deaths, marriages—in a Bible. You can see the blank pages left for just that reason. But there's so much loss here. Your poor grandma lost five children and two husbands. Then her only living child left and never came back. So, in the end, she lost all six of them, but her son did leave his three daughters behind."

Jo thought of how upset Ursula already was and regretted these tales of disease and death. Her eyes slid from Ursula, scowling and scared, to Ilsa frowning silently. Ilsa nodded. Ursula folded one arm across her belly, propped her other elbow on it, and covered her mouth with her knuckles, but didn't insist they stop.

"It explains a lot about why Grandma feared the outside world. I'd like to hear it," Jo said.

"Your grandfather's name was Nils Anderson. Your father, Josef, was the son of your grandmother's first husband. He was ten years old when your grandma married your grandpa. That's why you're named Nordegren. It was your father's name."

"S-so Grandpa wasn't our grandpa?" Ilsa clutched her hands together.

"He was." Ma reached out and rested one hand over Ilsa's. "Family is of the heart, and your grandpa loved you and raised you. That makes him your grandpa. It really makes him more like your father."

"There's so much death," Ursula said. "No wonder Grandma wanted to be up here. And no wonder she snapped at Grandpa so often. She blamed him for her son dying, and she feared he'd bring illness home again."

"There's a note that says your father, Josef, had a fever, too. Just a date and his name with the word *fever* put beside it. It's right under the name of his much younger brother who died. I-I think your Grandma must have expected him to die, too. It's like she wrote it in, expecting to fill in a date of death. But he obviously recovered, because he married a year later and had three beautiful daughters."

"Before he and our ma went to the lowlands again and died of something else," Ursula said, sounding gloomy.

"But Grandpa went down all the time and never died. He never got a disease," Ilsa said.

"Except maybe once, and he brought it home with him and killed his son." Ursula wasn't going to get over that.

"We're from the lowlands, and we're alive and well," Ma said.

"Except for your gutshot husband," Ursula growled.

"But he's healing well," Ma reminded her. "Not all sickness and injury kills. Your father survived a dangerous sickness, and if your grandfather did bring it home, then he survived it, too."

"We've never heard of any of these people," Jo said. "We've never even heard of Grandpa's last name. I always thought it was Nordegren. No one was here to call him anything but Grandpa. Even Grandma called him that."

"And then your grandma—it must've been her because the handwriting is the same and has been since years before she married your grandfather—wrote the date of your parents' marriage and the dates each of you girls were born and that's the end of it. No death listed for her, your grandfather, or your parents. It just ends."

Ursula spoke haltingly. "I think now, looking back, that Grandpa couldn't read, either. Grandma read to us when we were very little, and she must've just known the stories in the smaller Bible, because she didn't read them in an unfamiliar language. But they were always the same, word for word. And she held the book and turned the pages. I was eleven when Grandma died, so I was already telling the stories. I just knew them and . . . and said them as I'd learned them. I thought that was reading."

Ma said gently, "I can teach you to read. It's not a difficult skill. I taught my boys. There was no school close enough to attend."

"I want that," Jo said. "I want to be able to see all those names you've been talking about. There are pages of them."

"Yes, this Bible is very old. It has your grandma's birth listed, her name was Greta."

"I'm named for Grandma?" Ilsa said it on a breath, sounding very pleased.

"Yes." Ma touched Ilsa's hands again. They weren't in such a tight fist now.

"The world got all of them," Ursula said. "Sickness and danger. The lowlands are teeming with both."

"Your grandparents lived to a ripe old age. You can't say the world got all of them." Ma gently closed the Bible. "It's true that the world has dangers, but it has wonders, too. You can't stay up here, cut off, your whole life."

"I can and I will."

No one mentioned that she'd agreed to let the Wardens stay.

"But don't you want to marry? Don't you want children?"

"I have my sisters."

"But what if they leave? What if they want to marry and have children? Your grandma could cut herself off because she had her family already. But you girls have none of that."

"I want none of that."

"Do you speak for your sisters? They're adult women. It's very common to want to marry and have children."

"We're content," Ursula snapped. "And now it's late. I'll go prepare my room for three, and you Wardens can take over the rest of our house while you tell us our grandma's loss and grief aren't important."

Ursula stormed from the room.

"Ursula, please, I didn't mean—"

The bedroom door slammed shut.

Jo frowned at the closed door for a time, then looked sideways at her little sister. "It's going to be like sleeping in a room with an angry grizzly."

"No," Ilsa said.

"No what?" But Jo thought she knew.

"You can't bring your bow and arrow."

19

The three sisters didn't have to fit in the room because Pa took a turn for the worse.

"Ilsa, come quick. Quill's fever is up." Ma stepped out of the room she'd headed for to sleep at her husband's side, met Ilsa's eyes, and immediately went back in.

Ilsa was running on the first step. Mitch had gone into Jo's room to sleep, and he came banging out. Still dressed, he hadn't had a minute to get to sleep. Dave hadn't even picked up the rolled-up blanket he'd been planning to use on the floor before the hearth.

Jo rushed into the room behind Ilsa. Dave and Mitch met in the doorway and stopped. They were lodged in the door, trying to fight their way in.

Both stopped. "The room's too small for us anyhow," Mitch admitted.

Nodding, Dave backed up a step, and Mitch dashed in ahead of him.

A familiar, sneaky move that Dave remembered now from their childhood.

Dave reckoned that knack for trickery was how Mitch got so all-fired rich back east.

The room really was too small for all of them . . . and it was a decent-sized room, but this was ridiculous.

Dave took a long, hard look at his pa, then said, "I'll get cold water. We can bathe his forehead."

Jo looked up and smiled. She was on one side of the bed with Mitch beside her. Ilsa was on the other side near Pa's waist unwrapping his recently packed and bandaged wound. Ma was near Pa's head, holding his hand and speaking quietly to him.

Dave saw how much Ma cared, and how brave Pa was being, mainly for her. They were the bedrock he'd grown up on. He turned his back on the crowd, praying for all he was worth.

"Let me past."

He glanced back and saw Jo emerging from the room.

"I had to get out. There isn't room. Mitch should go, too."

"I'm not leaving this woman to care for Pa."

Jo, her back to the room, made a twisted face at Dave. He stepped out of Mitch's line of sight to grin.

From the room, Ilsa spoke, "It'd be a wonder if your pa could heal up without running a fever. This is to be expected. It didn't look suppurated when I changed his bandage earlier, so I think he'll be fine, just miserable for a while."

"Do they need anything but water . . . and prayer?" Dave went to a small barrel against the back wall. Jo hurried over with a tin basin. A big ladle was hooked over the edge of the barrel, and Dave dipped out plenty of water.

They'd used up all the hot water washing dishes, so now they needed to heat more.

Jo leaned close. "I know you want to be in there with your pa, but there really isn't enough room. Maybe we can . . . can . . ." Jo looked around, then shrugged.

"What we should do is get some sleep. We can take over after a couple of hours so the others can rest."

Jo nodded. "You could even sleep in my bed."

Dave stumbled and almost fell flat on his face. And he was standing still. He gave her a wild-eyed look and remembered a few unruly thoughts he'd had earlier.

Jo studied him. "What's the matter?"

"You . . . you . . . want me in bed with you?" Dave couldn't believe those words came out of his mouth, especially when he was standing only one room away from his ma.

"What?" Jo shouted. She looked stunned and then furious. She dashed the contents of the basin in his face.

Which, Dave had to admit, wasn't really that bad of an idea. Still, he was glad they were fetching cold water, not boiling hot.

"All right then, no, you did not mean that. Even though that's what you said."

"I said you can sleep in my bed," Jo hissed, then she jabbed one finger . . . which held a basin . . . so she jabbed that, too, straight at the room Dave and Mitch had been planning to share. "While I sleep in the room with Ursula and Ilsa." Her arm came around to point at the bedroom on the far side of the fireplace and whacked Dave in the head. The basin banged, and Dave found his thoughts clearing up nicely.

"Why are you beating on my brother?" Mitch chose a poor time to quit keeping an eye on Ilsa.

"She misunderstood something." Dave took the basin from

her, had himself a little tug-of-war, but he managed it. He refilled it. Handed it to Mitch with little regard for any water being sloshed. "Now I'm going to bed . . . uh . . . to sleep. Good night. Wake me if you need help. I'm as much a doctor as most of you." He headed straight for the bedroom, water dripping off of him and even squishing some in his boots. He needed a change of clothes, although sleeping soaking wet was an idea with merit.

He glanced around to see Mitch heading for Pa's room, and to see Jo ducking into Ursula's room with unusual haste.

Dave kind of wished he had that basin again so he could give himself another dousing. Maybe he should go throw himself in a snowbank for a minute.

It bothered Wax seeing that man perched high up on the mountainside watching him. Looking out at the deep snow that kept falling, he knew tracking the Wardens was impossible. And any trail they'd found would be filled in deep with snow.

But Wax could climb.

As soon as this snow quit falling, he was going up.

For now, his only work was tending his horse, which meant fighting his way through the storm to the barn once a day.

Some careful hunting turned up a copy of a deed in Quill Warden's name to the land Wax now stood on. There were bills of sale for cattle, horses, and supplies going back over twenty years.

Wax stopped in front of a mirror and stared at his waxed

moustache and the small, well-tended beard he'd waxed into a point. The wax darkened his naturally blond hair until, with the dark facial hair, his own mother wouldn't recognize him.

As he stared for a moment, he didn't recognize himself. Or what he'd become. A man needed money to make a start for himself in this world. Wax had always been too good with a gun. Too fast with too quick a temper. Now here he was right up against becoming a hired killer for real. He had a reputation. He was a known and feared man. But he'd always believed he was a decent man, too.

Now he had his chance to leave the gunman reputation behind, if he could outrun it, of course, and Pike's money was the last thing he needed. Wax wanted that money, but it felt like the price of it might be his life, and maybe his soul.

He thought of that man watching him from on high. Like God watches. Ma had always been a believer, but when Pa had gotten the switch, Ma had no power to stop the beatings. She'd held him after. Cried and prayed and bound up his wounds. But to stop Pa, she'd have to take the beating herself, Wax knew that. And it probably wouldn't spare him, it would just delay the pain.

He'd loved his ma and loved listening to her read Bible stories. But he hadn't taken up the habit of reading the Bible since he'd left home years ago, as a boy of fifteen, after Ma and his little sisters had died at the hands of marauders and set Wax on his first manhunt.

Wax had been living off his gun for ten years now.

It struck him that he'd laid down the Bible and picked up a firearm. He didn't think a man could carry them both. Well, soldiers did, and lawmen. Wax was neither.

Looking out at the deepening snow, he lifted his eyes to the hills and wondered about that man. And wondered if God was up there looking down. And if He was, did He like what Wax Mosby had become? And, if Wax stayed and took that money, could he do it and start a new life for himself that was clean and honorable? Did God forgive a man who hired out his gun? Or was that what the verse meant about an unforgivable sin?

What he needed to do was find out exactly what those folks had done to draw Pike's wrath. And for that he needed to talk to them.

His hand went to his holstered guns. He always wore two, tied down. Both hands slid over the butts with cool ease. They weren't going to want to talk, not after one of the fools who rode with Wax had shot Quill Warden. They were going to meet him with guns blazing.

20

"The fever broke in the night." Jo slipped out of Quill's room whispering. She'd heard someone moving around and wanted to share the news.

Dave was crouched low, stirring up the fire. He turned and smiled. "Really?"

Nodding, Jo said with quiet satisfaction, "Really."

It'd been five days of constant stomach-twisting fear.

Day and night, bathing Quill to bring down the fever, coaxing water and broth down his throat. Ilsa had packed bags of snow around him a few times when the fever was frighteningly high. And she had a potion she mixed up with dried rose hips, moss, juniper berries . . . Jo wasn't sure what all. Ilsa ground it down and steeped it into a dreadful-tasting tea.

Jo had had a fever or two in her life from a cut or other injury that went deep, so she knew this tea. It tasted like baked dirt scraped off the bottom of a hoof. But it worked.

The tea battled the fever and made Quill sleep.

He needed rest to fight the infection, and without the tea he was uncomfortable and restless. Convincing Mitch to let

Quill drink the medicine was a fight. For some strange reason, he took everything Ilsa said and did wrong.

Jo appreciated that Dave seemed to trust Ilsa. He and Ma had worked hard to persuade Mitch to go along.

The two men helped administer the awful stuff. Quill, in a delirium, seemed inclined to swing a fist when they came near him, so it was good to have strength on their side.

"He's better?" Dave rose from where he was crouched by the fire, his eyes flashing with excited relief.

Jo put one finger to her lips. "He's asleep."

"He's going to make it." Dave was exuberant but quiet as he took two long steps to reach her, swept her up in his arms, and whirled her around with a laugh.

"Shhh." She slapped his shoulders but couldn't help smiling. "Your ma has hardly had a wink of sleep for days."

Dave grinned. With Jo in his arms—her feet dangling above the floor, he walked to the door, set her down for a second, and grabbed two coats off the peg, hoisted her again, and took her straight outside into the cold dawn.

"What are you doing?" Jo's whisper was met with Dave's laughing.

"I can't be quiet." He walked until they were a fair distance from the house, then he set her down in the snow, glad they both had their shoes on. He thrust her coat at her, then pulled on his own, still smiling.

Then, with a sigh deep enough to make the branches wave, he said, "Thank God." He looked up to heaven and raised both arms high and wide. "Thank you, dear God in Heaven."

Jo dragged her coat on and stood in the beautiful snow,

listening to his joy, his prayers, watching him be so relieved and happy. She realized she was smiling like a lunatic.

"He's going to make it, Dave. Your pa is going to live." She threw herself into his arms.

He caught her and whirled her around so she was lifted high enough to look down at him.

They both laughed with pleasure and relief. She hugged her arms tightly around his neck. The whirling finally stopped. The laughter calmed, and she looked down at his sparkling eyes.

Slowly. Too slowly, he lowered her to the ground, their gazes locked. The wispy snow making the world all around them seem to recede until they were really alone, the only two people in the world.

His eyes left hers to flicker downward. Almost as if he were looking at her lips. It made her feel funny in a way she really didn't understand. Her lips felt dry so she licked them, and he noticed that for sure.

Her happiness was like a flame popping to life in a lantern. They stood together, just looking. Slowly, with not far to go, Dave lowered his head and touched his lips to hers.

A kiss. She remembered kisses. Not from her grand-parents—she didn't think they did such things. But her parents were known to share a kiss.

Her arms tightened around his neck. His nose bumped hers, and he tilted his head sideways. So lovely, to be in the arms of such a fine man, in the rising dawn, in the drifting snow. The cold driven back by his strong arms.

Dave raised his head slowly, still watching her, so close he wouldn't have to speak loud at all if he talked.

"Pa's gonna make it." Dave closed his eyes as if he couldn't contain the joy.

"Yes." She leaned close because it was nice. "He woke up soaked in sweat about an hour after I took over for you. He talked to me, his thoughts clear, his fever gone. I helped him drink a good amount of water. I tried some broth, and he got a few swallows down, but mostly he was just so tired. He fell back asleep, and then your ma fell asleep. I told her I'd sit up."

Dave hugged her and took another kiss. This one longer, deeper.

Jo's eyes fluttered open, and she fully registered the dim light of dawn and realized what it meant. "It's morning. This happened quite a while ago—much longer than an hour. I must've fallen asleep." It scared her to think of how long she'd neglected Quill. "But I felt his forehead before I came out here, and the fever has stayed down."

"You've been in there since I went to bed? Mitch should've taken over." Dave pivoted to stare at the cabin door.

"I've never had to wake him up." Jo looked at the cabin, too. "I was sitting in the chair by your pa's bedside and woke up with my head resting on the mattress. Mitch was just as tired. We are all worn clean out."

Frowning, Dave said, "Not Mitch. He's got more energy than all of us combined."

Jo saw him hesitate. She didn't blame him. Mitch was probably just really tired, but Dave took a firm hold of her hand and led her back inside. He took off his coat and helped her off with hers, which seemed strange. She needed no help.

One more sweet kiss, then he went to Mitch's door and swung it open.

His voice was quiet but teasing, when he said, "Mitch, you slept through your shift."

No answer.

Jo came up behind and watched Dave swing the door wide. The room was dark, with the shutters closed and the dawn still too new to give light around the tightly fitted window shutters.

Mitch was fast asleep, and Jo had been around him long enough to know the man was always fast to wake up. And he'd gone to bed right after dinner because his turn sitting with Quill came early. He'd been asleep near ten hours by now.

Dave walked up and grabbed Mitch's leg. Sounding like a mischievous boy, Dave shook Mitch's leg hard. "You slept through your work, brother. Stop being lazy."

No answer.

With a gasp, Dave went forward, and Jo whirled and grabbed a lantern, turning it up as she brought it in. Dave was on his knees beside Mitch, whose eyes were flickering open and shut like each eyelid weighed ten pounds.

"Whaz goin' on?" Mitch slurred his usual crisp words and raised one hand to shield his eyes as if the lantern hurt them.

"Jo, he's got a fever." Dave looked up at Jo, frantic. "Bring the light close."

Jo felt a fear she couldn't understand when she obeyed Dave.

"Look at his face. He's got spots all over it."

"What is it?" Jo's mind flashed through all the diseases her kin had died from. Typhoid, cholera, fever . . . Grandma had written all those in her big Bible. Quill just had a fever, and that didn't kill him. But what did Mitch have?

Fever alone could mean a lot of things . . . spots? The sisters had fevers from time to time, related to an injury, but no rashes. She remembered Grandma having a terrible fear of rashes.

Dave shoved himself to his feet and went running. He almost tripped over his ma, who must've woken from the ruckus. She was rushing out of Quill's bedroom. Jo had insisted she sleep after Quill's fever broke. Ma had been almost constantly at her husband's side all these days.

Ma must've gotten all the urgency because she turned to rush back toward Quill's room.

"No, Ma, in here. Mitch is sick."

"Sick?" Ma skidded as she turned toward the new trouble. She whisked past Dave, dodged around Jo, and went to Mitch's side.

Jo held the lantern high while Ma talked quietly with her prodigal son.

By now, Ilsa and Ursula were awake and coming to see what had happened.

"Quill's fever broke in the night," Jo said. She knew everyone's thoughts went to him when there was an upset.

Ma looked up. Relief washed over her expression, then faded away just as fast. "One man healing and another sick."

"He wasn't shot or injured, was he?" Ursula asked. Jo saw her big sister in the flickering lantern light and thought for one second Ursula was sick, too. In fact, Jo took a step toward her to feel her forehead.

Before she could take a second step, Ma charged right toward them, clogged in the doorway.

"Get out. Now." She got out of the bedroom as fast as she'd

gone in, closing Mitch's door behind her, and everyone fell back. "Jo, Ilsa, Ursula, you all have to leave, now. Without touching anything or taking one more breath. Dave, have the men finished work on our cabin yet?"

"No, I had them add a chimney to the one in the high valley. I thought we had time—"

"Go, now. Take the girls, then get back here."

"B-but why?" Jo didn't want to be sent away. "What is wrong?"

"I've been saying you're overly worried about being sick, but I'm not sure what my son has. Mitch is newly back from New York City. He's been home a week, but who knows how many people he saw and how long he's been traveling. Many sicknesses take time to show themselves. Somewhere, on his way home, Mitch picked up something that he is just now coming down with. He could spread it to all of you."

A door slammed, and Jo turned to see Ursula was gone.

"I'll stay." Ilsa took a step forward. "You can't tend two sick men by yourself."

"No, I can't." Ma swallowed hard. "Dave, I need you back here as fast as you can get the girls settled."

"Women, Ma," Jo said, cutting her off. "We are adult women. Not children to be sent running and hiding when there is trouble. You need help. We're not leaving you to a sickness that could hurt you and Dave, and in his weakened condition will almost certainly spread to Quill."

Ma turned haggard eyes on Jo. "I doubt you've heard this, but there is a disease called s-smallpox." She swallowed hard again.

Dave gasped and looked past her as if he could see through

the bedroom door where his brother lay fighting to wake up fully. He was a sick man and no denying it. "Smallpox? You think he might have smallpox?"

"I hope to God it's not. There are other sicknesses that leave a rash."

"You hope he's got something else?" Jo didn't want to be sent away. "Why is smallpox so bad?"

Ma turned to Jo, her eyes haunted with fear. Tears brimmed, and Jo wanted to hold her against the fear. But Jo knew Ma wouldn't allow it. Not after she'd told them to get out.

"Because if Mitch has smallpox, then there's a good chance, in the next couple of weeks, about half of us will die."

Jo gasped. Ilsa came to her side and hugged her.

Ma's eyes went back to Dave. "I don't think I can care for both of them alone. I hate asking you to come back, but what else can we do?"

Dave went to the pegs by the door and settled his hat firmly on his head, then pulled on his coat. "Let's go. Jo, Ilsa, we have to get you out of here. My cowpokes have a room and chimney added to your grandpa's cabin. You can stay there."

He shoved coats at both of them. Jo wanted to stay, but all the fears and dire warnings she'd grown up with were like blizzard winds buffeting her. Feeling like the worst kind of coward, she grabbed her coat, then her quiver and bow, and rushed out, running away.

Standing on the outside, watching life. Like always.

Ilsa was slower to come out. Her little fairy princess of a sister might be the bravest of the three. Or the most foolish.

Ursula was standing back, her arms crossed, a frown nearly cutting wrinkles from the corners of her mouth to her chin.

Dave headed for the barn, hollering for help saddling horses.

"I've never ridden a horse." Ilsa sounded excited.

"How can you be happy at a time like this?" Ursula nearly vibrated with fear. Her arms weren't just crossed, they were holding her together. "After a lifetime of being careful, we let strangers onto our mountain, and after only days, we are exposed to some dreaded disease."

Ursula had left before Ma had mentioned smallpox. Jo wasn't about to tell Ursula things could be far worse than even her darkest thoughts—or no, that wasn't right. Because Ursula's darkest thoughts were exactly how bad it could get.

Dave came out leading two horses. Alberto came behind with one more.

"Let's get you up there. Alberto and Jimmy Joe will ride with you, and they'll make sure you have supplies and plenty of wood for the fire. I'm not leaving Ma alone."

Jimmy Joe and another man emerged from the barn, each leading a horse.

Dave boosted Jo up. Ursula jumped back from him when he tried to guide her to a horse.

"Do you know how to mount a horse by yourself?"

Ursula shook her head tightly.

Looking around frantically, his eyes landed on a tree stump. The tree had been dead, and his men had cut it for firewood just a few days ago. It was fairly smooth on top and about the right height for Ursula to use to climb on the horse.

"Climb up there." He pointed to the stump.

Jo was surprised her big sister did as she was told. Her need to get away must have overpowered her need to fuss over everything Dave said.

"I won't touch you. Just grab the saddle horn." Dave waited.

Jo clamped her mouth shut to not distract Ursula from the first horse ride she'd had in years, probably since before Grandpa died.

Ursula grabbed the right thing, to Jo's relief.

Dave kept a firm hold on the reins and patted his horse's neck to keep it calm—or maybe to keep his hands busy so he wouldn't grab Ursula and get her settled. Jo could see he was crazed to get back in and help his ma.

"Now swing your right leg over the saddle and hang on for the ride. I'll tie the horses together in a string, and Alberto will lead you."

Ursula was awhile getting up, and she didn't look exactly comfortable, but she was balanced on the saddle and seemed stable. At least for right now.

Jo noticed Ilsa talking to her horse. Dave had to urge her onto the horse's back next.

At last the horses were strung together, each horse tied to the one in front of it. Jo could've probably handled her own mount, but everyone was hurrying as fast as the Nordegren sisters would allow. To save time, Jo let Dave arrange things to suit him.

Dave came to her side as Jimmy Joe swung up onto his horse.

Reaching up, Dave rested one hand on Jo's, which she had wrapped around the saddle horn.

"Jo, I don't want to send you away. But it's for your own safety and the safety of your sisters."

Wordlessly, Jo nodded. She didn't want to leave him, either.

"This morning meant a lot to me, but everything has to wait until Mitch is well."

"And until we see if all of us catch this sickness and . . . and survive it." Jo swallowed hard and fought the terrible fear Grandma had instilled in her. "I want to stay. You'll need help. You and your ma are already worn down to a nub from your pa's sickness. And Ilsa is the one who knows how to make more medicine. She's prepared a good supply though, and your ma knows how to make it into tea."

"We'll be fine. Getting you to safety, I hope in time to spare you whatever Mitch has, is important." Dave's hand tightened on hers for just a moment. Their eyes clung as surely as their hands.

Alberto took the leading rein, tied it to his saddle horn, and mounted up.

Dave let go. It was a good thing, because Jo might well have held on until she was pulled right out of the saddle.

Then Alberto led them away, Jimmy Joe bringing up the rear.

Jo looked back to see Dave watching them go. Their gazes held until the trail wound them into the trees and out of sight.

21

His hand burned from touching her. His heart burned from letting her go. He was fixed to the same spot until she faded into the woods.

Then Dave remembered Mitch and was running by the time he slammed back into the cabin.

Ma was in Mitch's bedroom with cool cloths. "Let me do that, Ma. Why don't you and Pa get out of here, too. You could go stay in that little shanty we built. You should—"

"Stop, Dave." Ma was calm in times of trouble. Always the one who kept things steady. Right now, he saw near hysteria. And it was all the worse because she was trying so hard to fight it.

"Your pa and I will go nowhere, and that's that. Don't suggest it again. I asked you to take the girls then come back."

"Alberto took them, no need for me to ride so far right now."

Nodding, Ma said, "I wanted to ask Ilsa to stay. She's a wise woman with good healing skills, and we could use her help. And Jo is a hard worker with a soothing way about her. But this is the Wardens' fight. It twists like a knife to let you stay. But I can't care for both your pa and Mitch alone. And they both need good care. This is our fight, and, win or lose, our cross to bear."

Silent for a long moment, Dave battled the urge to beg Ma to leave and take Pa. If not for her sake, then for Pa's, because he'd been brought so low. One more thing might be too much. Dave didn't say it because it was a waste of both their time. Pa wasn't up to leaving. Ma and Pa were here, and they were staying.

Finally, Dave spoke his worst fears out loud. "You really think it could be smallpox?" He'd heard the terrible stories of outbreaks that left a town with half their number dead, and those who survived maimed inside and out.

Ma's jaw clenched. "Do you know Dottie McDaniels?"

"The blacksmith's wife in Bucksnort?"

"Yes, that's her," Ma said.

Dave remembered how badly scarred she was. "She's got terrible pockmarks all over her face and on her hands, every inch of her you can see."

Nodding, Ma said, "She's the only person I've ever talked to who's survived smallpox. Honestly, she's the only person I've ever talked to who knows much about it, beyond the awful things you hear."

"I've never heard she had smallpox."

"It killed her whole family back east. Her parents and five brothers and sisters. Dottie was sick for a long time, but she survived. With her family dead and gone, and being only ten years old, she ended up in an orphanage. A couple of years later she got sent west on an orphan train and ended up in a little town south of Laramie, Wyoming. She married and they came here. The little I know about smallpox I learned from her. She said the pox have a dimple in the center of them. She said to look for that dimple if I was ever worried about smallpox. And they come on fast once the fever starts, so we won't have long to wonder."

Nodding silently, Dave looked between the doors to Mitch's and Pa's rooms. "Do you want to pick one and care for him, or should we trade off?"

"For the next few days, I want you to take care of your pa."

"Ma, I—"

She raised her hand so the flat palm faced him. "Stop. I'm your mother, and I've made this decision. I am trying to protect you, but there's more. I'm trying to protect your father, too. If I go back and forth between him and Mitch, I'll have a lot more chances to spread this to him."

"Mitch did his shift tending Pa just before we ate supper."

"I know," Ma snapped. "But we don't have to expose your pa over and over, do we? Now I want you to wash your hands in hot water and soap, then see to your father. There's stew from last night. Warm some up and get some solid food into him if you can."

Dave opened his arms, and Ma stepped back so fast she ran into the door to Mitch's room. Quietly she said, "You're a fine man, David. I'm so proud of the man you've grown up to be. And I need a hug right now almost as much as I need air to breathe. But we aren't going to touch each other for a time. You set food out for me. Until I am sure of what we're facing, you stay away from any spoon I eat off of, any glass I drink from, and any towel I touch. And that is even more so the rule about anything Mitch touches. In a few days, if Mitch is only going to be a little bit sick, I just might risk that hug."

Pa called out for water. Mitch started coughing.

"I'd better get Pa a drink."

Nodding, Ma said, "Consider Mitch's room off-limits, and I don't even want you washing his dishes. You keep things washed up that you and Pa touch, and Mitch and I will just go through the supply of things already clean for the next few days. By then we should know how much trouble we'll face."

Ma pointed to a small table near the front door. Mitch's room was right to the side of it, so she could get it easily when needed. "Put a glass of water on that small table right there. I'll use it then set it out for refills. When you pour water into it, don't touch it."

A shiver went down Dave's spine. "I reckon the Nordegren women will consider Mitch bringing sickness here proof that all their fears are right. I reckon Ursula will blame Jo and Ilsa for putting them all in danger."

"At least they're locked together in the only shelter anywhere. They may be at odds, but they will have to work out their troubles. In the end, I expect they are all glad to be away from here, and somewhere they can remember they love each other and put aside their arguments."

Jo dropped to the floor as a pan whistled over her head. Ursula reached for the next pot. This one full of boiling water and a good portion of their dinner.

"Not the potatoes." Ilsa leapt at her older and much bigger

sister. "You'll waste perfectly good food. You know Grandma wouldn't approve."

"Grandma wouldn't approve of Ursula burning me to death, either." Jo was disgusted with Ursula and her rage. And she understood why Ilsa invoked waste and Grandma to calm Ursula down, but it was a little annoying that burning your sister wasn't enough.

Leaping to her feet just as Ilsa wrested the pot away, Jo charged Ursula. "I am sick of you acting like this. You calm down right now, or I promise you, I will hog-tie you and stuff you under the table, and you'll stay there until spring."

Jo thought that was a lot nicer than boiling water in the face or kicking Ursula out in the snow to cool off. In fact, now that Jo thought of it, she said, "I'm going hunting."

She poked her nose right up to Ursula's and had to stand on her tiptoes to do it. "If you haven't stopped acting like a madwoman by the time I get back, you're going to sleep in a cave somewhere."

Ursula glared, but she didn't say anything more.

"An hour, Jo, no longer." Ilsa set the pot back on the fire, then with deft, experienced moves, she loaded potatoes and a couple of pieces of fried quail onto a tin plate. "It's a cold night out, and snow is coming. If you're out later than that, I'll have to come hunting you, and I don't want to."

She added biscuits to the plate and thrust it at Jo. "It's dinnertime now, so take it with you or you'll be starving to go with freezing."

Jo took the plate gratefully. "An hour isn't enough."

"You're on unfamiliar hunting ground, and the snow's let

up for now, but it could come back and cover your tracks. You could get lost out there."

"Thanks, Ilsa. Don't worry about me. You know a little cold doesn't stop me. I'll be back when you're both asleep. If you come looking, then enjoy the nice cold walk, because I won't be anywhere around." Jo grabbed her winter wrap and her bow and quiver of arrows, and slammed out with her hot supper. She didn't give Ilsa a chance to try and talk sense into her. She was in no mood for sense.

Once outside, she set her plate aside and took a few minutes to put her deerskin jacket on and pull on the leggings that kept her warm in weather far more bitter than this. She fastened a fur-lined hood over her head and pulled on buckskin gloves. Dressed like this, she could stay out all night—and had many times.

The snow had quit, but even with the sun up, the whole world was white land, trees, and sky. She got her quiver over her head and under her right arm. The arrows stuck up by her left shoulder so she could reach up with her left hand and snag arrows fast as lightning. Then her bow went next, over her head and under her right arm. The two straps crisscrossed right over her heart.

Once she was ready to go, she sat down on a tree stump out of the wind and ate her fill of the still-warm dinner. She let the chilly air cool her temper—it didn't work all that well because she kept thinking that if Ursula would just calm down, she wouldn't be eating out here in the cold.

Whether Jo was happy about it or not, she knew being riled up at her big sister didn't solve a thing. Ursula needed help. Jo wasn't sure how to give it, but something had to be done.

Warmly dressed, well armed, and with her belly full, she decided to let herself explore and forget the tension between her and her sister.

Looking around the valley, she considered all the new places there were to see, and that lifted her spirits and calmed her anger.

Cows grazed on the winter-cured grass that waved and danced in the breeze that hummed through the trees. The canyon walls must have blocked the wind and even calmed the snow, because it was nicer in here than it'd been on the ride up.

A spring calf butted another half-grown baby, and the two of them dodged and charged, then ran along side by side, kicking up the shallow layer of snow.

A stream tumbled and danced around rocks.

The valley wasn't free of trees, but it was a nice open stretch with good grazing.

Where to go?

Then she remembered Mitch speaking of coming in through a high valley. She'd never come in this canyon before, let alone gone higher.

That made her pause. She'd had this thought before. She'd never come in here. But why? It niggled in her head, but she just wasn't sure. Had Grandpa told her not to? That must be it. He must've wanted them to stay out so they wouldn't find his cabin. But it was a faint, long-ago memory she couldn't make come clear. She'd planned to ask Ursula if she remembered Grandpa saying anything about this valley, but finding a time to talk reasonably with Ursula wasn't likely to come soon.

All Jo really knew was, coming in here had scared her. She'd've never done it if not for Dave's hungry cows.

Well, she was here now, and according to Mitch there was more to discover. And a long hike suited her.

She set out in the dimming light. The days were short, and the sun was already low in the sky. Clouds hung overhead, and snow drifted down, whipped sideways now and then by a gust of wind. For all that, it was a beautiful day.

She could have galloped across this valley in only a few minutes. But she didn't know how to saddle a horse, nor what to do with a horse when she needed silence to hunt. So instead, she settled into her long strides. As she walked, her anger started to build again, and she knew that wily old enemy Satan was stirring up trouble in her heart. To push Old Scratch back, she ran. She couldn't go as fast as the horse, but she was a lot less likely to fall to her death this way.

Trying to think, trying to calm her anger, she prayed and thought on Scripture. As she walked, she thought of the story of the "Prodigal Son" and began speaking it aloud, "'And said he, a certain man had two sons: And the younger of them said to his father, "Father, give me the portion of goods that falleth to me." And he divided unto them his living.'"

Jo stopped herself as she realized that she knew those words just as well as if the Bible were open before her. She really did have it all memorized.

She could "read" the Bible with no book at all.

Except it was hard to do it out of order. When she thought of the Bible it was either stories like the "Prodigal Son" that she knew so well, or she started at the beginning. "In the beginning, God created the heaven and the earth."

But they didn't start at the beginning every night, of course. They worked their way through. She wondered if she even turned pages at the right time. How would she know?

Because she wanted to test herself, she began at the beginning and for a long time she "read" the book of Genesis while she ran for the high valley Mitch spoke of.

She spoke aloud for a time, then realized she could read just as well in silence, and she wouldn't spook any animals.

It was still light when she reached the rock Mitch had ducked behind when Jimmy Joe went to shooting at him.

Now, on land she'd never trod, she had to pay attention. So, she quit "reading" the Bible and woke her senses up wide to the wilderness around her. There was a narrow trail that twisted through rocks so scattered, the trail so steep, it'd take a bold horse to get through it. But nimble Rocky Mountain elk would have no trouble. Maybe she really could go hunting, though that hadn't been her true goal when she'd stormed out of the house.

She slowed, but kept pushing, climbing, skirting boulders. In sheltered places where the snow hadn't covered the ground, she saw prints. They had to belong to Mitch, so now she was backtrailing him. She'd come the right way.

How was he? Her prayers started up again. For Mitch, for Quill, for all of them if they caught what Mitch had.

The trail widened, and Mitch's boots had left a clear track. Jo saw elk prints, too. Plenty of them. Her heart sped up as she thought of what was ahead. Finding new hunting ground was one of her favorite things to do in the world.

She crested a peak, and the wind hit her so hard she stumbled to a stop. It made her turn back and look at the trail she'd climbed. She was amazed at how far she'd come, and how high she was.

The top of the world.

She caught her breath as she saw peaks in the distance, white capped and majestic. In the places where they were catching the light of the lowering sun, they were cast in the bright pink of a mountain rose.

It was the most beautiful thing she'd ever seen. The wind rustled past, but her coat had a hood, and the cold didn't bother her overly. Despite the noise of the wind, or maybe because it was so much a part of this scene, she felt like the whole world spread out before her in silence.

A high scream brought her head up. She couldn't believe there was anything higher than her, except the sunset and God in His heaven.

An eagle soared along the mountaintop where she stood. She thought of her Bible and the verse where God says He will raise you up on wings like eagles. She spread her arms wide and felt for a long precious moment like she was truly raised up by the hands of God.

As she stood above the landscape with only a bald eagle for company, it fit that she carried God's Word in her head and in her heart. It was all of a piece.

Jo was moved by the power of this moment until she could barely breathe.

She stayed too long because it was impossible to give it up, but a sound other than the eagle broke into her thoughts.

A bull elk bugled. It was a sound she'd heard many times at sunrise and again at sunset. It was especially common now during mating season. The sound rose high, almost like a woman's scream, but it echoed in a way no human voice ever did.

Borne on the wind, the sound bounced around her. A second elk cried out, then five. And all those sounds came from below.

She looked down from where she stood on Mitch's path and saw what had to be the high valley he spoke of. But she could only see the upper part because it was a bowl filled with fog. It held a haunting beauty, the hidden elk, the bugle cries, the fog below, and eagles and mountain peaks above. Down in that fog, elks were claiming land and herds. Others were ready to fight to create their own family.

Jo drank it all in for a long moment, and as part of it, she prayed.

Her pleas silently echoed with the elk cries. Then, when she'd reached high for God and let Him draw near to her, she asked first for Mitch, asking desperately that he not have a deadly disease, next that she and her sisters would escape the sickness. It wasn't even because she wanted to stay healthy. It was for Ursula because of the weight of all her fears. Then she thought of Dave. He'd kissed her. Her first kiss, and it was so sweet, so wonderful. She poured out her heart to God, the longing, the confusion, the reckless excitement of kissing Dave. When she'd wrung the joy and thrill out of her prayers, she thanked God for this moment of glory in the midst of trouble.

The elk bugle continued. Then somewhere far below her feet she heard the crash of antlers. A battle was in progress.

She touched her fingers to the spot on her chest where the straps from her quiver and bow crossed, then headed down. She was in no hurry to get home, and she wanted to be part of the beauty of a mountain valley full of fog and hidden beasts.

Listening carefully, watching every step, she still saw prints left by Mitch only a few days ago. This was a trail, worn down by centuries of critters claiming this valley. The fog swallowed her up. When she reached a level spot, she could see only a few feet ahead of her. She was no fool. A bull elk could be dangerous, and stepping into the middle of two bulls fighting was the act of a fool. She listened to the shrill music of their voices, the crashing of antlers, and she judged every step.

An elk bugled to her left, and the level spot, what she could see of it, spread out into grasslands. Cautious, she sidled right, away from the elk, until she realized she was on a new trail without Mitch's footprints. She must have veered off from the trail he took.

She walked along slowly, listening as much as watching. Enjoying the night, enjoying the feeling of being swallowed up in this mystical, fog-shrouded world.

A solid object loomed just ahead. She swung her bow around and notched an arrow before she gave it any thought.

Then she braced herself for an elk to swing its antlers her way and charge.

22

"Dave, I'm sorry, but I need you to help me get his fever down. I'm sorry. I'm so sorry."

Dave knew his ma thought she was bringing him to death's door.

"I can go, Dave." Pa swung his feet over the side of the bed, sat up, and pitched face-first toward the floor.

"Stop it." Dave caught his stubborn old pa and pushed him back in bed. And no one pushed Quillon Warden anywhere, so it spoke to how weak Pa still was.

"Let me go." Pa struggled against the hand Dave held firmly on his shoulder. "Let me in there, and I'll stay at Mitch's side. No sense in you being exposed to this."

"Pa, I'd let you go if you wouldn't just make more work for Ma." Dave kept his pa down and hated using his youthful strength and health against the finest man he'd ever known.

Ma was at the door. Tears coursed down her face, and Ma was a steady woman. She wasn't given to tears and other female takings.

"I need his strength, Quill. I'm sorry." Ma had said that

enough. "I need to bathe Mitch in cool water, and for that I need him rolled over, and he needs to sit up, all things I need Dave for."

"I can do it alone, Ma," Mitch called from his room. He was in the family fuss now.

Dave looked his pa in the eye. "Ma is trying to protect me and so are you, but I've been right next to Mitch ever since he came home. I'm exposed. Stop thinking you can prevent that."

Pa stopped struggling, his expression a mix of fury and regret. Then he nodded. "I would fall on my face. I'm sorry for making this harder."

"You're healing, Quill," Ma said. "The best thing you can do for us is to rest and drink water and pray like you've never prayed before. If you can get to your feet, maybe you can feed yourself. Maybe we can keep Dave away from you if he's helping with Mitch. You know getting sick right now is the most dangerous thing that could happen to you."

With a jerking nod of his chin, Pa said, "I can care for myself and leave food for you, even prepare some. I know how to make stew and biscuits."

Ma wanted to go to him. It was written in her eyes. Then she stepped back and left. Dave followed her out and into Mitch's room.

Mitch's fever was high enough he lapsed into silence, with his eyes closed, in a way that wasn't sleep, but not fully awake. He'd been getting hotter all day. Now the sun was setting, and a long, dangerous night spread out before them.

"Help me get his shirt off." Ma unbuttoned the woolen long johns. Mitch had been sleeping in them when he fell ill.

Ma drew the edges of the woolen underwear aside and gasped. "His chest is covered in a rash."

Dave felt his own chest itching, but he had been feeling like that all day, since he saw Mitch with spots all over. Dave had checked and found no rash, so it was likely all in his head.

"Isn't there any other way to know how serious it is?" Dave asked. "We just have to wait and see?"

"We have to wait a few days to know for sure by seeing how the blisters form." Ma wrung out a cloth in a basin of cool water and ran it over Mitch's chest. "But he could be sick for a solid two weeks."

Dave got his own cloth and began bathing his feverish brother. It was hard not to be a touch angry that Mitch had brought this danger home to them all. Of course, he couldn't have known, but Dave thought of the way the Nordegren sisters' grandpa had stayed off by himself after his trips to town and wondered if that wasn't a good idea. Had he ever gotten sick? Had he ever lay, itchy and feverish, in that little cabin for two weeks before it was safe to go home?

"If we don't see a rash with dimples in, he'll be sick for a spell, but we will be able to relax, even if one of us gets it."

Dave couldn't stand to see his fast-talking brother brought so low. But if Ma was right, Dave only had to face this fear for a few days, and what choice did he have? He'd pray for the best, work to head off the worst, and live with whatever happened.

"Ma," he said quietly as he worked, "those names in the Nordegren family Bible?"

Ma rinsed her cloth, wrung it out, and put it on Mitch's splotchy chest. "What about them?"

"All that death." Dave swallowed. "Is the family under a plague because of their strange beliefs?"

Ma shook her head, paused, then shook her head again. "Sickness is everywhere, Dave. Death is a part of life. I had two little sisters die the year after I married your pa. We'd headed west and left my family behind. I received a letter two years later telling me the town well had gone foul. Fever swept through every home."

"You've never told me that." Dave kept working, praying, and listening.

Ma gave a humorless laugh. "Too busy telling you to do chores, I reckon. And it was all so far away, a life that wouldn't ever touch you. No sense railing against it like the girls' grandma did."

"She got hit mighty hard. Too hard, I reckon. Seems like she went just the littlest bit mad from the grief."

Nodding, Ma said, "Grief is part of life, too. She'd've probably come around if she hadn't married a mountain man who took her way up here where she could convince herself it was safe."

"And I think there was an avalanche," Dave speculated. "The girls have cows up here and used to have horses, but there was no passable trail I ever found. I think it wasn't just Grandma being afraid. That trail was probably easily climbed when they moved up here. Then a rockslide cut the trail off. Grandpa had to do some hard climbing to get down, and I reckon it was easy for Grandma to just stay up here with her family. Tend to the home while her husband did the trading. It probably helped make her fears seem reasonable."

"Then her son left and evidently died. And here she was,

stuck with three very young children on a mountain she doubted she could get them down. Instead of moving through her grief, she nurtured it and let it take over."

"Ma, what if we bring fever and even death to Jo and her sisters?"

Shaking her head, Ma said, "If they get sick, even if they survive, we might drive them away from any human contact. I'm afraid Ursula is always going to be a solitary soul. But Ilsa and Jo seem eager to meet people and find friends, maybe get married some day and have children of their own."

Ma lifted her eyes to meet Dave's for a long second, and he had no idea why. He was busy feeling a strange pang at the thought of Jo, remembering their kiss. Wishing he could see her and talk through all the troubles with her. He didn't want to talk about Jo with his ma, so it was a good thing Ma didn't know.

"If that happens, they might just up and run."

"But run where, Dave? They sure aren't about to run to the lowlands, and there's not much higher they can go."

Dave didn't have an answer, but his gut twisted at the thought of how Jo moved through the woods, how silent and swift she was, and how well equipped she was to take care of herself. It would be a terrible hardship to Jo, but if she wanted to, she could vanish into the wilderness, and he'd never see her again.

Frozen, her arrow aimed, silent as fog, Jo waited, breathed silently, steadied her hands, and let go of all fear and tension as she always did when it was time to shoot.

She'd never understood the cool confidence she had about her bow and arrow. But after all these years, they fit into her hands as perfectly as her fingers. Her aim was true, her courage on fire. No doubt she could hit what she aimed at.

The dark object ahead didn't move. No attack. No bugle call. Not even the movement of breathing.

With her hearing razor sharp and her eyes keen—the fog notwithstanding—she knew what loomed ahead was not alive. Breathing in the night air, she caught no scent of animal nor man. Neither did it seem to be the trunk of a tree; it was too large. A rock wall, or a boulder in the path. Maybe it had rolled across the trail, because the trail she's been following led straight ahead.

Her arrow ready, she stepped forward, one step, two. Then ten, and she reached forward and jabbed . . . something . . . with her arrow. Then she lowered her weapon and reached out a hand. Stone. But it was squared off, and there were stones on top of stones to make a wall. She brushed her hand over the rough, sandy rock.

Another house? Did her grandpa build this one, too? What could he have been thinking? She decided to try to figure out Grandpa later. For now, feeling her way along, she came to a corner. Continuing her cautious advance, she reached something with edges that could only be a doorway. Whatever this building was, it was certainly deserted. No smell of people or meals cooked recently. No hint of ash from a fire, not even one gone stone cold. There was no door, just this opening. Working up all her nerve, she stepped in to . . . nothing.

Feeling her way along in the pitch dark, she fumbled in

her pocket for a flint and, in the pouch with it, a little bundle of crushed leaves that would catch easily.

The whole room smelled of dust. Feeling her way, her fingers became gritty with it, and she scratched her nose, then wondered if she was smearing her face with dirt.

She didn't want to start the fire with nothing to burn. It would only provide light for a few seconds. There was nothing she could identify as a hearth. She found walls again, and turned to walk along them. She came to an opening and turned again. She went along this way for another turn and another, and suddenly fear struck her so hard it had to be the hand of God.

Where was she going? Could she find her way back?

Near panic turned her around, and she rushed along the wall, found a corner, and turned. But was it the right corner? How many had she followed?

Suddenly she was furious at her whole life.

Up here, alone. She'd always run wild. She'd never before feared being alone.

Now she'd come into this mysterious place. For heaven's sakes, no one knew where she was. No one would find her if she became lost in some twisting, turning cave . . . though it had to be made by hand. This was no cave. These were walls.

Fighting down the fear so her brain would work, she evened her breathing and listened. The elk were still out there. She realized then the walls had no roof to muffle the noise. Climbing the walls wouldn't help now because the fog made it impossible to see, but if she didn't get out tonight, she would tomorrow. Spending the night outside wasn't something she worried about.

That thought calmed her. If she had to, she'd use the flint and leaves to light her way. Even a few seconds of light would help. She inched along.

As she began to move again, following the walls in the inky darkness, she came upon a corner and turned, moving toward the sound. The elk bugled, and the sound seemed to be straight ahead.

Jo vowed that this was the end of her wilderness living. Or at least the end of her cutting herself off from the lowlands. She vowed to herself she was leaving the lost world up here and going to a town. She was buying matches! She swore it.

Grandpa had even left them some money in a small wooden trunk long ago tucked under the bed he'd shared with Grandma. She knew nothing about money, so she didn't know how much a small case of gold coins was worth. And she'd found more in the cabin she was staying in with Ilsa and Ursula. Surely there was enough to pay for a few matches. She'd have to ask Dave.

But whether the gold was worth enough for matches or not, she was getting off this mountaintop. Hope Mountain. Until now she'd never thought much of hope, but now the name was right. She claimed that perfect name.

Maybe she wouldn't leave until spring. Maybe not until the trouble harassing the Wardens had been settled. But soon she was going. Dave had said it was a long ride to a town. And that town was probably New York City. Mitch made it sound very exciting, and she wanted to see it.

Her panic fully faded when she reached an opening that she knew from the wind and openness beyond was the outside. The fog was impenetrable. The starless night black as pitch. She wasn't going out there to find her way home. She'd stay here. Despite Ilsa's words, her sisters wouldn't worry. They knew her too well. And she wanted to see this high valley in the daylight.

Tomorrow she'd go back and get her sisters and bring them here to explore. Yes, Ursula included. Though Ursula ran the house for the most part, she did well in the woods and knew how to live with the mountains. She'd come.

It might keep their minds off the struggle for Mitch's life. The struggle that might yet rain death down on all of them.

23

Jo led Ursula and Ilsa toward the stone house. The snow came down more heavily than it had before. There was a foot of new snow overnight, but they could still pass.

They ran. The tireless, easy lope they'd all learned from having to travel through their mountaintop home on foot. They dodged around the skittish longhorn cattle, stomped through dry winter grass, and plowed through snowdrifts. Ilsa laughed aloud, and Jo felt the grin on her face. Even Ursula looked strong and free and wild. All her fears set aside for this one moment.

Jo hadn't bothered to braid her yellow hair this morning, but she always had her bow and arrow and a deadly aim that could protect and feed them.

Ilsa's black curls were flying wild around her like they danced for joy. She was always happiest swinging in the treetops, with her knife quick and always to hand.

Ursula was tidy with her white hair in a tight braid. But she had longer legs than Jo and Ilsa. And she was fast and prone to leading. The thinker, the planner, the watcher. Her mind as orderly as her braid.

Her fear of outsiders was a terrible exaggeration of her love for her sisters and her efforts to care for them, mother them.

She wasn't as good with a bow and arrow as Jo, but she was still very good and carried one with her most places. She wasn't as fast into the treetops as Ilsa, but she was plenty fast. She carried a handy knife, and knew her way around rugged land as well as any of them.

Smiling, Jo enjoyed the time together. There'd been so much unhappiness lately, but right now, in the cold, crisp air, with snowflakes swirling around them, they were a team, just as they'd always been. A group of three women who'd carved out a life in the highlands and done it well. Jo longed for her sisters to be close again.

But with the Wardens still in their lives. She didn't know if Ursula would let that happen. For now, Jo shoved aside the sadness that came on her and enjoyed being one of the Nordegren women.

The meadow filled with Dave's cows was behind them as they entered the deep woods and were swallowed up.

The three of them together. It made Jo's heart lift with the pleasure of her family.

The snow was deeper in the woods, knee-deep mostly, but drifted to neck-deep in places. It was light as powder, and they could plow through, sometimes nearly buried by it, but it didn't stop them. They followed a trail broken by Jo's trek out last night and back this morning.

The trees and snow slowed them, and they still had to keep a watchful eye. It wasn't too late yet for a bear to still be rummaging, and mountain lions never slept. And heaven knew wolves prowled all winter.

At one point, Jo glanced over to see Ilsa gone. She looked up and saw her little sister clambering up, then running along on branches so thick and so close together they were almost like a solid floor over their heads.

"I didn't see many tracks. It was too dark." Jo told them about the fog and the bugling elk. The clashing antlers and soaring eagles.

Ilsa and Ursula loved beauty and the outdoors just as much as she did, so they listened and asked endless questions.

The woods were so tight it cast the day into near twilight. Jo unslung her bow but didn't reach for an arrow.

"I can weave roots and hang them in these trees so I can swing," Ilsa called down from overhead.

"Look at the berries. There is food for the winter dried on the bushes." Ursula slowed further, learning this new land.

"And those dried stems, those are Indian potatoes." Jo pointed at a stretch swept bare by the wind. Ursula nodded.

"I've found an oak that didn't shed its acorns yet," Ilsa shouted. "We can gather enough for the whole winter from this one tree."

"And there'll be more on the ground if we need them." Ursula swung an arm across a mound of fluffy snow and laughed.

Ilsa knew how to slip through the woods silently, but today she was making noise, chattering like a bird in the trees. None of them made any effort to be quiet. Not only because they were enjoying themselves but also to alert any dangerous animals that there was something coming. Most animals would run. A bear, a wolf, a lion. They didn't understand people and even up here where maybe they'd never seen a woman, they'd choose to run away given the chance. But step too close to one and startle them, make them feel cornered, and they'd fight.

Their chatter was making the way safe for them.

Jo saw footprints in the snow and stopped, as if frozen. She tore her bow free, then an arrow. With a flash, she let loose one arrow, then another, and a third.

Rabbits. Big fat ones. "I got our dinner."

Ursula loped to the nearest one and picked it up by its hind legs. She got a second, and Jo fetched the third. Ilsa came down from the treetops, grinning. "We'll roast them and save the soft fur."

Content with their coming feast, they climbed the canyon and looked down on that valley, no longer shrouded in fog.

The three of them saw splendor.

Ilsa got there first and stopped dead in her tracks. Ursula came up beside her. Jo was last because she wanted to see her sisters' reactions.

And then she saw it. She'd headed home in the first light of dawn and known this valley was especially beautiful, but it was magnificent in the full daylight.

They stood, three in a row. Jo, Ursula to her right, Ilsa next, and they drank in the beauty. No one broke the silence. It was too perfect, a holy moment, as if they were closer to God up here. Finally, they were filled with the peace of the place, and Jo could speak.

"Look to the right." She pointed, and they all stared at the strange stone structure. It was a huge red-rock overhang, and in the gap between the overhead rock and the ground, someone had built walls. Windows were clearly visible. Some of the stacked, squared off stones had caved in. It had been built out from the overhang and had a roof at one time, but much of that was collapsed and gone, though the walls still stood in places. It was possible to believe the front of the structure was just fallen rubble. But behind that stood unmistakable walls built by human hands.

Ursula said in a hushed voice, "Someone had to stack those stones. But who?"

"There's no one here, and I went over it last night, then looked more this morning before I came home." Jo had slept here in the cold, bundled up and out of the wind. "I didn't explore for long though."

Ursula, who knew her very well, knew her curiosity, asked, "Why not?"

Jo glanced at her sisters. Ursula caught the look.

Jo grinned. "Last night, in the dark and fog, I was afraid I'd get lost in some twisting pathway and never find my way out."

"So you decided to let us get lost with you?" Ursula arched a brow, but her eyes gleamed with amusement.

"Yes, I thought you might as well get into trouble along with me. And that's why I didn't look much this morning. I wanted you with me when I explored." Jo's voice went quiet. "I wanted to share this with you, be with you when we discovered more about such an unusual place."

Ursula and Ilsa nodded quietly. They, too, felt the strangeness of these walls. They walked toward the odd building.

237

It was like nothing they'd ever seen before, nor heard of. Nothing they'd ever imagined.

When they reached it, Ursula ran her hand along the stones, and bits of gravel brushed off. She lifted her hand away to do no harm. "It looks so old."

Jo smiled at her, and Ursula smiled back. Yes, they'd been nearly at each other's throats last night, but today, when she'd rushed into the house, bursting with excitement, Ursula had forgotten her anger and come along.

Ursula liked exploring as much as Jo and Ilsa. Or maybe she'd just found a place even farther from civilization. Whatever it was, Ursula was smiling for the first time since Jo had told her about Dave.

"In here," Ilsa's voice echoed, and together Jo and Ursula walked down a hallway that had doorways opening off it.

"I can see why you didn't like this in the dark," Ursula said. "At least not the first time you went in."

They followed Ilsa's footprints in the deep dust. They found her in a room with a solid roof, no caved-in walls, doorways but no doors, no windows to let in the cold, and a fireplace with a tiny hole overhead for a chimney. You couldn't call it warm, but if they got a fire going, it might be decent.

Ilsa's bright smile was full of the excitement they all felt. "There are more rooms here, in a row, right up against the canyon wall. Look," Ilsa said, pointing at a wall. "That isn't made with these squared-off rocks, that's the side of a mountain. And the roof is that overhang. They'd created houses by using a cave with a wide-open front."

"The roof looks solid." Ursula studied over her head, her voice quiet with wonder.

"Who built this?" Jo's mind ran all around trying to understand.

"Has someone lived up here all this time?" Ursula's smile faded. "You said Mitch came from this direction. Has he talked about the trail that brought him up?"

"He said there was no trail, no way to bring a horse," Ilsa said as she crouched by the cold fireplace.

"Grandpa never wanted us to come up that trail where we brought Dave's cows. I've been thinking it was because he had that cabin in there, but could he have known people lived on past his cabin?" Jo saw scattered piles of sticks against the wall, maybe dragged in by creatures to build nests, though there were no animals to be seen.

Jo began gathering an armload of sticks, then took them to the fireplace. She leaned in and confirmed she could see the sky through the tight hole at the top.

Once she started, Ilsa and Ursula realized building a fire was a fine idea and pitched in to help.

Jo used her flint and bag of crushed leaves that she always carried and soon had a fire crackling. They quickly had the rabbits skinned and roasting with sticks propped at an angle to use as spits.

Together the work was fast, and the scent of the cooking meat and burning fire sent a savory smell through the room. It reminded Jo she hadn't eaten yet today, and she'd gone on a long run home and another long run back here.

Ursula sang her song of prayer. "The Doxology," Ma had called it.

Then they feasted on the meal in contented silence.

As they ate, Jo was reminded how much she loved her

sisters. They'd been at each other's throats since the Wardens came. But these two women were the people she trusted and loved most in the world. By welcoming outsiders, she'd driven Ursula away from her.

Ursula, who had always mothered them, who'd been the backbone and the heart of their family. Jo and Ilsa liked it best outside, and they wandered far and wide, day and night. But they always knew there would be a warm home with a hot meal and clean bed to sleep in.

Jo had taken advantage of Ursula's care of them for years. And she'd rarely said thank you.

Now she did. "Ursula, I love you. And Ilsa, I love you, too. The three of us working together made this meal, just as we've always survived by depending on each other. I've never been as grateful as I should be for all you've done for me. Ursula, you most of all. You've worked hard all these years to keep us going. So much of the responsibility landed on you when Grandma died. Thank you for being so wise and strong. Thank you for helping us survive."

"You're the one, Jo, who brings in meat. And Ilsa does most of the hunting for the roots and berries, the nuts and seeds, that help us get through the winters."

"And you tend the house," Ilsa said. "You cook the food we bring in. You tend the animals, the cows and chickens. And see that the garden is planted."

"It's always taken all of us." Jo went to the fire, tossed in the rabbit bones, and listened to them sizzle, smelled the rich meat. "I'm sorry for my part in the strife between us. I don't want us to forget we're a family. We always have been and always will be. Having the Wardens here doesn't change that."

"But what about the sickness the Wardens bring? What about the bullets and the trouble that could be following them?" Ursula turned to look at Jo, her brow furrowed, lines of worry cutting across her beautiful face.

Even knowing how much Ursula feared outsiders, Jo wasn't going to quit being around the Wardens. They'd added too much to her life. Dave most of all. But it struck her that Ursula felt betrayed and unwanted, and Jo couldn't blame her.

"Whatever lies ahead, there's no way to be alone on this mountain, not anymore. No matter how we act, they're not going away. We have to learn to live with them." They'd all lived their strange, lonely lives without much thought of changing. And now things were changing so fast, and Ursula, who had always sought to care for all of them, was hurt and afraid, and instead of treating her with kindness, Jo and Ilsa had ignored her and went their own way.

"How can we find out more about this place?" Jo shifted the topic. "Who would know what it is?"

"It's warm." Ursula sat before the fire, her hands reaching out to the flames. "The walls are thick and tightly built. The roof in this part is solid. If we had a door this place would be livable."

Staring into the flames, she said, "You two don't need me anymore. And I don't want to live near strangers. I might move up here and live by myself."

Ilsa gasped.

"You will not," Jo said firmly. "Cutting yourself off isn't the answer to your fears, Ursula."

Instead of speaking again of moving here, Ursula asked,

"Why is there an ancient, abandoned stone building with dozens of rooms on the top of the mountain? Who built this? Where did they go?"

Jo set her jaw tight and shook her head.

None of them had any answers.

24

"It's not smallpox," Ma whispered, but her expression spoke loudly. Her eyes begged him to agree with her.

"You said there'd be a dent in the center of each spot, and there isn't." Dave reached across the bed and caught Ma's hand as they stood on either side of Mitch, who was sleeping but still feverish. Dave drew Ma out of the room. "Just the opposite, they're forming peaked blisters."

Heaving a sigh, Ma looked behind her into the room where Mitch slept restlessly.

"He's going to be miserable for a few more days, I reckon," Dave said. "He keeps trying to scratch at those blisters, and his fever's hanging on. But it will go down soon, and the rash will fade."

Nodding, Ma said, "And if we catch it, we'll be miserable, but it's *not* deadly."

Pa came to his door. It was first light, but Pa had slept well last night and seemed more like his old self. He looked between them.

"How is he?"

Ma rushed to his uninjured side and hugged him, willing to risk it now. "He's going to be all right. I wouldn't be hugging you if he wasn't."

Pa slung an arm around her waist and gave her a tight one-armed hug. "Good to hear, Izzy. Mighty good to hear."

Ma straightened away and said, "I'm asleep on my feet." She looked over her shoulder at Dave. "I think we can rest for a time. Quill, can you lie back down at my side? I always sleep better lying next to you."

"I reckon it's early enough I can sleep another hour or two."

Dave watched them go. His heart caught at how much he loved them. How much he loved his brother. The family was together again, and they were going to be okay.

The door closed to their bedroom.

He didn't feel right about sleeping in the room Jo and her sisters were sharing. And Mitch tended to toss and turn.

Dave grabbed a couple of blankets and stretched out on the floor, so tired he was unsteady on his feet.

He blinked his eyes. Closed, then opened a moment later. Or so it seemed. But they'd closed in the firelit dark and opened to full daylight. He could tell by the way the sun came through a crack around the edge of the door that it was late.

Shoving himself to his feet, fearing the worst, he rushed to Mitch's room and found his brother snoring softly.

His face was covered in those ugly blisters, but he was also soaked in sweat. His fever had broken.

Dave eased himself out of the room. Sleep was the best

thing for healing. Ma came hurrying out. She must've heard his thundering feet.

He smiled and touched one finger to his lips to shush her. She looked behind her, smiled, then turned to shush Dave back. Pa must've been sleeping, too.

Dave jerked his head to the outside. She nodded and smiled, they went outside, coats in hand, and he hugged her tightly.

When they were far enough from the cabin to not disturb their patients, Ma said, "They're both going to live."

"We need to tell Jo and her sisters that this isn't a deadly disease. I'll ride up there."

"But stay well back. You could come down with it, re-member. But we'll be all right."

"I'll tell them that and make sure they stay away, but I want to pass on the news. Did you get enough sleep to man-age on your own for a couple of hours?"

"Yes, and knowing we can sleep well from now on . . . I hope . . . makes everything else simple."

Dave nodded, then gave her a smacking kiss on the cheek. Alberto came out of the barn at that moment leading his horse, a pack on its back. They had twelve men up here. The men had cleared space in the barn, a structure that held no hay and no animals—until the Wardens had brought their horses over. They'd been able to open a stretch of the ceiling and vent a campfire. They were living in there with a decent amount of comfort.

Striding over, Dave said, "Are you taking food to the Nor-degrens?"

"Yep, going over now. I've gone over every day, but I

haven't seen them since I left them that first day, when you sent them away."

"I warned them to stay back from us."

"They haven't even let me get a glimpse. But there's plenty of signs they're around. And the food and firewood are always gone."

Nodding, Dave said, "I'll go and tell them Mitch is better. He is past the fever from his sickness, and it's not smallpox."

Alberto gave a small sigh of relief. He'd been with Pa for years, and remembered Mitch from before he left.

"Pa is moving slow, but he's up and around. We're still at risk from catching whatever it is Mitch brought home, but it doesn't look to be real serious. Still, best to stay away from him. We'll try and keep him inside for another week or so. Thanks for taking up all the work Pa and I have left for you."

"The men have been working on your folks' cabin." Alberto shrugged off the thanks. He rode for the brand. If there was work, he did it. Dave had learned how a man conducted himself from his pa and from Alberto.

"Thank you. I've barely stepped outside all this time." Dave looked up at the dark, threatening sky. "There'll be snow again today."

"There's snow every day."

That was the pure truth. Dave managed a grin—he hadn't done much of that while Pa and Mitch were sick. "One of these times it'll come and bury us. We need that cabin."

Dave swung up on the horse, and Alberto turned back to the barn to saddle another. The rest of the men were all gone, working on the cabin, seeing to the herd, or standing sentry over the trail. Things were finally back to normal. Very soon he could turn his attention to wooing Jo Nordegren.

All three Nordegren women woke, ate breakfast, and packed for a long day on the trail.

Jo looked at Ursula several times, glad she'd come back. For a while, Jo was afraid she would stay at the stone building to live.

They were going back to that high valley today to explore more, but Jo noticed Ursula wasn't packing clothing, so maybe she didn't plan to move up there permanently. They set out walking across the valley, then heard hoofbeats. They turned, and Jo saw a horseman riding up.

"It's Dave." She took off running toward him. Over her shoulder, she called, "I have to see how Mitch and Quill are doing."

She didn't look back, and instead of rounding the edges of the valley to avoid the cattle, she ran straight through the widely scattered herd. They all gave way, trotting a bit to put space between them and her.

Dave swung down and took the pack of food to set by the door, then he added the firewood. As he raised his hand to knock, the moving cattle caught his attention, and he turned and saw her coming. He remounted and galloped toward her.

They met in the middle. Jo wanted to throw herself into his arms. He got down again and, smiling, said, "Better stay back. I might be carrying Mitch's sickness, but he doesn't have the worst kind of illness. You could catch it but, if you do, you'll be fine."

"I'm sure we've all been close enough to Mitch that we're at risk," Jo said.

"I hope not, but it's possible. You should stay up here for a while."

"Two weeks, like Grandpa used to?"

Nodding, Dave said, "That sounds about right. It'll go fast. But best to be cautious. Where were you headed?"

"Oh, Dave you'll never believe what I found." Jo told him all about the beautiful valley and the strange stone building. She told him about the soaring eagle and the bugling elk, the pink-tipped mountains, and the vast, grassy meadow.

"You have no idea who built that high cabin?" he asked.

"*Cabin* isn't the right word. It's a strange thing. Stone blocks stacked to make walls. The roof is mostly an overhang from the mountainside, but there were signs a roof had been built here and there, but those are mostly collapsed. It's all one big . . . house, I reckon." Shaking her head, she said, "You just have to see it. I've never known anyone to live up there, and the building is so old the stone is crumbling, much too old for Grandpa to have built it. Oh, and the part you'll like, it's in a huge valley, too, with lots of grazing. Enough to keep your cattle fat and happy all winter long."

His eyes took on a dreamy look, and she suspected his expression matched hers. "All that wild beauty." Then his eyes settled on her, and the words *wild beauty* seemed to be meant for her.

"Ursula wants to live up there."

His eyes saddened. "I'm so sorry she isn't happy with the changes the Wardens have brought to your lives. Do you think there's a chance she'll get over her fears and welcome newcomers?"

"I want to believe it. She's calming down a little. She hasn't thrown me out of the cabin for over a day."

Dave's mouth tipped up on one side in a weak smile. "I reckon that's a good sign. Maybe we'll win her over."

Nodding, Jo said, "It'll help if you stop being sick and don't get shot for a while."

"We'll sure do our best. And the work on our cabin is going well. We should be able to move out of your place as soon as Mitch is feeling stronger. Pa and Ma could go now, but Mitch's fever only just broke. It's likely to come and go for a spell, and we want him to go a few days with no fever before we risk taking him out in the cold."

Dave hesitated. "I'd like to ride up with you and see the high valley and that building you found, but I have to get back and help Ma. I had to tell you things were improving back at your house. Tell Ursula the Nordegren home probably saved Pa's and Mitch's lives. We are very thankful for the shelter and feel like God himself put you in our path in our hour of need."

"That's beautiful, Dave. I appreciate it, and Ursula will, too. I'm not sure she'll be able to calm down, but your thanks are very much welcome."

"I need to get back, but soon, Jo, you can take me up there to explore." This time he managed a full smile. "And maybe we can find time for another kiss."

Jo felt her cheeks burn as she met his smile with a shy one of her own.

Then he swung up on his horse and, with a tip of his hat,

rode away. Jo watched him until he'd climbed the canyon wall. At the top, he turned, took his hat all the way off his head and held it high, and swung it back and forth in a broad wave. Her happiness caught in her throat in a way that felt like it could lead to tears. Which would just be a pure waste of time. She waved back, just as high, just as broad.

He turned and rode around the curve that led out of the canyon.

It took every bit of her strength not to go running after him.

25

Dave came every day. There'd been no more kissing. Dave didn't think he should get that close to her, but he expressed a keen interest in the activity.

Jo returned that interest.

In fact, she grew more interested by the day. But even without touching, they got to know each other a lot better. They went riding for a stretch each visit. He was full of questions about her life and about how they found food during the winters up here. He wanted to know all about her memories of her parents and grandparents.

She never ran out of questions about his life. Seeing him again each day made the cold snow and blowing wind bearable.

For nearly two weeks, Jo and her sisters had lived up here. It was just past sunup on the fourteenth day when Ursula had awakened Jo with the sound of kneading bread with unusual vigor.

Lying on the floor by the fire, Jo looked up at her, and

from the back, she saw the rigid tension of her shoulders. Ursula was upset.

They'd gone up to explore the stone house almost every day and passed many hours enjoying the odd place. Every time they'd left, Ursula had talked of moving up there. She didn't say the words, but Ursula was considering being a hermit, a recluse. It hurt Jo's heart to see the longing in Ursula to cut herself off from the whole world.

Ilsa was still rolled up in her blanket. She'd slept in the bed in the main room. Ursula had the room the Wardens had added to Grandpa's cabin. Jo slept on the floor and never asked for a turn in the only extra room. Anything to keep her big sister happy. Jo remembered that she'd been happy when it was just the three of them.

Ursula had a gift for making a cabin a home. And she had a kind way about her when she was happy. The worry about the Wardens had eased since they'd gotten the good news that Mitch wasn't dangerously ill. It still hovered out there, but Ursula was full of music.

Now, when Ursula put aside her bread and covered it with a towel to let it rise, Jo slipped out of her blanket and caught her coat. Ursula, frowning, saw Jo jerk her head toward the door while she silently put on her boots. Bundled up, Jo went outside quickly so a cold gust of wind wouldn't bother Ilsa. Let her sister sleep. They'd been on a long, cold hike yesterday, exploring the canyon beyond the stone building. They'd found the place where Mitch had climbed up. It was sheltered enough in stretches that his footprints hadn't been covered with snow.

As always, Ilsa didn't walk when she could run. Exploring

that far canyon had Ilsa nearly running herself off her feet. When they'd gotten home, they'd eaten, and Ilsa had rolled up in a blanket and gone almost instantly to sleep. Jo and Ursula were only moments behind her.

Now morning had come, maybe the day they could move home. She was sure that was what had Ursula upset.

Jo admitted she was eager for it. That narrow canyon trail back to their home could fill in with snow, and they could be trapped up here all winter.

Oh, they'd survive. There were elk, and they'd eat one of Dave's cows if they had to. But she didn't want to spend the winter trapped with her sisters and away from Dave. Not to mention Ma's pies.

Ursula came out of the cabin, bundled up. She closed the door quietly, so she was thinking of Ilsa, too.

"I can tell you're worrying. What is it?" Jo hoped talking would ease Ursula's mind.

"The trail down will soon blow shut."

"I thought you wanted to get away from everyone. Being trapped ought to suit you."

Ursula crossed her arms and met Jo's eyes. She had the sad, frightened expression she bore too often these days. "I can't decide whether to worry about being stuck up here by heavy snow that closes the trail or getting out and having neighbors too close."

Ursula's voice rose nearly to a wail. "I don't know what I want, Jo."

"We haven't gotten sick." Jo was disappointed in Ursula, always fearful. That didn't seem very Christian. "Some of Dave's cowhands came down with a fever and rash, but they're already past the worst of it. When Dave comes today, I'm hoping he'll say it's time for us to come home."

"To a house full of strangers," Ursula scowled.

"No." Jo fought for patience, feeling as if she were fighting for her sister's very soul. "You know they're moving to their own cabin. We won't go back until they do. We'll have our cabin back and have it to ourselves. Why can't you be hopeful, Ursula?"

Ursula snorted, a very dark sound.

"Dave came only for a short time yesterday, he said they were pushing hard to get the cabin finished and warm and ready for Ma and Quill. They hoped to get moved so today they could bring us home. I'm sure they had to travel slowly because Quill is still fragile and Mitch still weak, but they are both on the mend, and we'll have our cabin back if not today, then for certain tomorrow."

Ursula opened her mouth.

"No, stop!" Jo's patience snapped. She held her hand up and nearly shoved her palm in Ursula's face. "Don't say whatever rude thing you're planning to say. Ursula, where is your Christian charity? Where is your hope? Where is the love God commands us to show our neighbors as ourselves? Stop this. You've let yourself get trapped by fear. You're not behaving as a Christian ought. Get control of your mouth and turn your eyes upon Jesus. Life and death do not matter if we belong to Him. 'To live is Christ. To die is gain.' You know all this, but you aren't living it."

Ursula's mouth opened, then closed. She did that again, twice. Finally, her mouth closed, then her eyes, and she lowered her head until her chin rested on her chest. It might have been to pray. Jo didn't speak. If Ursula was praying, then maybe God would allow Jo's words to reach her. For once, maybe Ursula would hear.

The silence stretched. Jo prayed for her sister and gave God time to work.

A soft coo of a mourning dove broke the silence. A stiff breeze buffeted their well-wrapped bodies.

Jo smelled snow on the wind, and the sharp scent of pine branches. Over that, the smell of woodsmoke puffing out of the chimney in their cabin.

Slowly, so slowly Jo wasn't sure it was even movement at first, Ursula raised her head, her blue eyes wide open and deeply calm.

"Every day. *Every* day, I have forced myself to come home with you from the stone building. I have this reflex in me to withdraw. I use reason and the love I feel for you and Ilsa to come back here, but inside me is something that is not reasonable, and it's got a powerful hold on me." Reaching out, Ursula clamped one hand on Jo's wrist. "You're right, Jo. 'To live is Christ. To die is gain.' I've been ruled by my fears, and that's a sin. I'm going to find courage and change. If I live, I'll live for Christ. If I die, it will be in the knowledge of the gain of heaven. I'm going to—"

A faint cry cut through Ursula's confession, her decision to change. Furrows appeared on Ursula's smooth brow. "What's that?"

"Ilsa." Jo's attention was pulled from Ursula, and she turned to the cabin, then rushed forward and swung the door open.

Ilsa was lying on the bed, wrapped tightly in her blanket.

Another cry came, and Jo rushed over to drop to her knees beside her little sister.

"What's wrong?" Jo reached to pull the blanket back and gasped.

Ilsa's face was covered with spots. Jo reached out to find Ilsa had a high fever. And even the pressure of Jo's hand on her forehead wouldn't wake her.

"I was a fool," Ursula snarled.

"Get cool cloths and hold them on her forehead." Jo pulled the covers away, fearing the heat in her sister's small body.

Ursula didn't move.

Finally, with the blanket pulled aside, Jo had a second to look up at her older sister, standing frozen with fear.

"Please, Ursula." Jo leapt to her feet and rushed to get the cloths herself to dip in the basin. "I need help."

Stumbling, Ursula went to a pitcher and poured it into a basin with shaky hands.

Jo was scared of handling this fever. She and Ursula knew too little of how to treat sickness. She needed Dave.

Jo thought of the daily delivery of food and hoped Dave came early. Then she heard the clop of hooves outside, and she raced for the door and flung it open.

Dave. Smiling and trotting toward the cabin.

Her expression made his smile melt like snow in August.

"We need help. Ilsa's burning with fever and covered in a rash. You remember how Mitch was."

"I'll go for Ma and bring medicine," Dave said, cutting her off. "I'll be back with all I need as fast as I can ride."

He whirled his horse around and galloped for the top of

the canyon. A man of action. A man of courage. He didn't hesitate to help, not for one instant.

Jo rushed back to the cabin to find Ursula holding a cool cloth to Ilsa's forehead and singing quietly.

The singing stopped. Ursula looked at Jo. "When he returns, I'll go."

"Ursula, no. We need you here. Ilsa needs you." Ursula had been a mother from the age of eight when their parents vanished. Then a few years later, with Grandma gone, she stepped in even more. Now she cared for Ilsa as if her little sister were indeed her own child.

It wrenched Jo's heart to think of all that had come true about Grandma's warnings.

"Do you remember how Grandpa went to search for Ma and Pa when they went away?"

"I remember a little." Jo dug around for memories. "I wanted to help him, too. I just remember Grandma saying no and that was that. But I was . . . five, maybe six when they left. Of course I couldn't go."

"I was three years older than you, and it was foolish for me to want to help, too. But I did want to. Grandpa left, and I used to sneak off, every day after he left, and go to the head of that trail and look down. I'd think about going."

"By yourself?"

"I was old enough to run around on my own, or at least I was allowed to. I'm not sure it was wise, but Grandma and Grandpa let us play far and wide."

Jo remembered that. "And you and I allowed Ilsa the same freedom." Jo looked down at her sick little sister. "We're lucky we weren't eaten by wolves the first week."

Ursula managed a weak smile. "I used to run off by myself and stand at the trailhead."

"The one Dave drove his cattle up?"

Nodding, Ursula went on. "I'd stare at that trail, and every day it seemed to lead to somewhere more dangerous, more deadly. I would imagine only black existed beyond where my gaze could reach. Some days I imagined going down it was like sliding into the belly of a snake."

"You were for sure too young to go down it, if you thought that."

"I imagined Ma and Pa dead. And Grandpa was gone a long, long time. I was sure he'd been swallowed by that snake, too. After a while, instead of sliding into a snake's belly, I was sure to go down that trail was to slide right into hell."

Jo gasped, but didn't interrupt Ursula. Her sister had never spoken of this before.

"It's not sensible. I suppose it's madness of a kind, but that's what I see when I look down the mountain. That's what I think is down there. And try as I might, I can't shake the feeling of not just a chance of death down there, but a sure trip straight to hell. And until I can get over that, I can't be around the Wardens. I can't be around you, Jo. Your choices are terrifying to me, and all I can do is want to save you."

"I don't want to be saved. I don't believe I need to be saved, not from nice folks like Dave and his family."

"I know, and having me close makes everyone miserable. Not just me, but you and Ilsa, too, and the Wardens. I'm going to go. I'll live alone and bother you no more."

"You have to stay until we're sure you're not getting sick."

Ursula lifted her head, her eyes shone like the blue at the

heart of the lantern light. "You're the one who said, 'To live is Christ. To die is gain.' What does it matter if I sicken and die alone?"

"Ursula, don't say such a thing."

"I'm going, and I don't want you to come after me. Now, Ilsa has some of her medicine up here. There's hot water. Brew some tea." Ursula went back to pressing the damp cloth on Ilsa's fevered brow.

"I will come after you. You're my sister, and I love you. I'll never allow you to cut yourself off from your only family. If you run, I'll come after you."

"So we know exactly how it's going to be."

"And now I'll brew the tea."

Ursula went back to her soothing song.

Jo and Ursula worked over Ilsa. Ilsa woke and spoke quietly to them. Her words were slurred, and they came slowly, but she was alert enough to understand she was sick, and she even gave instructions about how to steep the tea properly.

Then they heard pounding hooves.

Jo rushed to hang a pot of water over the fire to keep it warm. When she turned back, Ursula had left Ilsa's side and was pulling on her coat with jerky motions.

"I'm leaving." Ursula looked defiantly at Jo, then her eyes slid to Ilsa, but she wrenched them away. "You have all the help you need. I won't stay in this cabin with the Wardens. I'm going to the stone house."

She took her bow and knife and thrust supplies into a leather bag. Then she jerked the door open and glared back at Jo. "If you come after me, you won't be welcome."

She rushed out.

"Ursula, come back!" Jo reached the door to see her sister run as if chased by wolves across the open meadow. "Ilsa needs you!"

Ursula only ran faster, as if Jo's words were the wolves.

Coward. Betrayer. Weakling.

Jo fought down the rage in her heart. She couldn't forget it. Would never forgive this. But right now, she had no time. The Wardens, Dave and his ma, galloped toward the cabin. Jo didn't have time to wait for them, either.

Ilsa needed her. She went back inside and closed the door with a loud crack. Then she went to help her sister. Alone.

Ma galloped behind Dave like God himself might ride. She was so loving, such a great cook. So quick with a smile and a gentle hand, that Dave forgot just how tough she was, how long she'd been tearing a living out of a wilderness. The Wardens had come to this country right after the end of the Mexican-American War. They'd loved the land and turned toward the mountains after following the Santa Fe Trail. They'd built their first small cabin when there was nothing here.

They'd lived peaceably with the Utes, the native folks who were in the area. They traded with them, learned from them. They'd built a ranch and a herd with the strength in their backs and the wits in their heads. Ma and Pa had plenty of both.

Dave galloped straight for the cabin with Ma hard on his heels. He saw Ursula rush out, then Jo on her heels. But Ursula went on, and Jo gave Dave a look while he was still too far away to know what had happened, then Jo went inside.

They swung down, lashed their hard-breathing horses to

the hitching post outside the front door, and rushed for the cabin just as Jo swung open the door.

Dave halted, and Ma dodged around him, passed Jo without knocking her over, and knelt beside Ilsa before Dave could get moving again.

"Dave, bring in the supplies." Ma didn't even look in his direction.

He whirled toward the horses, both laden with heavy packs and filled saddlebags. Jo swung the door shut to hold in the heat and was at his side, helping him carry.

It took them two trips, but they had everything in. Jo already had a pot of water steaming in the fireplace.

"I've brought more of Ilsa's tea, but I see you have given her some already. I gave more of it to Mitch than Ilsa suggested, and it brought his fever down." Ma left Ilsa's side to begin brewing a new cup.

She soon had it steeping.

Jo eased cool cloths onto Ilsa's brow. "Her fever is higher than it was just an hour ago."

"Remember she wrapped up snow in heavy cloth, then packed it around Quill's head? I did that for Mitch, too. I brought a cloth we can use for that."

"I'll get it." Dave grabbed for the cloth and was back outside. He needed to help. He needed to do something, anything, to push back his fear.

He shaped the snow into a long, thin tube a little fatter than a snake, long enough to wrap from ear to ear over the top of Ilsa's head, and brought it inside.

Ma supported Ilsa's shoulders while Jo coaxed the tea down Ilsa's throat.

"Mitch is better now, isn't he? He didn't have the most dangerous kind of illness, what your worst fears were?"

Dave had told her that, but she needed to hear it again.

"No, he didn't have that, and she doesn't have smallpox, either. I'm sorely afraid you will catch it, too, Jo. And Ursula." Ma glanced over her shoulder at Dave. They'd both seen her run when they'd ridden up.

"She ran. She ran like the worst kind of weakling and coward." Jo kept her words gentle as she cradled Ilsa's head when Ilsa tried to turn away from the bitter tea.

"She waited until she knew help had arrived." Dave packed his tube of snow while he fought down the impulse to rage against Ursula. She was too adult to do something like this.

"Her fears got the better of her." That was as kind as he could be.

"And they shouldn't have. It's during hard times that we test ourselves, find out what kind of people we really are." Jo sounded disappointed, but she was quiet about it. Dave could see she was furious inside, but she didn't want to upset Ilsa.

Dave brought the packed snow to his ma.

"It's about more than how Ursula is feeling. What if she gets sick, and she's away from here, alone? She won't survive, not out in the cold with no one to care for her." Ma's eyes met Dave's.

"I'll go. I'll drag her back."

"No," Jo said. "Not yet. She was fine this morning, and she'll head for that stone building we found. She can build a fire there. And she can bring down a hog or a deer to eat. She's only in trouble if she gets sick. We do have to check on her soon. Right now, though, let's care for Ilsa."

26

Mitch the Itch.

Dave had given him that nickname about an hour after Mitch woke up with no fever.

Mitch was getting ready to make a fist and start swinging when Dave went riding off to deliver supplies to the Nordegren women.

Then he came tearing back with the news that Ilsa, that little pest, was sick. Dave went off with Ma, and left Mitch and Pa, neither of them feeling well.

The guilt was killing him, sitting in the brand-new cabin, safe and warm while his exhausted Ma and Dave doctored someone. "It's my fault. I had no idea I was sick. I don't remember anyone on the train who had a fever or spots."

Pa wasn't up to pacing, but he did hoist himself out of his chair to get coffee and a plate of the eggs Ma had just finished scrambling, then set aside to run off.

"It's not your fault, Mitch. You know that. It puts me in mind of Jo telling us her grandpa always stayed away awhile when he'd been to town. I've never considered such a thing.

We don't head into town that often. Maybe we oughta build a little cabin off a fair piece from our house."

Mitch shook his head. "So, riding to town gets every man stuck in a cabin by himself? That would make the idlers offer to run for supplies, and it'd make the hard workers who can't stand sitting around refuse to leave the ranch."

Pa was quiet awhile. "Not that different from spending time in a line shack."

Mitch decided food was an idea with merit, so he filled a plate and sat across the table from Pa. "I see no sign of spots on you or Ma or Dave, but what if you didn't catch it right away? You could still get sick. Of the four of us, I'm the one we're sure isn't contagious anymore. I should've gone to take care of Ilsa, not Ma and Dave."

"All those blisters have dried up and scabbed over. If you'd stop scratching, those scabs would heal up."

Just talking about it made him have to fight to ignore the itch.

"I should have gone." Mitch took his plate to the sink, then Pa's, and washed them good. Then he got them both a cup of coffee and a slice of the cake Ma had made yesterday. They ate while Mitch stewed.

When he was done, he made up his mind. "I can't go now, because that leaves you here alone."

Pa lifted his head from his cake, and their eyes met. Pa didn't talk, but Mitch knew two things.

Pa didn't care if he got left alone, and Pa wasn't going to say that because he didn't want Mitch to go.

"Doubt a long, cold ride is a good idea." Pa sipped his coffee. "What did you do with your company back east?"

"I sold out. I turned everything I had to cash." Mitch hadn't given every little detail about what brought him home. "I was involved with a woman. I thought things might be serious, and I was holding back on a proposal because I've always known I wanted to come home, and Katrina was no good fit for the frontier. I liked her though, thought I loved her for a time."

He saw sadness in Pa's eyes and even knew the reason why. If Mitch had married Katrina, there was every chance he'd've never come home, not even for a visit. It was a choice that would've cut Mitch off from his family for good. But Pa didn't mention that. He was a man who let another man make his own choices.

"Then I compared her to Ma and had made up my mind to break things off with her, but before I could get that done, someone tried to kill me."

Pa had the coffee cup raised to his lips, but he froze, then slowly lowered the cup. "So you said before."

"Yep, and then they tried again. I went looking for answers and found my business partner in cahoots with Katrina. They had plans to kill me and take over my property."

Mitch was silent for too long. "It's a humbling thing for a man to find out his judgment with women is faulty. My judgment with men, too, come to that. I trusted them both. I had to do some very quick and quiet work to sell my companies and convert the money I made into gold. I left a cache of gold coins hidden near the Circle Dash."

"And what of your woman friend and your partner? They won't try and find you?"

"I laid down a false trail so they'll think I'm traveling in

Europe. It gave me a good excuse to get things in order so my daily presence wouldn't be missed. Then I hired a man who looked like me to dress like me and get on that ship under my name for a six-week trip. I'm hoping they won't notice I'm gone for a long time. Then I headed west. I didn't go by Mitch Warden back east, anyway. I was Mitch Pierce."

"Your middle name, why'd you use that?"

"I had to do some things in the war that made me want to use a false name, and the name stuck. I had a commanding officer who helped me get started in business, and he knew me by the name I'd used while a spy. I never got around to correcting him. When I decided to come home, I sent that man to Europe under my middle name, then slipped out of town on horseback and rode a fair piece before I took a train under a different name, then I'd wait awhile, watch for someone following me. Then I'd travel on. Every time I changed trains, I changed my name. All so I could come home without bringing my past along."

Pa rubbed one hand over his head, his hair cut stubby by Ma's hand. "I'd scold you about living a life that drew gunfire if I wasn't right now nursing a bullet wound. It doesn't give me much room to talk."

Mitch smiled and relaxed a little. "I didn't do anything you'd call criminal back east. But many would say I had a ruthless streak. It wasn't the way I wanted to live out my days. I'm glad to be home, Pa. Dave told me about that high valley I climbed in on, the one he said has a house already on it. If it suits you to have me around, I think I'll buy it and set up my own ranch."

"It suits me, son. Right down to the ground." Pa nodded.

"I've got the deed to my land all in order, and Dave owns this meadow. This'll be his house once I'm back at the Circle Dash. I have some plans to get the ranch back that doesn't cost a bunch of my men their lives. They're good men, the twelve hands we've kept over the winter. And salty, a lot of former soldiers among 'em. But I don't want other men, no matter how loyal, dying for my land."

"Can you go to the sheriff in Bucksnort?" It was the nearest town and very small. The nearest good-sized town was days away.

"I know Sheriff Hale. He's a good man, but he's only got one deputy. He can't keep law and order all over the area. He gets paid to be the sheriff of Bucksnort, and he don't go beyond that, short of forming a posse to chase outlaws who come to town. It'll do no good to take this to him."

"So what plans?"

"I think I can get a message to the US Marshals' office. Maybe they can send enough men Bludge will just go away."

Nodding as he thought it over, Mitch said, "That might work."

"Whatever we decide to do can wait till spring. And we have to survive until then. It's a harsh winter up here."

"The Nordegren women have been doing it, three women alone, for ten years."

Quill smiled over that. "Indeed they have. Tough women. We'll need all their knowledge."

Mitch thought of that little imp Ilsa. She did have some useful knowledge, but she was so odd he didn't trust her.

"We have a roof over our heads, but I talked it over with Alberto, and we decided to build this house small and fast, then start a bunkhouse for the men. They'd done enough in here. Today they start work on a roof for their own heads. They did this for me, and I'm too useless to help them." Pa shook his head in weary disgust.

Mitch looked down at the dirt floor, one bedroom with no door. No furniture except a table and two rough chairs for four people. And yet Pa was right, the men needed a roof more.

"Then we need to scout windswept stretches where the cows can graze all winter. And considering we're fighting a man who's claiming I don't have a deed to my land, I want you to hold honest deeds to the meadow around the cabin the women ran to, and the one higher than that."

"The one I came through when I climbed onto Hope Mountain." He'd been too weary to look around much, but there'd been miles of grassland.

"It might risk our lives to go to town and buy it up. I hate the idea of waiting until spring just like I hate the idea of waiting until spring to reclaim my home."

"We'll get it all done, Pa. No one's gonna buy this land over the winter."

Pa didn't look satisfied by that, and Mitch couldn't blame him.

"What doesn't suit me," Pa said, "is being a burden. Sleep is pulling on my eyelids right now, and that's after sleeping the night through. I'm going to go rest and probably sleep until we eat the noon meal, which your ma already has on the fire. She said she might not be back for days."

Mitch thought again of Ilsa. Sick. And his fault.

"I'll sleep all day today, but this is the end of loafing. After today, I'm going back to work. If I can't do a lot, then I'll do a little, but I'm gonna help the men build a cabin for themselves like they did for me. And they can sleep in here on the floor with us in the meantime. Ma would've insisted."

Mitch smiled. "I'm afraid a nap is about all I'm up to myself. But maybe tomorrow. Especially with Ma and Dave gone to help those Nordegren women. Maybe tomorrow I can jump out of the wagon and help pull."

The snow quit falling, and the sun came out.

Wax had been trapped inside long enough.

Restlessness drew his eyes to that sheer wall where he'd seen that stranger perched.

He was new to this part of the country, but all he had to do was look at the snowfall they'd already had, and he reckoned he'd spend good chunks of this winter snowed in. There were no cattle to check, so his main job was feeding his horse. That'd take ten minutes a day.

The thought of it drove him nearly mad.

With another long look at that rock wall, and knowing himself for a headlong fool, he made a decision, and he was a man who trusted his own decisions.

He'd let the fire die overnight, and he didn't build it up. No sense heating a house that might be empty for a few days. He pulled on a heavy coat, his thinnest buckskin gloves, tied down the guns he wore on both hips, and tugged his Stetson down tight on his head. If it blew off, he wasn't going to have a spare hand to catch it.

He stepped out and was amazed at the beauty and wonder of this snow-covered world. Pines surrounded the ranch yard and scented the air. The cold smell of snow shot vigor through his veins.

He didn't bother with his horse even though it was a fair distance to the cliff he was planning to climb. And he didn't walk straight for the cliff. No sense leaving a tidy row of footprints to tell the world what he was doing, in case some of Bludge's men came riding in.

He picked his way along, stepping on spots swept clear of snow, walking along the tops of downed trees, wading through snow when he had no other choice. He was just past the tree line when he heard the sound of approaching riders.

He turned, eased himself behind a tree, and waited. Hooves were muffled by the snow on the unbroken trail. He expected Bludge's cowhands.

Instead, two strangers rode into the yard.

Two men, outfitted well. Dressed warm, with well-cared-for guns tied down—like his. One man led a packhorse. Their horses were magnificent. Sleek and tall Thoroughbreds. Not many horses like that in the West. A lot of money on the hoof.

He looked back and felt good about not leaving a trail. These men could find him if they worked hard, but just studying the yard from horseback, they wouldn't know there was anyone around. He'd kept his horse in the corral he'd found tucked away in the woods, with two other horses penned there. The corral was on a windswept slope, so there was grazing, and there was a flowing spring so the horses didn't need to be watered. He hadn't been out to see the horses yet today, and in fact, not since yesterday morning. It had snowed overnight and covered his tracks.

That well-hidden corral was yet more evidence that the

Wardens had built this place with a lot of effort and knowledge . . . and over a lot of years. Bludge Pike didn't know what winters were like out here, but Wax would bet anything the Wardens did.

The riders paused. One of them pulled his gun and fired it three times in the air. They were letting anyone around know they had visitors. Not men slinking around, sneaking.

They might be more gunmen hired by Bludge, and Wax oughta go out and say howdy.

He stayed where he was.

One thing he knew he wouldn't do was lead these men to that cliff, draw their eyes up, and pin himself against a wall like a duck in a shooting gallery. His climbing would wait for another day.

The smooth handling of that one gun told the whole story of great skill. The shooter was tall and thin. He wore a white Stetson and had gray hair showing beneath, a long black duster without a sign of wear, and he took care to reload his gun before holstering it again. Everything the men wore was new except their guns. Good guns, the finest money could buy, well cared for, but not new.

Crouching, wondering, he held his position. Movement, even through the branches of trees swaying in the mild breeze, might draw the eye.

"No one around." The voice was low, the same man with the white hat, the shooter. Probably the leader.

The second man was younger. He wore a black, broad-brimmed hat with a band beaded in white, blue, and red. He was dressed in buckskin but wore good boots on his feet. He had two guns like his saddle partner.

Wax saw a knife strapped across the younger man's chest when he dismounted. His coat swung open like a man not much bothered by the cold. He went to the cabin and studied the few prints Wax had left. Too new for anything but to be made this morning. The other man remained on horseback.

Who were they? What did they want? Were they after him or the Wardens? Were their intentions friendly or deadly?

Wax figured the way the one man was in charge of tracking meant he was the best. Which meant Wax needed to either go out and talk all friendly-like or get out of here.

Two easy-moving strangers, heavily armed, well mounted. There was no hard decision there.

He slipped away toward that hidden corral, quiet as a breath. By moving, he was leaving a trail. But the most important part of leaving a trail, in this case, was the leaving part.

27

"Her fever is higher." Ma dipped a cloth in the cold water, wrung it out, then pressed it to Ilsa's spotted forehead.

Dave's heart twisted at the sight of Ma's haggard face. They'd been fighting to get Ilsa's fever down all day, and Ilsa had only been awake a few times, confused, her words slurred.

Her blue eyes were glazed.

Jo brought tea when Ma asked for it, then she looked at her sister, terrified. They'd been fighting Ilsa's fever since Dave had gone running for Ma yesterday morning. No one slept.

Ursula hadn't come back. Jo said she'd probably gone to the cabin in the higher valley.

Yet another cabin. No, a stone building, that's what Jo had called it. Ancient and abandoned. Maybe that was right, or maybe the Nordegren women's grandfather was a building fool!

Or maybe he just kept moving farther and farther away from his crotchety wife.

"Ma, we need to start sleeping in shifts. We can't all stay up all the time. Ilsa's had her tea, and she'll sleep now."

Dave saw Jo's eyes go sharply to his ma. She got the message that he was worried.

Jo jumped in talking, "He's right, I want my turn sleeping, too, Ma. So, get started."

Dave bit back a smile as Ma returned Jo's snippy expression. Then a reluctant smile eased onto Ma's face.

"You're both right. I need sleep. So do you. But I'm an old woman while you're a couple of hardy kids. I'll take the first turn."

Jo stepped aside so Ma could get to her feet from where she'd been kneeling at Ilsa's bedside. Jo nodded toward the room Dave had added to this little cabin.

"We've been comfortable here thanks to you, Ma. And thanks to all the supplies you sent up out of your own stores. Blankets and food and firewood. You might as well use the new room."

Ma gave her a weary smile, and though he wanted to, Dave didn't hop up and help Ma get to her room. She wouldn't thank him for behaving as if she were too old to put herself to bed.

"Try and keep the noise down." Ma pulled the door shut to the new room and was snoring lightly just as the front door slammed open.

Big brother had arrived.

"How is she?" Mitch heard Ma's snores cut off. A second later she came to the bedroom door. He'd woken her. He winced with regret, but it was too late to leave now.

"Terrible," Ma said. "Her fever is higher than yours was. I'm afraid this is hitting her harder than it did you."

Jo gasped.

Mitch looked at her for a second, but it was all he could do to tear his eyes away from the tiny woman sleeping like a princess under a spell.

That led his thoughts in unexpected directions, so he turned to Ma. "You should go on home. Pa's all right, but you need rest, and I can help."

"I'm not going anywhere, it's absolutely out of the question."

Dave felt his brow furrow. His ma always scolded a little, but mostly she'd been acting like her only goal in life was to wait on Mitch and tell him how thrilled she was to have him home.

"Why's that?"

"Because I can't leave two young, beautiful women here alone with two young, handsome men. That would be outrageous."

"Oh." Mitch thought for a second. "You're right. It never occurred to me to think such a thing. It seems more like we're taking turns working in a hospital. But no, you can't go." He turned to his little brother. "You go."

This time Dave closed his eyes as if he were in pain. As if Mitch was a pain in the neck.

Having Mitch barge in here was a pain in the neck.

Ma needed sleep.

Jo needed to be doctoring.

Her little sister needed quiet.

Add to that, Mitch couldn't talk to Ilsa without snarling. Leastways not up until now.

Maybe having her be mostly unconscious would help that last problem.

Ma went in the bedroom and closed the door. Jo whispered, "Hush, try to be quiet for Ma's sake."

"Try harder, I can still hear you," Ma said from behind the closed door.

Jo flinched. Dave smiled. Ilsa's glazed eyes went to Mitch.

Dave was closest to a bedside table. He got a tin cup of water. "Take a drink," he said so quietly it was mostly his lips moving.

Ilsa sipped, then her eyes fell shut as if each lid weighed five pounds.

Jo hoped she'd sleep awhile because she'd been so fidgety from the fever that she couldn't be getting any real, deep healing sleep.

"Dave," Mitch said, "why don't you try and get some rest."

Dave straightened and frowned at Mitch. Jo noticed the man seemed to affect everyone the same way. "You're the one who's been sick. You shouldn't be out riding yet. You could end up back in bed."

Mitch looked at Dave for a long stretch. Jo noticed how much taller little brother Dave was. He was stronger, too, at least he looked it. He worked long, hard days fighting nature, wrestling cattle, breaking horses, mending fences. Near as Jo could tell, Mitch's work involved sitting at a desk and maybe getting up to count his money from time to time.

But from his attitude there was no mistaking who was the big brother.

Then Mitch closed his eyes, shook his head, and said, "You're right. I'm going to rest awhile. The ride really took the starch out of me. But I'm half-loco from lying around all day like a pine log. I'm here now. I'll rest. But later you'll need rest, too, both of you, and if she has a lick of sense, Ma will sleep for a long while."

"I can still hear you," Ma called from her room.

Mitch smiled and Dave matched him. Then, with a shake of his head, Mitch got to his feet, went and grabbed a blanket, and rolled up in it near the fire. The cabin was so small everything was near the fire, so that was no great trick.

Dave heaved a sigh of relief. Jo could tell he didn't like taking orders from his newly returned big brother. But he didn't like fighting with him, either. He must be content with the way this had worked.

Turning back to Ilsa, Dave's eyes met Jo's, and she saw deep concern for Ilsa. And beneath that the shared memory of their kiss.

She bathed Ilsa's head and neck over and over with the water, and still fever had her in its grip. Somehow that kiss seemed like a betrayal of her family. She'd chosen Dave over her sisters, and now Ilsa was sick and Ursula might be, too.

As the time passed and the fever worsened, all Jo could feel was regret that she'd befriended strangers. Ursula had the right of it. They should have hidden.

The Nordegren women were better off alone.

28

On the morning of the fourth day, Dave was bathing Ilsa's forehead, kneeling between the bed and the wall. Jo hadn't spoken one unnecessary word to him in days. She wouldn't look at him, nor Ma, nor Mitch.

She'd run off once for hours to check on Ursula and came back with the news that, at least for now, her crazy sister wasn't sick.

His heart ached to see Jo so upset, and he couldn't find a spare minute to talk to her, certainly not a spare minute to talk to her alone.

He noticed a bead of sweat pop out on Ilsa's forehead and trickle down her temples into her hair.

Catching his breath, afraid to believe it, he watched her closely, carefully. Then Jo was across from him, on her knees. "What is it?"

He didn't know what sound he'd made, but he'd awakened her from where she slept by Ma near the fire. She really looked at him for the first time in days, and she looked terrified.

She read his surprise as fear and thought her sister was dead.

He hurried to turn aside that heartbreak. "Her fever broke."

With a quiet gasp, she pivoted to study her little sister. Jo hesitantly reached her hand to touch Ilsa's cheek, almost as if she were afraid to hope. "When a sweat comes, that's the end of the fever, isn't it?"

Dave nodded. "Mitch's fever came and went for a few more days, but the worst was over."

"It's only been four days. He had five."

Mitch came to kneel beside Dave. "She had worse blisters. Maybe that sped things up. Maybe it's a little different for everyone who gets it."

Then Ma was there. On words as soft and quiet as a prayer, she said, "She's beaten the fever. She'll be all right now."

Jo smiled. Dave laughed out loud.

"Thank God." Mitch sagged back on his heels until his back rested against the wall.

Ma directed, "Get up, Jo. Give me a minute to check her over."

Jo got up, backed away, clenched her hands together into one big fist, and closed her eyes. A smile appeared on her face so angelic it made Dave's heart stumble.

He had to talk to her. Now. He'd left it too long as it was.

How would he ever have such a chance in this over-crowded cabin? And how could he hope she'd be able to even think of anything but her sister?

Drag her outside, that was all he could do.

Was his whole relationship with her to be handled in the snow?

Probably. Yes, it was the snow or nothing. And he wasn't willing to accept nothing.

Mitch bathed Ilsa's face, then lifted her with his arm under her shoulders as Ma handed him a glass of water. Dave had never seen his big brother be so gentle.

Right now, for just a few minutes, it looked like Jo didn't have much to do.

"Watch Ilsa. I need to talk to Jo." Striding the . . . two steps . . . to Jo's side, he caught her wrist and pulled toward the door. He pulled hard enough her feet left the ground for a second. He caught Jo's coat off an antler used for a hook and opened the door.

"No, there's nothing to say. I don't—"

Jo was still talking when the door slammed behind her. Dave thrust the coat into her hands. She glared at him, not putting it on. At least she was looking straight into his eyes, even if it was more glaring than looking.

"I need to find Ursula again," Jo said. "Ilsa made it through this with all our help. If Ursula is this sick, she might die without someone to care for her." She took a step toward the horse staked out nearby. Unsaddled, unbridled. What did she think she was going to do? She couldn't get the horse ready for riding.

"If you try and get on a horse before I have my say, I will tackle you into a snowdrift and sit on you while I talk. Now, do you want to do that with or without a coat?"

Her eyes narrowed, but she pulled the buckskin coat on. Her fur bonnet and doeskin gloves were in her pockets. He stood staring while she got herself bundled up.

"I'm sorry." Dave had been thinking for days about what to say and, honestly, "I'm sorry" hadn't even occurred to him. But that's what came out.

"I need to get to Ursula, or go back to Ilsa. I don't have time to listen to you."

"Ilsa's in good hands, and she's on the mend. And you're right, we have to check on Ursula. But there is time for you to talk to me for one minute."

Crossing her arms, the very picture of stubbornness, Jo said, "We have nothing to talk about. Once we've gotten through this sickness, if we are still alive, my family wants nothing to do with your family anymore. You've brought danger wrapped in friendship. You're a wolf in—"

He kissed her. Wrapping his arms around her, lifting her to her toes, he deepened the kiss, and he wasn't imagining that she was kissing him back. And he sure wasn't imagining her arms wrapping around his neck.

When she was fully cooperating, Dave pulled back only inches. He rested his forehead on hers and opened his eyes to see their breath mingle together.

"I am so sorry. So sorry Ilsa is sick." He pulled back far enough he could look her in the eye. "I'm sorry we brought you disease and danger. But Jo, don't say you'll have nothing to do with me. Please don't say that."

"Dave, we can't—"

He really wasn't going to let her say that, and to prevent it, he'd kiss her for as long as he had to.

She tightened her arms.

When the kiss ended this time, he lifted his head and studied her for signs of remaining resistance. Her eyes were a blue so deep and pure that he felt if he looked long enough, he could see his future. Her lips were swollen, her cheeks were pink, and her hair dangled wildly from beneath the bonnet. He had some memory of running his fingers into her hair. The bonnet hadn't stopped him.

On a whisper, he said, "You're not leaving me, Jo. You can't hide well enough . . . and believe me, I know how well you can hide. But not well enough to keep me from finding you. I'll just listen for the sound of my own heart breaking, and that will guide me to you."

Jo studied him. "How can I be with you when you nearly killed my sister?"

"Ilsa is healing. We didn't come anywhere near killing her." That seemed like such a weak defense that Dave decided to stop talking. But then he blathered on.

"Yes, she got real sick. But she beat it, and she'll heal and be her old self again."

"But it could happen again."

He reached for her and gently but firmly grasped her upper arms. "There are no guarantees for a long life untouched by sickness. We still have to face the men who shot Pa and ran us off his ranch. We have to go to the nearest land office and buy this land. If we do that, go down there, it'll expose us to the men who want us dead. We have to figure out where we're all going to live through this harsh winter. We have to find your crazy big sister and get her to calm down and come home."

"We'll have better luck with the gunmen." Jo's brows furrowed.

"None of this will be easy. But it's life, Jo. Life can be complicated and frightening. But it's also wonderful. Especially . . ."

He swallowed hard and forced himself to go on. "Especially when two people care for each other. And we do. One kiss is enough for me to know you're the finest woman I've ever known."

"It's been considerably more than one kiss."

A smile broke out on his face. "Yes, it has. I enjoyed our rides together last week, and working beside you helps me understand what a special, wonderful, hardworking, wise woman you are. I know all that about you, and we're only getting started."

Her eyes went wide. Her lips, shining from his kisses, opened enough to draw in a deep breath.

"I want to be with you, Dave. The way I feel when you kiss me, I want that. I don't want to be alone forever. But I'm so afraid." Tears welled in her eyes, and her lips trembled.

He drew her close and hugged her tightly. She clung to him with her face buried against his chest.

For a time, her arms were fastened like a vise, but at last she relaxed. He touched her chin with a gentle fist and raised her eyes to meet his. They were awash with tears and hope.

"With God, the worst thing to happen to us, things that lead even to our death, will only take us from this life to the next."

Nodding, Jo said, "You sound like I did when I was trying to convince Ursula to let go of her fears. I know it's a waste to live my life always afraid. That was the life Grandma and Grandpa chose for themselves, and they forced us into it. But it's not right—not faithful—to live in fear."

He lowered his head and kissed her, this time more gently and with love.

When he raised his head, Dave saw hope overcome her fear. "Say you'll marry me, Jo. Say you want to join your life to mine."

"Even if you bring danger to my life?" She swallowed hard, and he saw her throat work as if it'd gone bone-dry.

"Yes, even then. Because I'll also bring love, and a home we can share and fill with children."

Jo gasped. "Children. I've never even thought of that."

"Well, you need to start, because our love will grow into a family, babies will grow up, and we'll have to let them loose in the world, with all the risks and all the beauty. That's the world we live in. That's the world God created."

Jo kissed him quickly. "The only thing more frightening than letting you and your family into my life is thinking about a life without you. And I love your parents." Jo frowned. "I'm not sure why Mitch has to squabble with Ilsa so much though."

Dave shook his head. "My brother's just not adjusted to life out of the big city, I reckon. He'll calm down."

"And Ursula." Jo sighed deeply. "I doubt she has any plans to come back."

"It's time to check on her again, in case she's sick. Ilsa would've been in big trouble without someone to care for her. My brother, too."

"We should go now." Jo patted Dave on the chest then took a step toward the house.

Dave reeled her right back in. "Are you going to marry me, Jo? You never really said yes."

Jo shrugged sheepishly. "I don't know much about men, nor marriage. Come to that, I don't know much about talking to people other than my sisters. I think with most things, you're going to have to be really plainspoken, at least for a while."

That brought a smile to Dave's face. "It might not be a bad rule for our whole lives, and that has nothing to do with you and how much you know about people."

Dave took a step back, and holding one of her hands, he sank to the ground on one knee.

"What are you doing? You'll get your knee wet." Jo yanked on his hand, but he only grinned.

She was right. She didn't know much about people, nor the way a man went about proposing. Of course, neither did he. But he'd heard of this.

"I am on my knee because I want to humbly ask you to marry me. I want to beg you to say yes. And when a man begs, he gets down on his knees to do it. I want you to know that it would be the greatest honor of my life if you would accept my proposal of marriage."

"Really, you're doing all that?"

Dave laughed out loud. Then he kissed the gloved tips of the fingers he held. "Say yes, Jo. And you'll always remember this moment because of my strange act of kneeling."

She gave him a lopsided smile. "I don't think I'd forget even if you were on your feet."

He kissed the back of her gloved hand this time. "Say yes. I'll kneel here until you say it or until my knee freezes off, whichever comes first."

She tugged, and he stayed there in the snow. "I want you to stand up so I can kiss you and throw my arms around you and say yes. Yes, I'll marry you with great delight, great excitement, and great love. Kissing you is the most thrilling thing that's ever happened to me, and I once killed a grizzly bear with six arrows and a dull knife, so that's saying something."

Since the very thought of that nearly drove him mad, he distracted himself by springing to his feet, dragging her into his arms, and saying, "I want my first kiss as the man you're going to marry. Then we'll go tell my ma."

They were a long time giving anyone the good news.

29

Jo and Dave rode out to find Ursula as soon as they could get away.

Which wasn't that quick because Ma made a fuss over the coming marriage. A big fuss with a big smile. Mitch slapped Dave on the back and gave Jo a hug, which Dave put a stop to almost immediately.

Ilsa even said a slurred congratulations from the bed.

Finally they packed up a fine load of supplies for Ursula and headed for the stone building.

"If she's sick, we'll care for her," Jo said. She wanted to ride faster, but when she tried, the horse started to shake her off. Dave called it trotting and suggested they stop and practice, but Jo didn't want to wait.

"And if she's well, we'll try and convince her to come back," Dave said. He led the loaded packhorse.

"She can cut her own wood, hunt her own game. She was working on an elk-hide pelt to use for a door covering." Jo looked at Dave, worried half out of her mind. "She'll be alright if she doesn't get sick."

The stone structure came into view.

Dave pulled his horse up short. "What is this place?" he asked in a hushed voice.

"I don't know." Jo stopped beside him and looked at the dwelling Ursula had chosen over family. "The front part is falling down, but the rooms formed with that overhang as a roof are still standing. When I was here before, Ursula was in the first one we found with the working fireplace. It's not a bad place to live."

"If you don't mind being swallowed up by a mountain."

They studied the strange structure in silence for a long moment.

"Who built it? Not your Grandpa," Dave said quietly again, almost as if he didn't want to disturb this lonely place.

Jo kicked her horse into a walk again. "We have no idea. I hoped you could tell me."

Dave studied it with narrow eyes. "I've heard of cliff dwellings in a place they're calling Mesa Verde, not that far south of here. I've never been down to it, but I've heard talk. Stone blocks built into walls like these, some still standing, some tipped over and caved in. Mesa Verde isn't all on the ground though. It has rooms several layers up that are carved out of the sides of cliffs and natural caves. The bottom walls, though, and the shaped stones were done by human hand."

"There is at least one part that looks like it was a stack of rooms. Who lives in Mesa Verde?"

The wind whistled through the pines as they rode on. It crossed Jo's mind that she'd been assuming Ursula would still be here. What if she wasn't? What if she'd abandoned this place and found an even lonelier place to live? Could a place exist that was lonelier than this?

"No one lives there now. No one, not even the oldest native folks, have ever known anyone to live at Mesa Verde. There's no known mention of it in the most ancient tribal lore. Whoever built it and lived there vanished."

"So those folks who vanished may have spread up this far? Did they all leave together? Did they die in a war or . . . or in some disease outbreak?"

"No one knows." Dave's eyes were so fixed on the building that he fell silent.

That's when Jo heard her big sister singing. She heaved a sigh of relief. She was here and well enough to sing.

"That's Ursula." The song snapped Dave out of his intense focus on the building.

"Yep." They rode up to the stone dwelling, and Jo swung down off the horse. She was getting to be a good rider.

"Her voice and this strange, ancient place feel touched by God."

"When she's upset she sings." Then Jo realized that wasn't the whole truth. "When she's happy she sings. And when she's busy or idle or somewhere in between. She always has a song on her lips. She sings Bible verses and sings about weather and animals and cooking. She's been like that from my earliest memory."

Now the two of them stood outside the strange building and listened. The song was so sad it brought tears to Jo's eyes.

Not interested in nonsense like crying, and with no door to knock on, Jo hollered, "Ursula, I need to talk to you."

The song cut off. Ursula was utterly silent. She didn't come out.

Dave unloaded the packhorse, and Jo walked in. She came upon an elk hide hanging over an opening, so Ursula had gotten that much done. Jo heard the crackle of a fire. Ursula was just fine up here alone.

"Stay out, Jo."

Jo's fingers itched to shove aside the thick elk-hide door, grab her big sister, and drag her home. But it would do no good. They couldn't chain her to their cabin. They couldn't keep her prisoner forever. Ursula had to choose to come home.

Impatient with her own hesitation, Jo shoved the hide away and stepped in. "Ilsa is past the sickness. She's healing, and she's going to be fine."

Ursula let out a quiet whoosh of relief.

"Are you all right? Are you sure you're not feeling sick? We will take care of you."

"I'm fine. And I plan to stay here. I'll live alone, and I'll die alone."

The firm resolve in those words broke Jo's heart. "I want you to come to watch me marry Dave." There was only silence.

"Go away, Jo. You've made your choice, and I'm making mine. I'm not coming down, ever. Go away and don't come back."

Her sister was just afraid. Jo repeated that over and over to take the cruel sting from the rejection. "I'm leaving supplies for you. Some wood and some tools besides food stores. Extra blankets, and you left without any pans or dishes. We brought you everything we thought you'd need. Ma's making you a dress. We'll bring that up when it's ready."

"I'll throw it in the fire if you bring it. I want nothing from the Wardens."

Jo glanced over her shoulder at her beloved Dave. She wanted so much for him. For them.

"You're my sister, and I love you, and, well, whatever orders you say right now, it won't stop me from bringing more supplies. I'll be back. I have to come back since you won't come down. If you get sick, you'll need me."

Jo waited, wished, prayed, that Ursula would relent. But Ursula didn't speak again. Before she burst into tears, Jo turned and walked away.

Jo and Dave rode away in grim silence. They hadn't gotten far when the music began again. A mournful sound of grief and loss.

30

Dave had a cowhand Jo had heard called Parson Fred. It turned out he wasn't using *parson* as some strange Western nickname. He really was a man of the cloth—what cloth Jo wasn't sure; she knew very little about men, or cloth for that matter. But Dave said he was a man of the cloth, and whatever it meant, it turned out he could say some words that made Jo and Dave married.

They rode up to check on Ursula every day, fearful she'd start up with the fever. But so far she was fine. Cranky, but healthy enough.

She'd stoutly refused to come to the wedding. That hadn't stopped Dave from building a door onto her room or chopping a winter's supply of wood. Jo went hunting and dressed a deer and cut it up to dry for jerky. Ursula worked with her but refused to leave her lonely new house.

It took nearly two weeks for the wedding because they wanted Ilsa to get well.

As it was, Parson Fred performed the ceremony as soon as Ilsa was able to get out of bed. And that was literally true.

She stood on wobbly legs at her bedside after a full week without a fever.

Mitch was still covered with remnants of dozens of tiny scabs. He was best man. Something else that made no sense to Jo. He was nothing of the sort. She thought he was fifth, probably. After Dave and Quill and Alberto and Jimmy Joe. Parson Fred was a decent sort, too. So maybe Mitch was sixth best man.

But Dave called him best man, and Jo didn't bother to correct the mistake.

Ilsa was still very red and covered with blisters. She was the maid of honor—Dave spent considerable time trying to explain to Jo and Ilsa what *maid of honor* meant. It was hard because he admitted he wasn't sure.

Ilsa had heard of maids and maidservants from the Bible. She thought it sounded like she was expected to do the cleaning or maybe the cooking, and she just wasn't feeling up to that yet.

Jo thought Dave was saying Ilsa was more honorable than Jo and that seemed hurtful. Finally, Dave just said they needed an official witness to the wedding, and there was no cleaning, nor any judgment about anyone's honor.

If that was true, why had he brought it up?

Quill was strong enough to ride over for the wedding. Jo was sorry the man kept getting moved around. If he could just get a nice long rest, he might stop treating his side so gently.

Then she found out he was helping build a house for his cowpokes and stopped feeling sorry for him.

Ma made Jo another dress. "What am I going to do with two dresses, Ma?"

"It's good to have a spare so we can wash one of them while you wear the other."

"We never gave much thought to washing leather clothes. This kind of dress is going to be a lot of trouble." Jo frowned. It wasn't as warm as her leather shirt and trousers, either. But it was very pretty.

"It's a good color on you." It was bright blue made of a heavy fabric Ma called wool. "And warm. You can wear the leggings you're used to under it and the thick moccasins. We'll get you some proper boots when we get to town next time."

"Like the ones you're wearing?" Jo didn't say anything, but the boots didn't look half as warm as her thick moccasins. And Ma's feet clicked when she walked around. How was Jo supposed to sneak up on animals in them?

But all her worries about clothes flew out of her head when Ma made a cake the likes of which Jo had never imagined. The cake was white, and she stacked two circles of cake on top of each other. Ma called them layers. She spread fluffy white frosting between them and all over them. It was a thing of beauty and definitely the highlight of the wedding— although the part where she and Dave said "I do" was very nice.

Ma did all the sewing and baking with a huge smile on her face. She stopped cooking often enough to hug Jo and Dave and even Mitch.

She hugged Quill and Ilsa, too. Jo just loved her more every day. She'd've married Dave just to get into the same family as Ma.

After the wedding, Ma and Pa—Quill finally gave Jo

permission to call him that—stayed at the little cabin. They tried to send Mitch away, but he chose to stay and sleep on the floor.

He seemed swamped with guilt over Ilsa getting sick and wanted to help care for her, which included him nagging her to be careful and eat and rest. He seemed to think all his cranky, bossy ways were indispensable, especially now that Dave and Jo were riding away.

The days were short, and Ma and Pa were exhausted. Everyone was but Mitch. He seemed to be at full strength. They ate an early supper in the last light of the day, and Dave's parents went to bed early.

Dave and Jo left the cabin to the sound of Ilsa and Mitch bickering quietly while Ma and Pa snored loudly in the added-on room.

They were moving to the Nordegrens' cabin for their wedding night, with plans to live there. Ilsa would join them when she was up to it.

Even with the arguing and snoring, Jo missed them all the minute they rode away.

Dave felt light-headed with relief when they rode away from that noisy cabin full of people.

"You know, one of the happiest days of my life was when Mitch came home. I've missed him every day he's been gone. And now the new happiest day of my life is leaving him behind to ride off with my brand-spankin'-new wife."

That was mostly because of the wife, but his brother was a caution, and it was hard getting used to his bossy ways.

Everyone's sleep had been so disrupted for so long that he'd forgotten how loud his parents snored when they got into a really deep sleep.

As he rode, he fretted over whether he was such a loud sleeper.

Ma had told him plenty of times he didn't have their snoring habit, but who could be sure of such a thing? He was worried Jo might be kept awake.

Shoving aside his concern for something he didn't know how to fix, he just enjoyed the quiet as he rode beside his wife in lightly drifting snow. They'd traveled a good part of the way in silence when Dave's ears finally calmed down enough to want to add talking.

Maybe he should offer to sleep in the barn if he snored. He didn't want to sleep in the barn.

"Finally, we're alone together, Jo."

"Why do you think Ilsa and Mitch fuss at each other so? I don't know him well, but Ilsa isn't a person who argues much. I suspect as soon as she can, she'll get away from your brother and stay away."

"She needs a few more quiet days before she can move to our cabin." Dave didn't want company right away.

"Well, there will be no quiet days with Mitch staying there."

"I suspect Ma will kick him out come morning no matter what he says. Maybe he and Pa will go back to the new cabin our cowhands built. From the sound of things, the men can use the help finishing the insides of the cabin and bunkhouse and making furniture."

Dave added, "Pa's still moving slow, but Mitch can go back to work. And Pa's got some plans for the Circle Dash.

He's thinking of going down the mountain right now and taking it back."

"But you said we couldn't go down, that even if the trail is passable, the horses would leave fresh tracks that anyone could follow straight up here."

"He's considering doing it anyway. He wants us to buy this land up here, and he wants to see if the US Marshals will be able to send men to the area to enforce the law."

Jo didn't comment on that. Instead, still thinking of her sisters, she said, "I certainly hope Mitch goes back to work. Ilsa needs peace." Jo looked back like she was considering fetching her sister right now.

"Let's trust Ma to take care of her."

Jo nodded. Maybe because she trusted Ma and maybe—Dave hoped—because she wanted to be alone with him for a day or two.

They enjoyed their time together in the setting sun.

Riding into the tight canyon mouth that hid the Norde-grens' cabin, Dave realized everyone had left. He knew the evening chores had been done; Parson Fred promised to do them on his way home. They had a few head of cattle, all tame as housecats. And chickens aplenty.

The hands were all down at the bunkhouse by the cabin they'd built for Ma and Pa.

Everyone who'd invaded the Nordegren home was gone—with Dave the big exception—and he wasn't going anywhere. They put up the horses and went inside to find a fire burning, and the cabin warm and ready for the newly married couple.

They hung up their coats, and Dave pulled her into his arms.

"I thought we would never be alone." He kissed her.

Jo's arms wrapped around his neck like the ties that bind.

"Marrying you is a fine thing. We'll make a good life together."

"We have to try and save Ursula from her strange ways," Jo said. "I reckon that'll be a trial. She's so stubborn. She'll never give up that stone building atop Hope Mountain."

"We'll get her to come down, or at least we'll do our best. Maybe Ma can help. Or maybe a winter alone up there will do her good." Dave thought it would probably do Jo and Ilsa some good to be away from Ursula's dire warnings.

"And she's probably sleeping on the floor. I can build her a bedstead, though she'll probably try and block me from bringing it in."

"You didn't put a lock on her door. That was wise of you. We'd never get in if you had. What if she's—"

Dave cut off her worries with another kiss. A long one, a deep one.

When he raised his head, her eyes opened slowly, she blinked, and her arms slid around his neck.

Smiling, he said, "We'll take care of her. She'll be as fine as Ursula can ever be. And now, I don't want to talk about your crazy sister anymore."

He swept her up into his arms and paused. Mitch had taken Jo's room when he was sick. Dave didn't like that. He looked and saw the bedding all fresh, the blankets tidy, and decided Mitch wasn't going to be allowed to ruin a room in this cabin. He carried her in and laid her on the bed.

"Is it bedtime then?" Jo propped herself up on her elbows.

Dave's heart twisted with longing at the beautiful sight of

her, all his. He sat down beside her. "I love you, Jo. I will be a good husband to you. I will honor and cherish you in good times and bad, in sickness and in health, whether we have plenty or are in want. And I will keep doing all that, for all the days of my life."

"We took those vows only a short time ago."

"Yes, but I want to say them to you now, here, while we are alone. What we said before Parson Fred and our family are the usual wedding vows, but I want you to know I mean every word of them."

She sat up and reached for his lips with one finger. She rested it on his mouth. He felt the calluses on her fingers from using her bow and arrows with such skill and frequency.

"I meant them, too, but the vows seem to be overly about bad times. I want to hope we have no sickness, we have no want."

He took her hand in his. "We'll hope and pray for that, but those vows are there to remind us that if there are bad times, the marriage holds. It's the foundation upon which we will build a life, and that foundation, with God as the cornerstone, can never be broken. I swear before God I will keep my vows."

Nodding, Jo said, "It's like the Bible story that says—"

Dave stiffened, afraid of what strange parable she'd make up this time.

"—there is no greater love than a man laying down his life for his friend. I want to promise that to you." Jo touched Dave's lips gently. "Think of that. I do lay down my life for you, Dave. Yes, I would die for you. I'd face all of life's dangers for you. But also, I will spend my life doing my best to make our marriage joyful, faithful, and happy."

With that he relaxed. Yes, she had some confused ideas about the two Bibles. But she surely did know the one. And she knew what faith was. What she didn't know, she'd learn, just as he'd learn. Together they'd be better people.

She smiled. "I've had a lonely life, Dave. And I've been content with it, but now, adding you and your family, even that strange Mitch, have made me rich in the things that matter. And if we are ever in want, I'll just go bring down a wild boar or some such. That's my vow to you. And if you ever get sick, I will stay by your side, not run off in fear as Ursula did."

"Now I've got something to tell you about married life that has nothing to do with our troublesome brother and sisters, nor arrows and sickness."

Her eyes arched in surprise. "You do? What have we left out about our married life? Tell me."

"How about I show you instead." He lowered his head and kissed her.

The long winter night passed. The crackling fire burned low. The snow fluttered softly down outside. Though when they'd met, neither had been aiming for love, they found it, and now, together, they began a life on a mountain called Hope.

About the Author

Mary Connealy writes romantic comedies about cowboys. She's the author of the KINCAID BRIDES, TROUBLE IN TEXAS, WILD AT HEART, and CIMARRON LEGACY series, as well as several other acclaimed series. Mary has been nominated for a Christy Award, was a finalist for a RITA Award, and is a two-time winner of the Carol Award. She lives on a ranch in eastern Nebraska with her very own romantic cowboy hero. They have four grown daughters—Joslyn, married to Matt; Wendy; Shelly, married to Aaron; and Katy, married to Max—and five precious grandchildren. Learn more about Mary and her books at:

maryconnealy.com
facebook.com/maryconnealy
seekerville.blogspot.com
petticoatsandpistols.com

Sign Up for Mary's Newsletter!

Keep up to date with Mary's latest news on book releases and events by signing up for her email list at maryconnealy.com.

More from Mary Connealy!

Set on the landscape of Lake Tahoe and the Sierra Mountains in 1860, three rugged mountain cowboys must overcome dangerous obstacles that threaten their lives while fighting the attraction that draws them to the women who step into their paths.

HIGH SIERRA SWEETHEARTS: *The Accidental Guardian, The Reluctant Warrior, The Unexpected Champion*

You May Also Like . . .

On her way to deliver vaccines to a mining town in the Montana Territory, Ingrid Chastain never anticipated a terrible accident would leave her alone and badly injured in the wilderness. When rescue comes in the form of a mysterious mountain man, she's hesitant to trust him, but the journey ahead will change their lives more than they could have known.

Hope's Highest Mountain by Misty M. Beller
HEARTS OF MONTANA #1
mistymbeller.com

Gray Delacroix has dedicated his life to building a successful global spice empire, but it has come at a cost. Tasked with gaining access to the private Delacroix plant collection, Smithsonian botanist Annabelle Larkin unwittingly steps into a web of dangerous political intrigue and will be forced to choose between her heart and her loyalty to her country.

The Spice King by Elizabeth Camden
HOPE AND GLORY #1
elizabethcamden.com

As part of a bargain with her wealthy grandmother, Poppy Garrison accepts an unusual proposition to participate in the New York social season. Forced to travel to America to help his cousin find an heiress to wed, bachelor Reginald Blackburn is asked to give Poppy etiquette lessons, and he swiftly discovers he may be in for much more than he bargained for.

Diamond in the Rough by Jen Turano
AMERICAN HEIRESSES #2
jenturano.com

◆ BETHANYHOUSE